Then You Happened

Sandi Lynn

Then You Happened

Copyright © 2014 Sandi Lynn

Cover Design by Cassy Roop @ Pink Ink Design

Cover Photo by Voyagerix

www.dollarphotoclub.com

Editing by B.Z. Hercules

Dedication

Then You Happened is dedicated to all of my die hard romance fans! Thank you for taking a chance and reading something new from me. I've stepped outside the box to hopefully give you some laughter and fun!

XOXO

Quotes

"Give a girl the right shoes and she can conquer the world." ~
Marilyn Monroe

"Clothes are like a good meal, a good movie, and great pieces
of music." ~ *Michael Kors*

"A girl should be two things: classy and fabulous." ~ *Coco
Chanel*

Sandi Lynn

Table of Contents

Prologue

Do you remember when you played with your Barbies as a child? You had a beautiful, blonde-haired Barbie doll that you dressed in the most elegant dress because Ken, the hottest male doll ever made, was coming to pick her up and take her to the most magnificent ball. She'd be up in her room, in the townhouse, looking at herself in the full-length mirror. While butterflies stirred, Barbie would be all giddy with excitement for her date with Ken. The doorbell rang and Barbie would take the elevator down to find Ken, who was looking hot and sexy in his black tuxedo. He would lean in closer for a kiss and whisper in her ear, "Barbie, I'm going to marry you and buy you a dream house where the two of us can raise a happy family."

Barbie would smile at Ken as she jumped up and down in excitement, but still waited for that ring on her finger. She would hook her arm in his and off they would go to the ball.

Once they arrived, Barbie would look around and thank Ken for bringing her to such a glamourous event. She would feel like the luckiest Barbie on Earth to be on the arm of the most handsome male of them all. Barbie was a queen and Ken was her king.

All would go well until Teresa Barbie showed up at the ball with her long, silky, black hair and eyes like a cat. Her skin glowing with a luminous tan as she strutted her little body in her silvery, short, glittered dress past my king. I watched as his head turned and the smile on his face grew wide.

"Excuse me, Barbie. I'm going to get us some drinks from the bar."

He walked away and I noticed he approached Teresa. Tears filled my eyes as I watched them talk and laugh. He grabbed her hand and off they went. My king, stolen by another woman. I ran back to my townhouse, as my world was now shattered. The love of my life. My king. My Ken, dumped me for another Barbie. My life would never be the same.

And that was where it all began. Somehow, we knew, even as children who played innocently with Barbies, that men would ultimately betray us and fill our hearts with promises they never intended to keep, leaving us alone and wondering what the other Barbie had that we didn't.

What's the moral of this story, you ask? It's simple. Men suck, Barbies suck, and there's no such thing as true love. Does life go on? Sure it does, but with plenty of tequila. This is my story.

Chapter 1
Sierra

I stirred when I heard my phone beep and I opened my eyes. The smell of his cologne first thing in the morning was nauseating. I rolled out from under his arm and picked up my phone, which I left sitting on his nightstand last night. Shit, I thought as I read a text message from Kirsty.

"Where the hell are you? I'm at your house, sitting on your unslept bed. Did you forget about the meeting you have this morning with the Dickson Brothers? They already aren't fond of you. This is your last chance."

"I didn't forget. Get out my black pinstripe pant suit and my black lace push-up bra. You know, the one with the extra lift? I'll be home soon."

"Look what I found!" Royce said as he held up the leather strap.

"Good times," I said as I gave a fake smile and put on my bra.

He got up from the bed and walked into the bathroom. "Grab a cup of coffee on your way out. My maid bought some to-go cups," he said as he peed with the door open.

I rolled my eyes at his generosity and pulled on my skirt. I grabbed my purse and put on my sunglasses. "I'm out of here, Royce. Thanks for last night."

"Have a good day, Sierra. We'll talk soon. Last night was fun," he yelled as I walked out the door.

James, my driver, was waiting for me at the curb. "Good morning, Sierra," he said as I took the cup of coffee he held in his hand.

"Morning."

James had been driving me and my father around for the last five years. He was accustomed to me and my behaviors. The thing I loved about him was that he didn't judge me, unlike my mother, Delia. He knew my patterns and he knew my men. Shit, he knew my secrets. He was there for me during the toughest times in my life and he got me.

"Tough night, Sierra?" he asked.

I yawned before I took a sip of my coffee. "Isn't it always, James?"

He cocked a smile and pulled up to my house located in Hollywood Hills. As he reached his hand out the window and punched in the three-digit code to the gate, I watched as Kirsty came running out of the house with her hands up in the air.

Kirsty and I were the same age and we met back in college when we were roommates. Delia was appalled that I actually stayed in a dorm freshman year because the Adams were better than that. I wanted the rounded freshman college experience of living on campus, even if it was just for a year. I hated every minute of it and my dad refused to let me move because he said that it would be good for me to see the other side of life. After my freshman year, my dad moved me into an upscale apartment and I moved Kirsty in with me. She became like a second daughter to him. Not only was she my assistant, but she was also my best friend. She grew up in a small town in Missouri and attended UCLA on a full-ride scholarship for business. She was incredibly smart and she tried to her best to keep me grounded. She had a thing for James and I'm pretty sure he had a thing for her. Who wouldn't love her five-eight stature and size two waist? Not to mention her gorgeous long, brown, wavy hair and big brown eyes. She was one of the funniest and sweetest people I knew and I loved her more than the world. When my father passed away two years ago, and I took over as CEO of Adams Advertising, I brought Kirsty on as my assistant. She already kept my life in order, so why not pay her for it? As for her and James, there was a twelve-year gap in age between them. She was thirty and he was forty-two. She didn't see anything wrong with it. I did because my parents were twelve years apart and it didn't turn out well.

My parents, Carl and Delia Adams, divorced when I was nine years old. They shared joint custody of me because my dad wouldn't have it any other way. I was his little angel and the only angel in his life. He got my mom pregnant at the age of eighteen and they thought they were doing the right thing by getting married. Obviously, it wasn't, because they always fought. During my weeks with him, he would make me come to the office to sit and observe. He always told me that Adams Advertising, one of the largest advertising agencies in the world, was going to be mine someday and he wanted to make sure I was ready for it. I learned the ropes, the tricks, the lingo, and then attended UCLA, where I graduated with a Master's degree. As soon as I graduated, I became his right hand.

He was diagnosed with prostate cancer at the age of fifty-two and lost his battle four years later. I became the CEO of Adams Advertising when I was just twenty-eight years old and had been running it for almost two years. It was tough being a young corporate woman where nobody wanted to take you seriously. That was why I devoted my life to my career and my company. There were other reasons, but I'll get into that later.

"It's about time? Do you see what time it is?" Kirsty snapped.

"Yes, I do," I said as James helped me out of the limo. "Are my clothes ready?"

"Of course they're ready. All laid out nicely on the bed, waiting for you to change into them."

I walked into the house, set my coffee on the counter in the kitchen, and said hello to Rosa, my maid.

"Good morning, Sierra."

"Morning, Rosa. Toast a half of bagel for me please, light cream cheese. I'll grab it on my way out."

"No problem, *senorita*."

I walked upstairs and opened my bedroom door. There, lying on the bed, was my pinstripe black suit and my push-up bra. Kirsty followed behind and sat on the bed while I changed.

"So, how many last night?" she asked.

I turned to her and smiled as I threw my shirt at her and put on my push-up bra. "Three."

"Damn. The only orgasms I've had lately were compliments of *moi*."

I laughed as I slipped on my jacket and buttoned the only button there was, exposing the lace on my bra and the enticing cleavage it created. I twisted up my long, blonde hair with a clip and turned to Kirsty. "Well, if it makes you feel any better, I pictured George Clooney fucking me in order to achieve them."

She giggled. "You have the most perfect tits. I wish I had tits like you. All I have are these size B cups," she said as she looked down and pushed them together through her top.

"Get a boob job?" I smiled as I put my feet into my black Jimmy Choos with the four-inch heels.

"I just might."

"Bullshit. You're too scared," I said as I left the room and she followed behind.

"True. But then maybe James would notice me more."

I sighed. "Give it up, Kirsty. He's too old for you."

"Only by twelve years. When you're our age, that doesn't matter anymore."

I rolled my eyes, grabbed my bagel and briefcase from Rosa, and headed to the car. James opened the door for me and I slid in while Kirsty got in on the other side.

"We're going to be late," she said.

"We'll be fine," I replied as I pulled out my phone. "Hmm. I have a text message from Don. He wants to meet up tonight. Apparently, there's a new art gallery opening and he wants me to attend it with him."

"I don't like him," Kirsty said.

"You don't like any of the guys I know."

"True. But he creeps me out. He has those creepy eyes. You know; like a child molester's."

I smacked her on the arm. "He does not. He's a good guy. Rich, successful, and a no-strings type of playboy."

"Child molester," she said as she shook her head.

Chapter 2

The Dickson brothers were exactly what part of their last name was: dicks. They were twins and owned an acne treatment line called "Zip, Zap, and Away." Did the shit work? Hell if I know. I didn't care if it did or didn't. My job was to make sure they were happy with the advertising jingle my company came up with. Apparently, they weren't and that was why this urgent meeting was called.

"Morning, Sasha," I said as I took the cup of coffee she had waiting for me in her hand.

"Morning, Sierra. The Dicks, I mean, Dickson Brothers are waiting for you and they're pissed you're late."

I sighed and put on my fake smile as I entered my plush office.

"Good morning, Brad and Tim. You gentlemen are looking spiffy this morning."

"You're late, Sierra. How many times do we have to tell you that our time is precious?" they both said in sync. Weirdos. Plain weirdos.

"I'm sorry, but the LA traffic was brutal this morning. I can't help traffic. I wish I could," I said as I sat down behind my desk. "Now, what's going on with your account?"

"It's shit," Brad and Tim said together.

I looked at them with knitted eyebrows. "Do either one of you ever speak alone?"

They both looked at me and leaned back in their chairs. Kirsty was sitting in a chair across the room, holding up her pinky finger. I did everything in my power not to burst out into laughter.

"If you can't handle this account, then we will find someone who can," Tim said.

"Hold up, guys. You've been with Adams Advertising for what, three years now?"

"Yes."

"We made it work then and we'll make it work now."

"Your father made it work, Sierra." Brad scowled.

Sexist pigs. That was what they were. I folded my hands and brought them up to my chin. "Let me call Terry and bring him up here." I smiled as I picked up the phone. I picked up the sketches with the slogans from my desk and looked at them. My face twisted as I read the slogans.

"I think they're catchy," I said as I got up from my chair and walked over to them. I looked at Kirsty as she sat there, pushing up her tits. I walked over to Brad first and handed him the first sketch. I bent over, making sure my cleavage was all up in his face.

"*Zip, Zap, Away; your zits aren't going to stay*," I read as I pointed to the slogan. "See; that's catchy. I would totally buy your product and so will every acne-ridden teenager in America."

I walked over to Tim and did the same, making sure he got a full view of my cleavage. "As you can see here, there's a happy teenager looking at herself in the mirror. So what do you both think?"

"They're absolutely beautiful."

"Excuse me?" I said as I stood up straight.

Both of them came back to reality with looks of horror on their faces. Brad cleared his throat.

"We mean that the sketches are beautiful."

"Yeah, they are, aren't they?" I smiled as pushed my shoulders back and walked to my desk.

Terry knocked on the door and then poked his head in. "You called for me, Sierra?"

"Come in, Terry. It seems that Brad and Tim aren't happy with the slogan for Zip, Zap, Away.

"Really? We all thought it was great," he said.

"It doesn't matter what you think, Terry. It's what our clients think and they think it sucks." I got up from my desk and held my pen in my hand. I walked over in front of Tim and Brad and dropped it between them.

"Oh dear. Excuse me," I said as I bent down and picked it up. Instead of standing back up, I knelt down with my arms on their chairs so when they looked at me, all they could see were my tits. "So, I'll have Terry come up with something else."

"Umm. No need," they both said together. "We've decided we like it."

"Fabulous, gentlemen." I smiled.

They got up from their seats and I shook their hands. "See; I knew we wouldn't disappoint you."

"No, you certainly have not!" They smiled before walking out of the office.

Kirsty walked over and high-fived me. "Brilliant!"

"They're pigs." I laughed.

"That may be true, but they're pigs who you made very happy and gave them something to jack off to." Kirsty smiled.

I sighed as I opened the small closet in my office and took out a cami. I slipped it on over my bra and sat down behind my desk. Kirsty left to go do assistant work and I picked up my phone and sent a text message to Don.

"Hey, I'd love to go to that art gallery opening tonight. I'll meet you there around eight?"

"Hey, gorgeous. Sounds good. After the opening, we can grab a bite to eat and then head over to my place so I can fuck you senseless. Sound good?"

"Sounds great," I lied.

I only dated rich men who wore expensive suits, drank the finest wine, left big tips, and who were as fucked up as I was where relationships were concerned. No relationships, no strings, and no bullshit. It was the easiest way to avoid heartbreak. I don't think there's any other pain in the world that hurts as bad as heartache. I'd had my share. Besides turning two of my ex-boyfriends gay, the man I thought was the love of my life left Los Angeles to go on a trip and never came back. Since then, I rarely went out. I buried myself in my work and occasionally, okay, more than occasionally, had sex with the businessmen that were in my own powerful world. I was a huge fan of art, so attending the opening of a new art gallery was enticing to me. Don wasn't all that bad in bed, even though he called himself "the king." As long as I pictured George Clooney, I was good to go. If I ever had to step into reality and focus on the guys that were fucking me, I'd probably join the convent. I was happy in my little sex world with George, and nothing or no one was going to change that.

I needed to go home and get ready for tonight. I grabbed a bunch of files from my desk and called James to meet me out in front. As I left my office, I turned to Sasha and told her that she could go home for the day. When I stepped outside the building, James wasn't there yet, so I decided to run across the street to Starbucks and grab a coffee for the way home. They had a sign on the door that said *"Open during construction." When the hell did this start?* I walked up to the counter and was greeted pleasantly by Anna, the barista girl.

"Hello, Miss Adams. The usual?"

"Hi, Anna, and yes."

As I looked around the shop, I noticed a man staring at me. He was dirty, covered in dust, and he was wearing one of those yellow hard hats. Besides all that, the one thing that caught my attention beneath all that dirt and grime were his green eyes. It was the way they looked at me. If they caught my attention from that far away, I could only imagine what they'd do to me up close.

"Here you go, Miss Adams," Anna said as she handed me my coffee.

I pulled out my wallet and paid her. "What's going on here?" I asked.

"We're expanding."

"Oh. I see. Well, happy expanding."

I glanced over one more time and he was no longer looking at me. Instead, he was giving orders to one of the other workmen. When I walked out the door, James was waiting for me with the limo door open.

"How did you know I was here?" I asked.

"I saw you through the window," he replied.

"Oh. Good job."

James shut the door and, before he pulled away, I looked out the window and saw green eyes staring at the limo from the door.

Chapter 3

Cameron

Wow, I thought to myself as I watched the limo pull away. She had to be the most beautiful girl that I'd ever seen. I was blown away by her eyes when she caught me staring at her.

"Give it up, man," Paolo said as he patted me on the back. "She's way out of your league. I mean, way out."

"How do you know that?" I asked.

"Did you see what she was wearing? That expensive tailored business suit and not to mention those Jimmy Choos."

"How the hell do you know she was wearing Jimmy Choos?" I asked.

"Trust me, man. I know Jimmy Choos when I see them." He smiled as he walked away.

I laughed as I shook my head and then walked over to the counter. "Hey. That woman that was just here. The one in the suit. Do you know who she is?"

"You mean Miss Adams?"

"Was she the one in the business suit?"

"Yes. That's Miss Adams. See that building across the street?" she said as she pointed across the shop.

"The one that says Adams Advertising?"

"Yeah. That's her company. She's the CEO."

I gulped. "Wow. Thanks."

"No problem."

I walked back to where Paolo was standing and he put up his hand. "I heard. Sorry, man, but I told you. Way out of your league."

"Yeah. Yeah. Yeah. Anyway, I want you guys to finish this wall before you leave. We have to stay on schedule."

"Are you done for the day?"

"Nah, I'm going to head over to the Marino's place to make sure Joey's on schedule. I'll see you guys back here in the morning."

I hopped in my truck and, before I pulled away, I stared at the building across the street. I couldn't get her eyes out of my mind. A corporate woman. A beautiful corporate woman who was indeed way out of my league.

✳✳✳✳

Sierra

I pulled out my Chanel black dress from the closet. When I walked out, I was startled when I saw Kirsty sitting on the bed.

"Jesus, you scared me. How many times do I have to tell you not to sneak up on me like that?"

"Oh, please. I'm not sneaking up on you. You were buried deep in the depths of that monstrous store you call a closet. It's not my fault you can't hear anything when you're in there," she said as she thumbed through the *Cosmo* magazine I had sitting on my nightstand.

I rolled my eyes as I held up my dress. "What about this?"

"Perfect. Why am I not surprised the price tag is still on it?"

"I haven't had a chance to wear it yet."

"I saw James downstairs." She smiled.

"And?"

"He's so hot. Why do you have this paged marked?"

"What page would you be referring to?" I asked as I leaned over the counter and touched up my mascara.

"*Your best sex ever: 20 moves from cuddly to crazy.* Are you planning on getting wild and crazy with your suits?"

"Stop calling them suits, and no, I am not going to get wild and crazy. I was tired and I didn't want to lose my place in the magazine."

"Sure."

"Don't you have somewhere to be?" I asked. "Like maybe downstairs with James?"

"Good idea," she said as she jumped up from the bed.

I finished touching up my makeup and I ran my fingers through my wavy hair. I slipped into my little black dress, put on my Jimmy Choos, grabbed my evening bag, and headed downstairs. James whistled as I walked into the kitchen.

"Two nights out in a row. I think I deserve a raise." He winked.

"Very funny." I smirked.

Kirsty was sitting at the table, swooning over James. She looked like a lovesick puppy dog.

"Who is it tonight?" James asked.

"Don."

"That guy? There's something off about him."

"Right? That's what I told her. But she insists he's okay," Kirsty interjected.

"Are the two of you finished? I have an art gallery to get to."

James and Kirsty laughed as I walked out the door. Kirsty yelled, "Make sure to show Don your twenty wild and crazy sex moves."

I flipped her off as I climbed in the limo. I couldn't stop thinking about Green Eyes. I kept picturing the moment I looked over and saw him staring at me. He definitely was hot, and the way his t-shirt clung to his body showed off his muscular arms and a hint of ripped abs underneath. That was from a distance. I could only imagine what that body looked like up close. The suits I dated, their bodies were okay. Nothing to write home about, that was for sure. They were in shape. They had some muscle tone, but nothing compared to Green Eyes.

"Earth to Sierra," James said as he looked back at me.

"Huh?" I said as I snapped out of my daydream.

"Your date is waiting for you outside the gallery. Look."

"It's not a date, James."

24

"Whatever you say, Sierra."

He opened the door and helped me out. "I'll be going home with Don tonight, so pick me up in the morning around seven."

"Will do, Sierra. Have a good night." He smiled.

I looked at Don, who gave me a small wave, and then I looked at James and rolled my eyes. I put on my fake smile as I walked over to him.

"Look at you, sexy beast." He smiled as he tried to kiss my lips. Thank God I had quick reflexes. I turned my head so his lips hit my cheek.

"Hello, Don. Shall we see what this art gallery has to offer?"

"Of course." He smiled as he put his hand on the small of my back.

We toured the gallery and mingled with some very influential people. I was known in L.A. Actually, I was known around the world. I was the youngest female ever to be put into a CEO position of a top advertising firm. Hell, any firm, for that matter. Every time the waiter would walk by, I grabbed a glass of champagne and downed it.

"Are you ready to be fucked senseless?" Don whispered in my ear. "I've been staring at that pussy all night and I want to spank that hot, firm ass of yours until you scream so loud, I come."

Seriously? I thought to myself. "There will be no spanking tonight, Don." The truth was that I was still a little sore from Royce's not-so-tender hand last night.

"Behave yourself or no kinky sex," I said. I almost gagged myself.

We climbed into his limo and he couldn't wait. His tongue traveled down my neck as his fingers forcefully made their way into me. I gasped.

"I'm surprised you're not wet," he whispered as his tongue slid down my cleavage. "I'm as hard as a rock already."

My mind traveled to where it always did with these guys: George Clooney.

"Yeah, there you go, baby. Now you're dripping. I want you to fucking come. Do you understand me?"

"Yes, Geo—Don." Oops. I almost slipped up.

"Good," he said as his fingers fiercely probed inside me.

"Ah. Oh my God. You're so hot. I'm going to come. Don't stop. Don't stop Geo—Don."

"Yeah, baby, say my name. You know I love it when you say my name."

I couldn't scream out his name for the fear that I'd yell out George's name. I tightened my thighs around his hand as my orgasm took over.

He pulled out his fingers and got down on the floor of the limo. He forcefully pushed my legs up, pulled my panties down, and went to town. I lay back and rolled my eyes. For a split second, Green Eyes popped into my head and, suddenly, I was about to come again. *What the fuck!* I thought.

"Don, don't you dare stop. I'm about to come again," I said with bated breath.

"Already? Fuck. They don't call me 'the king' for nothing."

Green Eyes. Green Eyes. I thought of him as Don's mouth was clamped around my pussy, his tongue flickering in and out. My body shook as I came again.

We pulled up to Don's house and he got out and opened the door for me. "I need to fuck you right now. I need to come right now. I fucking need your pussy wrapped around my cock," he yelled.

"Whoa, Don. Settle down, big boy. First, we need to do a couple shots of tequila," I said as I walked through the door. "You know the routine."

"Come on, Sierra. Do you really need the tequila?" he whined. "I think you had your fair share of champagne at the art gallery. We can do the shots after I fuck you."

"No. No. No," I said as I waved my finger. "No shots, no sex."

He sighed as he walked over to his bar and set two shot glasses in front of me. He took the bottle of tequila and poured it into each glass. I took one glass, held it up, and threw it back. The burn felt so good. I picked up the other glass and did the same. Don stepped out from behind the bar and pulled down the straps to my dress, exposing my tits. He grabbed them forcefully as he kneaded them and pulled at my hard nipples. He led me over to the chaise lounge.

"Get on here and stick that beautiful ass up in the air. I'm fucking you right here, right now."

I got into position as he straddled me and slapped my ass. I flinched. "No spanking," I commanded.

"Sorry. It was begging me to, baby."

I rolled my eyes and got my head in George mode. Don took down his pants and I heard the condom wrapper tear. He forcefully entered me as he thrust in and out as fast and hard as he could. "Baby, oh baby, your pussy is amazing," he kept saying over and over again. Of course it was George I pictured saying that to me.

"Oh my God, the king is about to come!" he screamed. "Come with me. That pussy better come with me!" he continued.

I began moaning in a high-pitched voice. Faking an orgasm when needed was my specialty.

"Call me 'the king' as you come!" he exclaimed.

"Oh. Oh. Oh my God. King!" I screamed as I faked an orgasm.

"Oh yeah," he moaned as he pushed deep inside me and stood there. He pulled out and rolled the condom off his cock, then walked over to the trash can behind the bar and disposed of it. I climbed off the chair, grabbed my dress and panties, and went upstairs to his bedroom. I was exhausted and I just wanted to sleep. He followed behind me and climbed into bed.

"Oh, by the way, I just want you to know that I'm getting married," he said.

I rolled over and looked at him. "WHAT!" I yelled.

"I know, baby. Don't be upset. I still want to fuck you from time to time. This won't change things."

"I didn't know you had a girlfriend!"

"Yeah. It's a status thing. I really have no choice. It's kind of like a business deal. You understand, right? But don't worry your pretty little head; she's not that great in bed. In fact, I think the king is too much for her."

Fucking unbelievable. I just fucked a guy with a fiancée. That went against my number one rule. I got up from the bed and grabbed my phone from my purse. I sent a text message to James.

"I need you to pick me up at Don's house now!"

"Sierra, it's two in the morning."

"NOW!"

"Leaving."

I slipped on my dress as Don lay there and watched me. "Baby, what are you doing? Get that pretty little ass of yours back in my bed."

I turned around and pointed my finger at him. "You listen to me. I don't have sex with guys that have wives, girlfriends, or fiancées. I've been that woman and I know what it feels like," I yelled as I left his room and stomped down the stairs, looking for my shoes. "You're all alike. A bunch of fucking scum-sucking bottom feeders who think you can just have any woman you want. Oh, and by the way," I said as I turned to him before opening the front door. "That last orgasm; I totally faked it!"

All I heard as the door shut was, "No you didn't."

I sat on the bench in the middle of some flowers and waited for James. About ten minutes later, he pulled up. He got out of the limo in a pair of sweatpants and a sweatshirt. I got up from the bench, wiped my teary eyes, and climbed into the limo.

"What happened?" James asked.

"Why are you in sweatpants and a sweatshirt?"

"Sierra, it's two thirty in the morning. I was asleep."

"Sorry," I said as I looked down. "I'll make sure to include a bonus in your next check."

"No need to do that. You know I'll always pick you up no matter what time it is. It's not like this is the first time and I'm sure it won't be the last." He smiled.

I stared at him. Kirsty would be dying right now if she saw him like this. "He told me that he's getting married, so I high-tailed it out of there as fast as I could."

"What an asshole," James replied.

"I know. He said that it wouldn't change anything and that we could still have sex. Do you believe it?"

"To be honest, coming from someone that calls himself 'the king,' I do believe it." James chuckled.

"I hate men. No offense."

"None taken." He smiled as he looked at me through the rearview mirror.

James opened the gate and pulled up the driveway. He got out, helped me from the limo, and walked me up to the door. "Listen, Sierra. You need to stop doing this shit with these guys. You deserve better than them and you most certainly deserve to be treated better."

"Shut up, James. You're my driver."

"I'm your friend," he said as he kissed my forehead. "Good night. I'll see you in about five hours. Sleep off that tequila."

I rolled my eyes as I shut the door and leaned against it. I clutched my purse tightly against my chest. I took in a deep breath and headed upstairs. As I slipped into bed, the feeling of loneliness crept in. What was I chasing?

****

"Wake up, sleepy head. It's time to rise and shine!" Kirsty said.

"What the fuck time is it?" I asked in a pissed-off tone.

"It's six a.m. and it's a beautiful day," she said as she walked over to the window and pulled back the curtains. "Damn, I will never get used to that view."

"Go away and shut the fucking curtains!" I said as I put the pillow over my head.

"Nope. By the way, I thought you were spending the night at the king's house."

"He's a fucker and it's a long story. I need coffee. Lots of strong black coffee and some aspirin. Tell Rosa to fix me some dry toast. Whole wheat."

She walked over to the intercom. "Rosa, Sierra needs strong black coffee, dry whole wheat toast, and some aspirin."

"Coming right up, Miss Kirsty," Rosa replied.

I moaned as I rolled over, holding the pillow tight against my throbbing head. Too much champagne. It wasn't the tequila. Tequila didn't let me down. It was that damn champagne. Two glasses and I was fine. Five glasses – I was feeling it the next day.

"Sierra, you need to get up now," Kirsty whined. "I want to hear all about last night."

"Just give me thirty more minutes. I'll give you a raise if you just give me thirty."

"As tempting as that sounds, I'm afraid I can't."

I heard the door open and Rosa's voice as she set the tray on the dresser.

"Come on, *senorita*. It's time to get up."

She grabbed one arm and Kirsty grabbed the other as they pulled me into a sitting position.

"Ugh. You two are fired."

"This is what happens when you drink too much." Rosa scowled as she put the tray in my lap. "Now eat the toast, take the aspirin, and drink the coffee. You'll be okay in a bit. And hurry up and go to work. I have to change your bed sheets today and I don't want to get off schedule. This house is big and it takes me longer to clean."

"Don't forget that I doubled your pay when I moved here. I know it's a lot bigger than the apartment I was living in."

"That's why I can't get off schedule. Now hurry it up," she said as she walked out of the room.

Kirsty laughed as she sat on the bed next to me. "I love her. So, tell me what happened last night and why I found you sleeping in your bed when I came over."

"He told me he's getting married," I said as I took a bite of toast. "And that it won't change our sex relationship."

"What? What a douchebag! What did you say to him?"

I popped three aspirin. "I told him that I don't have sex with guys who are in relationships. Then I told him I faked the last orgasm as I walked out the door."

"Good for you." She smiled. "Did you really, though?"

"Yes." I laughed.

"I had a date last night with my boyfriend on batteries. What does a girl have to do to get laid by a real penis?"

I spit out my coffee as I looked up and saw James standing in the doorway with his arms folded, staring at Kirsty. The look of horror on her face was priceless.

"Please tell me you didn't hear that," she said in embarrassment.

"Hear what?" James smiled.

"Morning, James."

"Morning, ladies. It's kind of a turn on seeing the two of you in bed together." He winked.

I threw my pillow at him. "Get out of here. I'll be down in a bit."

He laughed as he shut the door and Kirsty grabbed my arm. "Great. Now he probably thinks I'm some horny whore."

"Well, you are. Not a whore, but horny." I smiled as I got up and got in the shower.

Chapter 4

Sierra

When I got out of the limo, I turned around and stared at the Starbucks across the street. I wondered if Green Eyes was in there today.

"Kirsty, do me a favor and go to my office and make sure the campaigns are ready for the meeting. I'm going to hit up Starbucks. Do you want anything?"

"No. I can go for you."

"No. I'll go myself. Just go up to the office. James, I'll see you later," I said as I walked across the street.

When I stepped through the door, I didn't want to make it obvious by looking around for him, so I stood in line with about fifteen other people. This was why I hated Starbucks and always sent either Kirsty or Sasha. I wondered if he was here. I pretended that I was looking at the pictures on the wall. As I scanned each wall, my eyes diverted themselves over to the construction area and *bam*! There he was, except he didn't notice me today or at least he wasn't looking my way. Maybe he didn't know I was here. Maybe he didn't see me walk in. Maybe he was just too busy to know what was going on around him. The line was moving rather slowly and, as I was looking up at the drink menu on the wall, I felt someone put their hand on the small of my back.

"Excuse me, miss. I need to get through here," the warm and deep voice spoke.

I turned my head and saw Green Eyes smiling at me as he pushed his way through the crowd of people. His light touch sent chills running throughout my body. *Holy shit!* He was even sexier up close. He stood about six feet tall. Maybe six one. His light brownish-sandy blonde hair was short and sexy. Did I mention the scruff? Good lord, the scruff on his face was perfect. Not too much and not too little. When I looked at him, he smiled at me and his green eyes looked into mine. I was brought back to reality by the text tone of my phone.

"Where the hell are you? Are you still in line across the street? You have a meeting in ten minutes."

"Tell them I'm running late and I'll be there soon. I'm the fucking CEO, for god sakes. I can be late!"

It was finally my turn and I ordered my coffee. Green Eyes walked by and the girls behind me started to giggle.

"He's so hot," one girl said.

"I know. I love a hard-working man who gets all dirty and sweaty," her friend said.

I rolled my eyes because they had to be all of eighteen. But they were right about the "hot" part. As for the dirty and sweaty, not my cup of tea. I grabbed my coffee from the counter and, as I approached the door, Green Eyes opened it and held it for me.

"Thank you." I smiled.

"You're welcome." He nodded.

****

Cameron

I looked over and there she was, the girl that was way out of my league, standing in line to get coffee. I tried not to make it obvious by staring at her the way I did yesterday, but I caught myself stealing little glances. I had to use the bathroom and it was on the other side of the shop. There was a line of people and I needed to get through, so I decided to cut in between the corporate woman and some young girl. This was my chance to get closer to her, even if it was only for a split second. As soon as I said "excuse me," she turned and smiled at me as she moved up. I was right; she was even more beautiful up close. Damn her. Why did she have to be so beautiful? I needed to get some tools out of my truck and, as I approached the door, so did she. I held it open for her and she thanked me. Her voice was soft with a happy tone to it.

As I opened the back of my truck, I watched her walk across the street and into the building. She walked with confidence. I could tell just by her actions that she was a strong woman and not a force to be reckoned with.

"You still gushing over that CEO lady?" Paolo asked as he put his hand on my shoulder.

"Nah. I don't gush. Let's get back to work."

****

Sierra

The meeting was a success and we landed a new client.

"Sasha, come in here, please," I said through the intercom.

I walked over to the bar, got out three glasses and the bottle of tequila. Sasha walked in and smiled.

"Are we celebrating?" she asked.

"We sure are," I replied.

Before I cut up the limes, I handed the salt to Sasha and Kirsty. After I poured the tequila, I handed them their glasses, poured salt on the back of my hand, and got my lime ready.

"Here's to landing another account and continuing to grow this company! Woo hoo!" I said with excitement as all three of us drank the shots. "Damn, that's good." I smiled.

My phone began to ring and I walked over to my desk, only to see that it was my mother calling. "Party's over, girls. Delia's calling."

"Hello, Mother," I answered.

"Sierra, darling. Tell me you don't have plans for tonight? Silly question, I know, because you don't ever have plans. Anyway, Ava and I are coming over for dinner. I've already called Rosa and planned the menu, so you don't need to worry about a thing. Dinner is at seven sharp, so please don't be late. See you later, darling. Love you." *Click.*

And just like that, she was gone. I looked at my phone and then at Kirsty. "You're coming to dinner tonight at my house at seven sharp. You are not leaving me alone with that woman."

"Hell, no. I have plans tonight."

"What plans do you have? Because I know damn well that if you had plans, you would have told me. You tell me everything."

"Well. Uh, I forgot."

I set my glass down on the bar. "Oh well. Looks like I'll have James to keep me company."

Her ears perked up like a dog's when it hears a noise outside. "James is coming?"

"Yep. Too bad you have plans."

"No big deal. I can cancel them."

"Are you sure? Because I wouldn't want you to miss out on something special."

"No...no. It's fine. I'll be at your house at seven sharp." She smiled as she opened the door and left.

I sat down in my chair behind my desk and turned it so I was facing the window. I sent a text message to James.

"Dinner. Tonight. My house. Seven sharp. You'll be there or else."

"Delia?" he replied.

"Yep."

"Okay. I'll be by the office to pick you up around six thirty."

"I'll be waiting with a bottle of tequila in my hand."

I stared out the window of my office and at the city of Los Angeles. Actually, I stared at the Starbucks across the street. That's right; my window faced Starbucks. I sat and watched for any sign of Green Eyes. I couldn't get him out of my head, especially when his hand touched the small of my back and he held the door open for me. *What the hell is it about him? Why do I feel like a stalker right now?* This was not me. But I sat there in my big, oversized executive chair and watched and waited, even to catch a glimpse of him. My phone rang, and when I looked at it, I saw Don was calling. I hit ignore and it rang again. I hit ignore, and it rang again. For fuck sake.

"What do you want, Don?" I answered.

"I don't want you to be upset about Milania."

"Who the fuck is Milania?" I asked in anger.

"My fiancée. I promise nothing between us will change," he said.

I rolled my eyes. "What part of goodbye do you not understand? Don't ever call me again. Before I let you go, let me give you one piece of advice. If you're going to marry this woman, at least have the decency to stay faithful to her or don't marry her at all. Goodbye, Don." *"Asshole,"* I said out loud.

I was startled when I heard someone clear their throat from behind. I turned my chair around and nearly stopped breathing when Green Eyes was standing there, staring at me. I suddenly became heated and nervous. The butterflies began to flutter and my heart started to pick up the pace. My lips wouldn't form any words, so I just sat there and smiled.

"Asshole, huh?" he chuckled.

"Oh, yeah," I said as I looked at my phone. "Just a guy I know who cheats on his fiancée, repeatedly."

"Yeah, then he's an asshole. A big one, in fact."

"Can I help you with something?" I asked.

"Sorry," he said as he reached in his pocket. "You left your credit card across the street. I overheard the girl saying that she was going to bring it by later, and I was heading over here anyway to the deli down the street, so I told her that I'd drop it off."

"Thank you. Thank you so much. I didn't realize that it was missing."

"You're welcome," he said, and then looked at my card. "Sierra Adams."

He walked over to my desk, and when he handed me the card, our fingers touched. I swear a bolt of electricity penetrated my body. Then that awkward moment happened. You know; the one where you both stand there and don't say anything because you don't know what to say? Yeah. That happened.

"I need to get going." He smiled as he pointed behind him.

I got up from my desk and walked over to him. He sure was sexy. Holy shit. I stuck out my hand.

"Thank you again—" I stopped and looked into his green eyes.

"Cameron. Cameron Cole." He smiled as he shook my hand.

The intensity of our hands clasped around each other was overwhelming. Just as we were saying goodbye, Kirsty walked in.

"Thank you again, Cameron."

"No problem. I'll see you around." He smiled and walked out.

Kirsty stood there with her mouth wide open. "Who in the name of Adonis was that hot-looking guy?"

"I don't know. He's doing some work across the street. I left my credit card at Starbucks and he brought it back to me."

She stood there and stared at me with her hands on her hips and tapping her foot.

"What?" I asked.

"Something's off with you, and I think it has something to do with that hot guy."

I rolled my eyes and sat down at my desk. "The only thing that's off is you. Now get back to work before I fire you."

"You always threaten that, but think of how screwed up your life would be if I wasn't around."

I looked up at her. "True."

She left and I sat there pondering. Green Eyes wasn't Green Eyes anymore. He was Cameron Cole.

Chapter 5

I stepped outside the building and, before I got in the limo, I looked across the street and saw Cameron by his truck. He gave me a small wave and a smile. I returned the favor and climbed inside.

"Who's that?" James asked with curiosity.

"His name is Cameron and he was nice enough to return my credit card that I left at Starbucks this morning."

"Ah, leaving-the-credit-card-where-the-hot-guy-is-working-so-he'll-bring-it-back-to-you-trick. Clever, Sierra." He smiled.

"Very funny, James. I'm done talking to you right now," I said as I put up the privacy window. I looked at him and he was laughing.

I dreaded dinner with my mother. Ava is my sister and she's fifteen years old. Delia met Clive, her current husband and Ava's father, sixteen years ago after her second divorce. She got pregnant three months after they started dating. I swear she did it on purpose to trap him. Clive is in real estate and finance and he's worth millions. Which is good, because Delia wouldn't accept anything less. He's a womanizer. My mother either doesn't see it or turns the other cheek. Personally, I think he's a dog. But, Delia seems happy and my father always said she was nothing but a gold digger, so it is what it is.

I looked at the clock on my phone. It was six fifty. I had ten minutes to get in and get changed before Delia arrived. Just as we walked through the door, Kirsty pulled up. The aroma in the house was amazing.

"Rosa, what are you cooking?" I yelled from the foyer.

"Chicken cordon bleu with asparagus and red skin potatoes lightly tossed in lemon and oregano."

Kirsty and James followed the smell to the kitchen, and I ran upstairs to change into more comfortable clothes, aka, yoga pants and a tank top. As I was coming down the stairs, the doorbell rang. *Here we go,* I thought to myself. I opened the door and the first thing Delia did was look me up and down.

"Hello, darling. That's what you're wearing for dinner?" she asked as she kissed both my cheeks.

"Hello, Mother, and yes. It's my house and I'll dress any way I want." I smiled. "Hey, Ava," I said as I hugged her. "No Clive tonight?"

"He's on business trip in Monaco," she replied.

I looked at Ava and she rolled her eyes. She made finger quotes and mouthed, "Business trip, my ass."

I couldn't help but laugh as I put my arm around her and we went into the kitchen. Ava was a very active fifteen-year-old. Delia tried to mold her into everything *she* always wanted to be. Since she claimed she failed with me, poor Ava was getting the brunt of it. She was in beauty pageants, multiple dance classes, tennis lessons, swim lessons, and private voice lessons. She was a beautiful girl. Tall, long legs, long, blonde hair, and big, beautiful blue eyes. I wouldn't be surprised if she was crowned Miss America one day. Don't get me wrong; Delia tried all those things with me, but my heart was in the business world, thanks to my dad. He kept me somewhat grounded and out of the limelight that my mother so badly wanted me in. Clive didn't care what Delia did to Ava because he was too busy with other things. My thought was that he just let her do what she wanted to keep her quiet.

"Hello, Kirsty. Hello, James," Delia said as she walked in the kitchen. "I didn't know you'd be here tonight."

"I invited them, Mother, since it's my house and my housekeeper that cooked this meal."

She shot me a look and then raised her eyebrow at me. "It's fine, Sierra. Stop getting all defensive."

"Dinner is ready. Everyone take your seats in the dining room," Rosa said as she looked at me and rolled her eyes.

We did what Rosa asked and sat down. "I thought you were having some things redone in this house?" Delia asked.

"I just moved in three months ago and I haven't had time to look into anything yet. I do work for a living."

Ava laughed. I could tell that Kirsty and James were uncomfortable. Delia and I never saw eye to eye on things. She blamed my father for that. She claimed that he corrupted my mind with all things corporate. Her belief was to let the men handle the business world while we stood by their sides and looked pretty. She resented my father for taking me into the world of advertising and now I thought she resented me as well. Our relationship wasn't exactly perfect. When Ryan left me and never came back to Los Angeles, I was torn to pieces and all she could say was, "You must have done something wrong or couldn't be the woman he wanted you to be, or else he wouldn't have left." We didn't speak for three months after those words flew out of her mouth. She did ultimately apologize for hurting and upsetting me. But she never apologized for what she said.

"Rosa, can you please get me a glass of water?"

She looked at me and smiled. "Of course, *senorita.*"

Rosa and I had a code. When I asked for water that meant to fill the glass with tequila.

"Rosa, this chicken cordon bleu is too die for. If you ever consider leaving Sierra, you can come work for me."

"Rosa isn't going anywhere, Mother. Stop trying to steal my help."

She went to set the glass on the table, but before she could, I took it from her hands. "Thank you." I smiled as I drank half the glass.

Once our eventful dinner was over, Rosa brought out a strawberry cake with buttercream icing and fresh strawberries on top.

"My favorite, Rosa! Thank you!" Ava exclaimed.

"None for Ava, Rosa. She has her swimsuit tryouts tomorrow and I can't afford her putting on any weight."

The look on Ava's face was pure disappointment and I could see the fires of Hell in her eyes. I felt bad and I wish I had more time to spend with her. I pulled Kirsty and James aside and asked them to take Delia outside in the back and complain about my landscaping.

"I'll be out in a minute. Ava, come here." I smiled.

I cut a huge piece of strawberry cake and put it on a plate. I grabbed a fork from the drawer and I took Ava's hand.

"What are you doing?" she asked.

"You'll see. Follow me."

I took her to my bedroom and I set the plate on the desk. "Eat." I smiled.

"But—" she said.

"No buts, Ava. Just eat the damn cake. Forget about Delia and your swimsuit tryouts for one night. Be a kid and scarf down that cake!"

She smiled at me as she looked at the cake. "You're the best, Sierra," she said as she threw her arms around me.

"So are you, Ava."

I left Ava in the bedroom and went out on the patio to join the Nazi, Kirsty, and James.

"The yard looks good, Sierra. I think the only thing you need to do is add more lighting around the pool and hot tub."

Did my ears just hear Delia compliment something of mine?

"I will definitely look into that," I said as I sipped on my "water."

We sat outside for a while and listened to Delia spew about Clive and how much money he made last week and how they were going on a family vacation to Belize next month. I'd put money on it that Clive would get the family down there and then take off on a "business trip" for a couple of days. He had a pattern and I wasn't stupid.

"Come on, Ava. We have to be up early in the morning for your tryouts," Delia spoke as Ava stepped outside.

I hugged them both goodbye and, when I shut the door, I let out a deep breath and lightly banged my head against it. Rosa looked at me and smiled.

"She may be a big pain in the ass, but she's your mother and she endured a lot of pain to bring you into the world."

"I know that, Rosa. She constantly reminds me of that. Good night. I'll see you in the morning." I smiled.

When I went to go back outside, I stopped in the doorway and watched as James and Kirsty were sitting down, talking and laughing. She was throwing her head back and he was all smiles as they seemed to be engaged in some heavy conversation. Maybe they would make a great couple, despite the age difference. I stuck my head out the sliding door wall.

"Hey, I'm heading up to bed. You two stay and talk. Lock up when you leave."

"Night," they both said and then turned to each other and continued their conversation.

I changed into my nightshirt and climbed into bed. I reached over and grabbed the *Cosmo* magazine from my nightstand and flipped through the pages. My mind went to Cameron standing in my office. His eyes had gotten to me and his smile was becoming an addiction.

Chapter 6

It was eleven-thirty on Friday night and I was still at the office. It was better than having to sit at home. I had the options to go out with friends, suits, whoever. But, the way I saw things, it was easier to keep busy and bury myself in my company. It had been three years since Ryan left. We had started dating when I was twenty years old. Seven years of my life wasted on that asshole. We met in college and then, once we graduated, he moved into my apartment with me and Kirsty. We had our ups and downs like all relationships. I was never the first priority in his life; his friends were. I always came second, sometimes third; no matter what. The last two years of our relationship were rocky. I wanted to get married, he didn't. I wanted to at least get engaged, he didn't. It was always one excuse after another.

I picked up my phone and called for a car service. I didn't want to bother James. I grabbed my purse, turned the lights off in my office, took the elevator down to the lobby, and said goodbye to Alex, the security guard.

"Have a good night, Miss Adams. I'll see you Monday morning." He smiled.

"Have a good weekend, Alex." I waved.

I exited the building and was pissed off when the car wasn't there yet. *Shit.* I looked at my watch and it was eleven-fifty. When I went to go back into the building, I heard someone call my name. I turned around, and standing across the street was Cameron.

"Hey," I said.

He stood at the curb with his hands in his pocket. "Are you still working?"

"I was. I'm waiting for a car. You're not still working are you?" I asked.

"Actually, I just finished. We had a mishap today and I wanted to fix it to stay on schedule. If you want, I can give you a ride home."

"Are you sure?"

"Of course I'm sure. I promise my ride is a lot better." He smiled.

"In that?" I pointed.

"Yep."

"What do I do if the car shows?"

"When he doesn't see you standing there, he'll leave."

He was convincing and I was tired. As I walked across the street, he went and opened the passenger door for me. I started to get in, and then I stopped.

"What's wrong?" he asked.

"How do you get up in this thing?"

"Climb up. Here; let me help you. It doesn't have running boards. If you grab hold of that handle up there, you can jump up."

"For real?"

He chuckled. "For real."

I took off my shoes, threw them in the truck, and climbed in. Cameron helped me by holding on to my arm.

"See? That wasn't so bad, was it?" he asked.

"Truth?" I asked.

"Truth."

"It sucked and it wasn't very classy."

"Well, that's because you're in high heels and a skirt."

As soon as he pulled away from the curb, we watched in the mirror as the car pulled up to my building. I put my hand over my mouth and began to laugh.

"Oops." Cameron smiled. "So, where are we going?"

"Hollywood Hills."

"Ah, the Hills. I haven't been to that area yet. Can you give me your address so I can punch it into the GPS?"

He pulled over on the side of the road and I rattled off my address. "Thank you for taking me home."

"You're welcome." He smiled as he looked over at me.

His smile seemed to brighten my day. As weird as that may sound, I felt different when I saw his smile. His smile made me smile. Even if I had no reason to smile, I did. This wasn't good. He wasn't my type.

"So what kind of mishap did you have today?" I asked to make conversation.

"One of the guys put a half wall in the wrong spot when I went to check on another job. So I had to take it down and put another one up. If I would've waited, it would've thrown off our schedule."

"What company do you work for?"

"It's mine and my dad's. Actually, it was my dad's, but now he's retired, so I run it. It's called Cole's Remodeling and Construction."

"Sounds like me." I smiled. "My dad owned the advertising firm until he passed away a couple of years ago. When he died, he left the entire company to me."

"That's a lot of responsibility. Is that why you were still there on a Friday night at almost midnight?"

"Yeah. Something like that," I said.

I wasn't about to tell him that I preferred to work over having a social life.

"So you do remodeling? Is it only business remodels or do you remodel homes too?" I asked.

"I do both. Why? Are you looking to remodel?" He smiled.

"Yeah. Actually, I am. I just moved in three months ago and there are some things I wanted redone."

"I can take a look for you and give you an estimate."

He pulled up to the gate and looked at me.

"You can just drop me off here," I said as I opened the door and got out of the truck. I walked around and punched in the code for the gate and he rolled his window down. "How about if you come by tomorrow morning and I'll show you what I was thinking."

"I can do that. What time were you thinking?" he asked.

"How about nine o'clock? Just push the intercom button on the gate and I'll let you in."

"Okay. I'll see you at nine." He smiled.

"Thanks again for the ride. You were right; it was better than a car."

"It was my pleasure, Sierra. Have a good night."

I smiled and walked up the driveway to the house. He pulled away and I walked inside. I grabbed a glass and the bottle of tequila and had a couple of shots before falling asleep.

****

Cameron

The whole ride home, I couldn't stop thinking about her. I hadn't felt this way in a very long time. Normally, I don't let a girl consume my head, but there was something about Sierra that couldn't be helped. I couldn't put my finger on it, but since the day I saw her standing in line at Starbucks, I couldn't get her out of my head. Her house looked amazing from what I could see of it in the dark. I grabbed the mail from my box and headed up to my apartment. There was a letter from the landlord. I opened it.

"Mr. Cole, I'm sorry to inform you that the apartment building has been sold and the apartments are being renovated into condos. This is your 30-day notice to either

vacate the apartment or purchase it. For pricing and details, please stop by the office."

Shit. Were they serious? It took me forever to find this apartment that I could afford. It's not exactly cheap to live in Los Angeles. I threw the letter on the counter and climbed into bed. I smiled at the thought of going to Sierra's tomorrow and seeing her house. To think that she wanted me to do some remodeling for her gave me a little bit of hope. Hope that maybe one day, she'd go out with me. Maybe I was being delusional. But for tonight, I had hope and that was all I needed.

Chapter 7
Sierra

"Oh shit!" I exclaimed as I looked at my clock and saw that it read eight forty five. How the hell did I sleep that late? I never slept that late. The thought of Cameron being here in fifteen minutes terrified me. I looked like shit. My hair was sticking up every which way and I had mascara stains under my eyes because I was too tired to take off my makeup before bed last night. I jumped out of bed and ran into the bathroom. There was no time for a shower. I poured makeup remover on a washcloth and washed my face. Damn it! I couldn't let him see me with no makeup on. I tore off my nightshirt and threw it on the ground. I grabbed a maxi dress out of the closet and put it on. Shit. I forgot a bra. Oh wait; this dress had a built-in bra. I heard the intercom buzz. SHIT! I ran down the stairs and pushed the button.

"Cameron?"

"Good morning," he said.

"I'll open the gate. Let yourself in. I'll be down in a few minutes. Just make yourself comfortable."

"Okay," he replied.

I opened the gate and flew back up the stairs. I quickly brushed my hair and threw it up in a high ponytail. I dabbed on some concealer to hide the bags under my eyes and then a light coat of BB Cream. I ran a soft pink shadow across my eyelids and brushed on a coat of mascara. I dabbed my cheeks with some pink blush and looked at the final product. Not too bad, but not too good either. SHIT! After I composed myself, I walked downstairs and saw Cameron standing in the foyer holding two cups from Starbucks. He looked at me and smiled. Suddenly, my day just got brighter.

"For you," he said as he handed me the cup.

"Why, thank you." I smiled. "You didn't have to bring me coffee."

"I had to stop by Starbucks and pick up my measuring tape that I left there last night, so I asked Anna what your usual was and she made it."

"Thank you, Cameron. That was very sweet of you."

"You look great," he said. "I'm not used to seeing you out of business suits."

I looked at him and narrowed my eyes. "So are you saying that I don't look great in business suits?"

"Oh my God. NO! That's not what I'm saying," he said in a panic.

I took a sip of my coffee and smiled. "Relax. I was just kidding."

"Very funny," he smirked. "So show me around your palace and tell me what you're thinking about having done."

"First and foremost, I need to show you my bedroom closet. I need more shelves put up for my shoes," I said as we walked up the stairs.

He walked into my bedroom and looked around. I gasped when I saw my thong and nightshirt lying on the floor. Too late, he saw.

"Don't mind this. Rosa, my maid, is off on the weekends," I said as I picked them up.

"You have a maid?"

"Yeah. Being a CEO of a company doesn't exactly allow time for cleaning."

"I sort of get that." He smiled.

He walked into my closet and flipped the light switch. He stood there and looked around. "You seriously want to expand this? It's bigger than my apartment. Actually, it's probably bigger than two apartments."

"Yes. I have a lot of shoes and they need to be displayed properly."

"Does one really need that many pairs of shoes?" he asked with a smile.

"A girl can never have too many pairs of shoes. If you're going to walk the path of life, you might as well do it in style."

He looked at me and then raised one eyebrow. Fuck, he was sexy. "I guess I never looked at it that way before."

"See, now you know!" I smiled.

He took out his measuring tape and I heard my phone ring. "I'll be right back."

I picked my phone up from the nightstand and it was Kirsty.

"I can't talk right now. I'll call you back," I whispered.

"Why? What are you doing?"

"Someone's over."

"Who?"

"The builder guy, Cameron. The one who brought me my credit card to the office."

"Oh, Mr. Sexy man with the green eyes. What's he doing there?"

"I may have him remodel the house. Now I have to go," I whispered.

"Wait."

"No, I can't. He's coming." *Click.*

He walked out from the closet and then took some measurements on the outer wall. "Well, the good news is there's enough room to expand. I can bring this wall out to about here, and then line it with shelves for your thousands of pairs of shoes." He smiled.

"Perfect." I smiled back as I sipped my coffee.

"Was there anything else?" he asked.

I motioned for him to follow me downstairs. I took him into the living room.

"See where that door wall is?" I pointed. "I want that entire wall filled with windows. I love the backyard and the pool. But I also love the view. So I would like to be able to sit on my couch and look out and see that beautiful view. I also need a corner bar put in. I was thinking about here. And I want the fireplace spruced up."

"Spruced up how?"

"I don't know. Maybe stone or something."

"Okay. I think I have an idea you'd like. Anything else?"

"You saw the spiral staircase in my room, right?"

"Yes."

"Let's go back up there. I want that space turned into an office."

We walked back to my bedroom and then up the spiral staircase. "The view up here is amazing. This is what made me fall in love with this house."

"It is beautiful up here," Cameron said.

"I want this wall all windows too and I want wood floors put in. This carpet is nasty."

Cameron chuckled. "Okay. Got it."

"Follow me." I motioned with my finger. "We're not done yet."

We went into the hallway where the two guest bathrooms were. "I want both bathrooms completely redone. New tub, fixtures, tile, everything. Start from scratch." I smiled.

He wrote it down on his pad of paper and then looked at me. "Anything else?"

"No. I think that should do it for now. So when can you start?"

"I haven't even given you an estimate yet. I have to draw up plans and price it all out."

"Doesn't matter. I trust you and I know you won't rip me off. How soon?"

"You're not very patient, are you?" He smiled.

"No. Actually, I'm not. How soon?"

He rolled his eyes and shook his head as he laughed. "I don't know; maybe next week. Maybe. I need to finish up a couple other jobs first and then go apartment hunting again."

"I'm starving. Have you had breakfast yet?" I asked.

"No."

"Then let's go grab something to eat. There's this great little café just around the corner. We can walk."

"Okay. Sounds good." He smiled.

I couldn't believe I asked him to breakfast. It just fell out of my mouth. But I was starving and he wasn't leaving. As soon as I opened the door, Kirsty was getting out of her car.

"Hey!" She smiled with a big wave.

I could have killed her at that moment because she knew I was with Green Eyes.

"Kirsty, this is Cameron. Cameron, this is my assistant and best friend, Kirsty."

"Nice to meet you, Kirsty." He smiled as he shook her hand.

"What are you doing here?" I asked.

"The question is, where are the two of you going?"

"We're just going to get some breakfast. Would you like to join us?" Cameron asked.

I shot her a look. The look that said, "Come with us and die, bitch."

"Um. No, I already ate. But thanks anyway. I'm just going to use the pool."

Good girl, I thought.

"Okay, enjoy the pool. I'll see you later," I said as Cameron and I headed down the driveway and to the café.

"Oh, don't you worry. I will!" she yelled.

Chapter 8

Cameron

We reached the café and I held the door for her. We sat in a booth and the waitress handed us the menus.

"Coffee?" she asked.

"Yes, please," we both said at the same time.

I looked across the table at her as she opened her menu and looked it over. She was by far a very beautiful woman and I enjoyed being around her.

"You mentioned earlier that you had to go apartment hunting. Why?" she asked.

I closed my menu and set it down. "I received a letter yesterday that they are turning the apartments into condos and I either have to buy it or get out."

"Ouch. That won't be cheap," she said.

"I'm not staying in Los Angeles for any length of time, so I'm not buying it. The thing that sucks is it took me a long time to find that apartment. It's the cheapest I could find."

"Where are you from?"

"A place I can guarantee you've never heard of." I smiled.

"Try me."

"Robbinsville, NC. My parents own a house on Lake Santeetlah."

"You're right. I never heard of it," she said.

The waitress finally came over and took our order. I ordered a big breakfast and Sierra ordered two scrambled eggs and fruit.

"So what brought you to L.A.?" she asked.

"Work. Things were a little slow in North Carolina, so I bid on a job here remodeling a restaurant. I got it and then it led to a couple home remodels, the Starbucks remodel, and now your lovely home remodel. I was supposed to leave after the restaurant remodel, but then other work started popping up."

"Do you like it here?"

"In L.A.? Yeah. It took some getting used to. I don't think I'll ever get used to the traffic. I've never seen anything like it. How about you? I'm assuming you were born and raised here?"

She flashed me her beautiful smile. "Yeah. I've lived here all my life. I'm a big city girl. L.A., Chicago, New York. If it's big, has lots of traffic and people and, most importantly, more than ten shoe stores, I'm there."

I couldn't help but laugh.

"You think I'm kidding?" She smiled. "I'm very high maintenance."

"I can tell."

Her mouth dropped and she made the cutest face. She threw her napkin across the table at me.

"Now that's not very lady-like, you big city girl."

"Who said big city girls are lady-like?"

The waitress smiled as she set down our plates in front of us.

"Have a piece of bacon," I said as I held it up.

"Hell, no. Do you know how much fat is in that piece?"

"That's what makes it so good." I smiled as I shoved it in my mouth.

As we ate our breakfast, she kept checking her phone over and over again. "Do you ever take a day off?" I asked.

"Huh?" she said as she looked up. "Oh, sorry. I had to answer a couple of emails. Everything's urgent in the corporate world. Unfortunately, this is my job and it goes with me everywhere I go."

I gave her a small smile and the rest of our breakfast consisted of me eating and her picking at her food and sending emails. I felt out of place with her. I guess I wasn't used to corporate women. I only dated small-town girls. Once we finished our breakfast, we walked back to her house. I opened the door to my truck.

"I'm going to head on home. I'll draw up the plans for the renovations and I'll have a final price for you on Monday. I'll drop it off at your office."

"Before you leave, can you come in the back with me for a minute? I want to show you something," she said.

I followed her into the back. Kirsty was in the pool.

"Hey, you two." She waved.

"Hey." I waved back.

"I have a guest house." Sierra smiled.

"That's nice. Do you want that remodeled as well?" I asked.

"No. Not right now, at least. At breakfast, I did some research. The apartments are slim pickings right now. The cheapest one I could find, even twenty miles away, is over $3,000 a month. So, since you'll be doing work at my house for what's going to seem like forever, I'd like to offer you my guest house to stay in."

"You said you were answering emails." I laughed.

"I didn't want you to know that I was looking up apartments for you. Plus, I did send a couple emails out to some contacts of mine who are in the real estate business. Unfortunately, things aren't looking good for you, apartment-wise."

"Thanks for the offer, Sierra. That's really nice of you, but I can't stay in your guest house."

"Why not?" Kirsty said as she walked over to us. "What's wrong with the guest house?"

"Nothing's wrong from what I can see. It looks great on the outside."

"Well, hold on a second and I'll go grab the key," Kirsty said.

A moment later, Kirsty came back and inserted the key into the lock. She opened the door and flipped the switch. We walked inside and I was surprised how much bigger it looked on the inside.

"Look; you have everything you need. Living room, small kitchen with appliances, excluding a dishwasher, a not overly small bathroom, and a bedroom that is fully furnished with a queen-size bed and dresser."

I looked over at Kirsty and smiled. "Are you sure you're not in real estate? I think you'd be good at it."

"Hush your mouth. She's my assistant and, without her, my life would be complete chaos," Sierra said.

"I appreciate your offer, but I don't know."

"Well, it's up to you. I was just trying to help you out and since you'll be working here, I thought it would be convenient. Excuse me; I have to take this call."

She walked out of the guest house and Kirsty slapped me on the chest. "What the hell is the matter with you?" she asked.

"Ouch. What was that for?"

"Listen to me. This whole thing has me freaked out. Sierra doesn't do shit like this. All she does is work. She barely goes out. She only dates suits."

"Suits?" I asked in confusion.

"You know, businessmen. Powerful, corporate businessmen. Her life has been turned completely upside down since Ryan left and I'm trying like fuck to get her back on track. So you are to move into this guest house because she offered it to you. Plus, I won't have to worry about her as much for a while if you're right in her backyard."

"Why do you worry about her?"

"I just do."

Sierra walked in and told Kirsty that she needed to call a client. Kirsty let out a big sigh before leaving.

"What's the verdict?" Sierra asked.

"Yes, I'll take you up on your offer, but you will charge me rent. I won't stay here for free."

A big smile fell upon her face. "That's fine. I can charge you rent. I'll have Rosa clean this up first thing Monday morning and you can move in Tuesday if you want. Feel free to use the pool and hot tub whenever you'd like and you can use the barbeque."

"Thanks, Sierra. I appreciate your help."

"No problem, Cameron." She smiled.

I said my goodbyes to her and Kirsty and drove back to my apartment. I couldn't believe that a few days ago, I saw this beautiful woman that was out of my league standing in line at Starbucks and now I was moving into her guest house. I sure hope I had made the right decision. It was bothering me what Kirsty said about Sierra's life being turned upside down by some dude named Ryan. Also the fact that she only dated rich, corporate men. I needed to put Sierra out of my mind for the rest of the weekend.

Chapter 9

Sierra

I couldn't believe that I offered up the guest house to Cameron. What the hell was I thinking? I needed to remember that it was only temporary and once my house was remodeled, he'd be moving back to North Carolina. He did say that he wasn't here permanently, so this was only a temporary arrangement.

"Good morning, Rosa," I said as I strolled into the kitchen.

"Good morning, Sierra."

"I need you to clean the guest house and change the sheets. There will be a guest staying in there while the house is being remodeled."

"Guest? Who is this guest?"

"His name is Cameron Cole and he's the one who will be working on the house."

"Why is the builder guy staying in your guest house?"

"It's a long story, Rosa, and I don't have time to get into it. He'll probably be moving in tomorrow."

"Is he cute?"

I smiled at her. "Yeah, he's pretty cute." I wasn't about to tell her that he was drop dead gorgeous.

"He better be clean. I have enough to do around this big house," she yelled as I walked out of the kitchen.

When I climbed in the back of the limo, Kirsty was already waiting for me.

"We have a lot to go over today," she said.

"Can we start with a good morning?" I smiled.

"Why are you smiling? You never smile first thing in the morning. What's going on? James, why is she smiling?"

"I couldn't tell you, Kirsty."

"I can't smile? Is there a law that says Sierra isn't allowed to smile in the morning?" I asked in confusion.

"Have you been drinking already? Let me smell your breath," she said as she leaned closer to me.

"Get away from me and go back on your side. I have not been drinking."

While Kirsty rattled off the events of the day, I found myself thinking about Cameron. He was the reason for my morning smile. I didn't want to think about him, but I couldn't help it. *Damn him.* James pulled up to the curb of the building and opened the door for me. As I climbed out, my eyes took control and looked across the street. I didn't see him. In fact, I didn't see his truck. I walked into the building and went straight up to my office. As I passed by Sasha, she handed me a cup of coffee.

"Good morning, Sierra." She smiled.

"Not particularly," I growled and stepped into my office.

"I see you're back," Kirsty said as she followed behind.

"What are you talking about?" I sighed.

"Your smile's gone and you're back to your usual morning self." She smiled.

God, she was irritating me. "Kirsty, don't you have a meeting to plan or trips to book or something?"

"It's him. Isn't it?"

I walked over to the bar, opened a travel size bottle of Kahlua, and poured it in my coffee. "Is he what?" I asked.

"Builder boy. I saw you look across the street and the instant change on your face when you didn't see him or his truck."

"You saw nothing. Drop it."

"Fine. You'll talk when you're ready. By the way, Royce will be here soon for a meeting."

"Ah, shit! I forgot about him."

"I figured as much. Good thing you have me." She winked and left my office.

I sat down at my desk and turned my chair to face the window. I still didn't see his truck. This was unusual for him because he was there every morning.

"There's my pretty lady," Royce said as he walked in unannounced.

I turned my chair around and glared at him.

"Sasha wasn't at her desk," he said.

"Come on in, Royce. Have a seat. Can I get you some coffee?"

"That would be great." He smiled.

He did look quite handsome in his black Armani suit and the way he wore his jet black hair swept to the side. But that fucking cologne. I filled both cups with coffee and discreetly poured the rest of the Kahlua in mine.

"Here you go. Now, let's get this meeting over with. I have a lot of work to do today."

He held his cup up and flashed me a big smile. "I agree."

Royce's company was one of the tech companies we worked closely with for our digital advertising. He had a problem with commitment and the minute a woman suggested a relationship, he kicked her to the curb. He told me he had mommy issues. Most of these CEOs did. Shit, I had mommy issues. As soon as we wrapped up our meeting, he sat across the desk from me, leaned back in his chair, unbuttoned his suit coat, and smiled. I tilted my head and stared back. I knew what the fucker wanted. He got up from his chair and took off his jacket. As he walked over to me, he held out his hand and helped me from my chair. His lips caressed my neck as his hand grabbed my tit.

"You're so sexy. I really need to fuck you right now," he whispered as he took off his shirt and laid it across my desk.

His hand slipped up my skirt and his fingers pushed my panties to the side as they plunged inside me, causing me to gasp. He unbuttoned my shirt with his other hand and slid it off my shoulders. His teeth took down one of my bra straps, exposing my bare breast and his mouth engulfed my hard nipple. His fingers moved in and out of me and, instantly, my mind went to George.

"Ah," I moaned.

"Mhmm, you're so fucking wet, baby."

Suddenly, George was no longer in my mind and, in a flash, Cameron popped up. Before I could even think about anything else, Royce turned me around, pulled down my panties, lifted up my skirt, put on a condom and pushed himself deep inside me. All I envisioned was Cameron from behind. I could hear his moans each time he thrust in and out of me. His hands kneaded my tits and his fingers played with my nipples.

"You're coming, baby. I can feel you coming!" Royce exclaimed as he pushed deep inside me one last time and moaned with pleasure. "That was nice, baby. Thank you," he said as he pulled out and slapped my ass.

I opened my eyes and snapped back to reality. I sighed when I saw him walk to the bathroom. He was no George and he was certainly no Cameron. I grabbed some tissue from my desk, cleaned myself up, pulled up my panties, and pulled down my skirt. I sat down in my chair and there was a light knock on the door. As Royce walked out of the bathroom, buttoning his shirt, Cameron walked into my office. I froze. He looked at Royce and then at me.

"Hey, your secretary wasn't at her desk."

"Hi," I said in a panicked tone.

"I can come back if you're busy."

"No need. We're finished here. Thanks again, love." He smiled as he walked over and kissed my cheek. I'll call you soon."

Cameron looked at him and they nodded at each other before Royce walked out of the office. I could tell he was feeling uneasy.

"I just wanted to give you the drawings and the price for the remodel. Everything is here on these papers," he said as he put them on my desk and then began to walk away.

"Cameron, wait," I said as I got up from my desk. "He's just—"

"It's none of my business, Sierra. Don't worry about it."

"I didn't see your truck across the street this morning."

"I had to close out a couple of jobs so I could start on your place tomorrow."

"Are you moving in tomorrow?" I asked.

"Yeah. I don't have much, only a couple of bags, so I can be there in the morning, and then, as soon as I get settled, I'll start on your closet."

I smiled. "Thanks. I thank you and my shoes thank you too."

"I'll see you around," he said with a disappointed look and walked towards the door.

"Cameron," I called out.

"Yeah."

"Do you want my phone number in case you have any questions while you're working?"

"Sure. I guess I'll need that."

He pulled out his phone and, as I rattled off my number, he punched it in. I didn't dare ask him for his at that moment. I was humiliated and unsure of what he thought of me.

****

Cameron

I walked out of her office and I didn't know what to think. Seeing that guy walk out of the bathroom, practically naked, really pissed me off. I had no reason to be pissed, but she just confirmed my decision. A woman like her would never go for a guy like me. I was stupid as shit in the first place for even thinking it. She was way out of my league and now I saw it with my own eyes. She slept around with rich, high-powered men. Men who were on her level. Men who she had things in common with. She liked rich. I liked simple. Why did she have to be so damn beautiful? And that smile. Why did my face light up when she smiled at me? Fuck. I was going to focus on remodeling her home and that was it. She'd be gone at work all day and by time she got home, I'd make sure I was done for the night. That way, we wouldn't really have to see each other. Small conversations and that was it. Nothing more and nothing less. Why did I feel so bummed out?

Chapter 10

Sierra

I opened up the papers that Cameron left me. I looked at the designs and then the total price. I honestly thought it would have been more than what he charged me. I felt like a whore who just got caught by her mommy.

"Sasha, send Kirsty in here, please."

"Sure thing, Sierra."

"What can I do you for, ma'am?" she said as she walked in.

"First off, you can stop calling me 'ma'am.' Second, I feel like a whore."

"Why? Because you fucked Royce but have a thing for Cameron?"

"I don't have a thing for Cameron. How did you know I fucked Royce?"

She rolled her eyes. "Please. You always fuck Royce when he comes to the office."

"That's not entirely true," I said. "Anyway, Royce came out of the bathroom, buttoning his shirt, and Cameron walked into the office."

"So? You just said you don't have a thing for him, so who cares?"

I rolled my eyes at her and put my hand on my head. "I care because he's a nice guy and he shouldn't have seen that. I don't need the guy who's doing work on my house thinking I'm a slut."

"Then stop fucking guys in your office. It's simple. Now come on. We have to go."

"Go where?" I asked.

"Your mother's dinner party."

"No," I whined. "I don't want to deal with her. Especially not tonight."

"You don't have a choice, Sierra."

"Tell her I'm sick."

She walked over and grabbed me by the arm, pulling me up from my chair. She grabbed my phone, my briefcase, and my purse, and pushed me out of the office.

"You're a bitch," I said.

"Yeah, your bitch." She smiled.

We walked out of the building and before I climbed into the limo, I looked across the street and saw Cameron's truck.

"Get in the car, Sierra," Kirsty said as she looked up at me from inside the limo.

I climbed in and James shut the door. "What was all that about?" he asked.

"Sierra fucked Royce in her office and Builder Boy walked in while Royce was buttoning his shirt. Now she thinks Builder Boy thinks she's a slut."

"I see," James said. "He shouldn't think anything, actually. The two of you have a business relationship. It's none of his business who you're fucking and not fucking."

I didn't say a word the rest of the ride home. The only thought going through my head was how drunk I was getting tonight.

****

Kirsty and I stepped into the foyer of Delia's house and were immediately greeted by a hot waiter carrying a silver tray filled with glasses of wine. I politely smiled as I grabbed one from the tray and sipped my way through the house and to the living room where the party was taking place.

"Tell me exactly why she's having this party," I said to Kirsty.

"It's an art auction to raise money for women of domestic violence. The money raised will go to Haven Hills."

"Oh."

We entered the living room and, immediately, Ava ran over to me.

"Thank God you're here."

"Hey, sis. What's wrong?"

"Delia. That's what's wrong. She's been driving me nuts all day. You know how she gets when she decides to host a party."

Delia glanced my way and slithered her way over to me. "Sierra, darling. Thank you for coming. Hello, Kirsty."

"Hello, Mother," I replied. "Nice turn out."

"Yes, it is. I sure hope you're going to buy some art, since you can certainly afford it. It's for a good cause."

I looked at her and put on my fake smile. "I don't understand why you even have these things. You can certainly afford just to hand over a huge donation to the shelter. Why go through all this?" I deserved an Oscar for my performance.

"It's to make people aware, darling. Now if you'll excuse me, I think we're about to start."

"To make people aware, my ass. It's to make her look good," I said as I polished off my wine. I looked over at Ava, who was laughing at me. "Where does she keep the tequila? The really good, expensive kind?"

"Downstairs, locked in a cabinet. I don't know where Clive hides the key."

I motioned for Kirsty and Ava to follow me downstairs. I looked around the room to see if I could figure out where Clive was dumb enough to hide the key. My eyes darted to the corner where a tall, fake tree sat. I walked over to it and lifted the bottom. Hot damn, there was the key.

"How did you know that was under there?" Ava asked. "I never would have thought of that."

"I remember growing up that Delia would always hide shit under plants."

I took the key and inserted it into the cabinet. I took out the bottle of Rey Sol Anejo Tequila. It cost a mere four hundred dollars a bottle. I pulled off the cap and inhaled its sweet, savory scent. Now, if Royce was wearing this when I saw him, George might never have to come to mind. I grabbed a wine glass and poured some tequila in it.

"Would you like some?" I asked Kirsty.

"No. I'll stick with the wine."

I pointed my finger at Ava. "You don't ever drink this and you forget that key is under there. Understand?"

"Yes," she sighed.

We walked back upstairs. The auction was just starting. We took our seats in the back and patiently waited for the first painting to be auctioned off. I glanced over and almost had a heart attack when I saw Don walking towards me with a woman on his arm.

"Hello there, Sierra." He smiled as he sat down next to me.

"Go sit somewhere else," I whispered with a smile on my face.

"These were the only two seats left. Look around."

"That better be Milania you're with."

"It is." Don cleared his throat. "Milania, baby, I would like you to meet Sierra Adams. She's the CEO of Adams Advertising."

"It's nice to meet you." She smiled as she held out her hand.

Poor woman. She had no clue what a cheating whore her fiancé really was. Two paintings were auctioned off; the third was one I was very interested in. The bidding started at $1,000. I raised my hand and then Don outbid me. No big deal at first because it was for charity. We were up to $8,000 and he leaned over and whispered to me.

"Fuck me one last time and it's yours."

"It's mine regardless, and when I win it, I am going to shove it up your ass."

He looked at me and bid one last time. When I bid $10,000, I placed my hand on his and held it down while I dug my fingernails deep into his skin.

"Sold to Sierra Adams."

I let go of his hand and smiled. "Don't fuck with me or I'll spill the beans to your pretty little fiancée." I finished off the tequila and got up from my seat. I snagged one of the waiters and took a glass of wine from the tray. As I was drinking it, rather quickly, Delia came up to me.

"Thank you for your contribution, darling. It's a lovely painting."

"It is. Isn't it?" I slurred.

She shot me a look and walked away. Five glasses of wine later, and Kirsty had to help me to the limo. James met us halfway down the driveway and picked me up and carried me.

"In you go," he said as he put me inside. "Too much of a bad day for you, Sierra?"

"It was a bad day, James."

****

Cameron

I grabbed my bags and looked around the apartment to make sure I didn't forget anything. All looked good. I spent last evening cleaning up so I could get my deposit back. I also thought about Sierra; one time too many. I walked down to the rental office and handed in my keys. I wasn't sorry to be leaving because this place wasn't exactly what I would call home. It was old and not well kept, but it was the cheapest place I could find. I climbed in my truck and headed over to Sierra's house. Her guest house was bigger than my apartment, so I was looking forward to having more room. Plus, with her house being behind gates, I didn't have to worry about someone stealing my tools from my truck. I pulled up and rang the bell at the gate. Suddenly, I heard a voice.

"Who are you?" she asked in her accent.

"My name is Cameron and I'm staying in the guest house."

"Oh, you're the builder boy. I'll let you in."

I chuckled at her response. The gates opened and I pulled in the driveway. As soon as I got out of the truck, a woman came from the house.

"I'm Rosa, Sierra's maid. I'll show you to the guest house," she said as she looked me up and down. "You're cute. You have great muscles and you're tall. I like tall men."

"I'm Cameron Cole. It's nice to meet you, Rosa."

A car pulled in the driveway and Kirsty got out. As she stomped up the driveway, she looked at me and Rosa.

"Where's Sierra, Rosa? She's not answering her phone."

"She's not up yet. I tried to wake her, but she yelled at me to go away."

Kirsty rolled her eyes. "Oh, hi, Cameron."

"Hi, Kirsty." I waved. "Why won't she get up?" I asked.

"Let's just say that she drank too much last night at her mother's dinner party."

Rosa told Kirsty to go inside while she took me to the guest house. She opened the door and handed me the key.

"I hope you're not sloppy. I have enough to do around here without having to work extra hard and cleaning up your mess. Bed sheets are changed every Monday morning. I will be in here twice a week to dust, vacuum, clean the bathroom, and mop the floors. So don't leave anything lying around."

"Yes, ma'am." I smiled.

Rosa went back to the main house and I took my bags to the bedroom. So, Sierra drank too much last night. I got the impression she liked to drink. I bet she was really adorable when she was drunk. I shook my head to stop thinking like that and went to the main house. That was when I saw her coming down the stairs in a short, pink satin robe. Her hair was a mess and her eyes were tired. But, damn, if she didn't look amazing.

Chapter 11

Sierra

"Fuck me," were the words that flew out of my mouth as I stopped midway down the stairs and saw Cameron standing there.

"Excuse me?" He smiled.

Oh what the hell, I thought. This was me on most mornings after I drank, and with him going to be working on my house, I was sure this wasn't the last time he'd see me like this.

"Sorry. I look like shit. Get used to it and I need coffee."

He chuckled as I walked past him and he followed me into the kitchen.

"Coffee?" I asked.

"Sure."

"Rosa, two coffees."

She rolled her eyes at me as she took two cups from the cabinet. "No looks today, Rosa."

"Maybe you shouldn't have drank so much last night and then you wouldn't look like this," she said as she moved her hand up and down in front of me.

Again, Cameron chuckled. "Aren't you supposed to be at the office?" he asked.

"I took today off. I have work I can do at home, but I think I'm just going to relax by the pool today."

"Yeah, she just took the day off as of fifteen minutes ago. You just can't do that, Sierra. I have meetings scheduled," Kirsty said with irritation.

Rosa handed me my cup. "Listen, I'm the CEO. It's my company and I can take a damn day off. I'm hung over and just need to relax by the pool. Cancel the meetings. Reschedule them. I'm not going in today."

Kirsty sighed. "Fine. I'll be at the office if you need me."

As Kirsty walked out, I heard her yell from the hallway. "Your painting is here."

"Oh good. Tell them to bring it in the kitchen," I yelled.

A handsome-looking man walked into the kitchen with the painting I bought last night. "Are you Sierra Adams?" he asked as he looked me up and down.

"Yeah. That's me."

He had a smirk on his face. "Can you sign here, please," he said as he handed me the pen.

"What's that look for? Haven't you ever seen a woman hung over before?"

His eyes widened and Cameron looked at me. "Sorry, miss. I think you look good."

"That's better." I smiled as I handed him the pen and paper back. "Thank you for delivering this. Have a good day."

He walked out and Cameron began to laugh. "What?" I asked.

"You totally had him flustered."

"Well, then, he shouldn't have looked at me like that."

"You're right; he shouldn't have. But look at the way you're dressed. He couldn't help it."

I bit down on my bottom lip because I thought Cameron was telling me in a subtle way that I looked sexy. I took the wrapping off and revealed my painting.

"Do you like?" I asked as I looked at Cameron and Rosa.

"It's pretty. What is it?" he asked.

"The streets of Italy. See this café right here?" I asked as I pointed to the painting. "That's the last place my dad and I had breakfast together before he died."

Cameron looked down. "I'm sorry. It's a beautiful painting."

"How much did that cost you?" Rosa asked.

"Ten thousand."

"Ten thousand dollars for a painting! You're joking, right?" Cameron asked.

"No, I'm not. Not only was the painting special to me, but the money is going to Haven Hall for domestic violence."

"Oh. That's a good cause, but still."

I didn't expect him to understand. I was sure ten thousand dollars was a shit load of money to a guy like Cameron.

"Can you hang it for me?" I asked.

"Where do you want it?"

I walked over to the empty wall by the table. "Right here. That way, I can stare at it when I eat breakfast and think about my dad."

"You don't eat breakfast in here," Rosa said.

"Well, I'm going to start."

"You two need to scatter. I'm not used to having people in the house while I'm trying to clean. Now go. You're throwing off my mojo."

"I'll go get my tools and hang that painting for you. Then, I'll get started on your closet. Paolo should be here soon with the drywall."

"I'm going to get dressed. Just make sure it's centered," I said as I walked out of the kitchen and upstairs to take a shower.

****

Cameron

I went to my truck and grabbed my tool box. The thought that she paid ten thousand dollars for that painting still filled my mind. I walked back to the kitchen and Rosa poured me another cup of coffee.

"This is the last of it," she said.

"Thanks, Rosa." I smiled.

I was digging through my tool box, looking for the anchors and nails to hang the picture, when Rosa walked up behind me.

"Do you have a girlfriend?"

I turned my head and looked at her. "No."

"Hmm," she said. "Why not? You're a handsome, hardworking man."

"Thanks, Rosa." I laughed. "I just haven't found the right girl yet, I guess. Plus, I'm not staying here in California for long, so it would be silly of me to meet someone here, form a relationship, and then have to leave."

"Hmm. We will talk more later on. I have work to finish."

She was nice lady. The way she and Sierra went back and forth was funny. I hung the picture on the wall and took a step back to view it. That was when I heard her voice.

"Thank you. It looks great there," Sierra said.

I turned around and she was standing behind me in a sun dress. Her hair was still wet and wavy, and she had put on some light make-up.

"You're welcome. Are you done upstairs?"

"Yeah. Do you need to get started up there?"

"I want to get the plastic put down before Paolo gets here with the drywall," I replied.

"Rosa's up there, cleaning up my mess. So give her a few and then go up. I'll be doing some work by the pool if you need me."

There was a knock at the door and it was Paolo. "Hey, man." He smiled.

"Hey, Paolo. Did you get the drywall?"

I walked with him to his truck and we carried in the sheets of drywall. "Be careful; there's a lot of stairs," I said.

We made it up the stairs and into the bedroom. "Wow, look at this room," Paolo said.

"Wait until you see her closet." I laughed as I shook my head.

Paolo walked in and looked around. "Why are we expanding this? This is like another bedroom."

"She needs more shelves for her shoes."

"More shoes? My God, look at all the shoes she already has."

Just as Paolo said that, Sierra walked into the bedroom. "I'll tell you what I told Cameron. If you're going to walk the path of life, you might as well do it in style."

He walked out of the closet with a smile on his face. "I like the way you think."

"Thank you." She smiled back.

I introduced them and then Sierra walked back out. She just needed to get a rubber band for her hair.

"Wow, dude. She's really hot. Shit. I'd tap that ass. Out of my league or not."

"Don't talk like that and I don't want to talk about her. Let's get to work."

Chapter 12

Sierra

So much for my day. Instead of canceling my meetings, Kirsty turned them into phone conferences. I sat in the lounge chair by the pool with my phone on speaker. Cameron and Paolo had been working all day on my closet. Once I finished the last meeting, I got up and went into the kitchen for a bottle of water. Rosa was cooking dinner.

"Builder Boy doesn't have a girlfriend," she said with her back turned to me.

"So."

"I think he's a good man."

"You've known him for a few hours. He could be a serial killer, for all you know."

"Listen to your nonsense."

My phone rang and it was Delia calling. "Hello," I answered.

"Are you home, darling?"

"No, I'm not. I'm still at the office."

"Really? Because I was just at the office and they said you worked from home today."

Shit. "Just joking. Of course I'm home."

"Good. I'm on my way over. I have something to talk to you about."

F.U.C.K., I mouthed as I pounded my fist on my thigh. "Okay, Mother. See you soon."

Rosa stood there, staring at me with a wooden spoon in her hand. "Is she coming now?"

I nodded my head. Instantly, I had a headache.

Cameron and Paolo walked into the kitchen, as they were finished working for the day.

"It was nice to meet you, Sierra." Paolo smiled.

"It was nice to meet you too, Paolo."

Cameron smiled at me and then started to walk out the door to the guest house.

"Excuse me, but where are you going?" Rosa asked.

I wanted to burst into laughter.

"I'm done for the day. I was going to take a shower."

"When you're done, come back here. I cooked dinner for you."

"Oh, Rosa, thank you, but—"

Oh boy, here it comes. You don't turn down something Rosa did for you. Big mistake.

"Excuse me, young man? I slaved over this stove all day to cook a meal for you and you're going to refuse it?" she yelled as she shook the wooden spoon at him.

He looked at me and I shrugged my shoulders.

"No, Rosa. I swear, I'm not refusing it. It smells delicious. Just let me go shower and clean up real quick and I'll be back."

"Okay. Hurry up," she spoke calmly.

I was dying and bursting with laughter on the inside. "Good job, Rosa. You probably just scared my builder off and now my house will never get done."

"Nonsense. Did you want to be alone with Delia?"

"Have I told you that I love you?" I smiled.

"You can thank me in my next check." She smiled as she handed me a glass of tequila.

I took a couple sips when I heard the doorbell ring. Delia had already opened the door and let herself in before I got there. My stomach tied itself in knots.

"Hello, darling," she said as she kissed both of my cheeks. "Did your painting arrive?"

"Yes. I hung it in the kitchen," I replied as she followed behind.

She stood there and looked at it with her finger on her chin. "Do you think that's the best place for it?" she asked.

I rolled my eyes. "Yes I do." I didn't want to tell her the meaning behind the painting. She wouldn't understand and she'd just make some rude comment about my father.

She said hello to Rosa and walked over to the stove to see what she was cooking. A few moments later, Cameron walked through the patio door. He looked at Delia and smiled.

"Sierra, who's this man that just walked into your house?"

Here we go. I sort of felt bad for Cameron, having to be subjected to the likes of Delia. I walked over to him and hooked my arm in his. He looked at me strangely.

"Mother, this is Cameron. He's the escort I rented for the week. He'll be staying in the guest house. He's here to fulfill my needs."

The horrified look on her face was priceless. Rosa was holding back the laughter and Cameron's eyes grew wide as he looked over at me.

"Oh. I see. It's nice to meet you, Cameron. I'm Delia, Sierra's mother."

She looked at me with that stuck-up look she always had on her face. "I didn't know you did things like that."

"There's a lot of things you don't know I do." I winked and then took a drink of my tequila.

Cameron was at a loss for words, but I think he got the hint when I squeezed his arm.

"We're just about to sit down for dinner. Would you care to join us?" I asked.

She cleared her throat and sat down at the table. "No, thank you. I'm going to make this quick, since you're obviously busy." She glared at Cameron. "I have my doubts that Ava is going to make it into the final round for Miss Teenage

California. She isn't focusing and I think it's because of a boy."

I reached my hand across the table and touched her arm. "Oh my God, a boy! No way!"

"This is no time for jokes, Sierra. I'm serious. I want you to have a talk with her. Tell her that boys are no good and they just will get sick of you and throw you away, like Ryan did to you. You have experience. Share it will her."

Ouch. That really stung. Cameron looked at me and then looked down. I picked up my glass of tequila and finished it off. Rosa turned her head and looked at me with sadness in her eyes. She walked over and grabbed my glass from the table and refilled it. I was at a loss for words because what my mother said stabbed me so deep in the heart that I felt it ache all over again.

"I'll talk to her," I said as I took another drink.

"Thank you. I knew I could count on you. Now, I must go. I'll speak to you later darling. Ta ta, Rosa. It was nice meeting you, Cameron, I think."

She left and Rosa set our plates of food on the table. There was complete silence in the kitchen. I couldn't even bring myself to look at him. I was humiliated. Suddenly, Rosa spoke up.

"Go on; eat your pasta. I'm going to go home now. I'll see you both in the morning. Sierra, don't give what that woman said a second thought. Brush it off, girl. You know how she is."

I forced a small smile as Rosa left. "Now you know why I drink," I said as I held up my glass.

"Water?" Cameron asked in confusion.

I handed him the glass and he sniffed it. "Oh, that's not water."

"I've had to live with that shit all my life."

I realized what I'd just said and stopped. I wasn't about to revisit my past with Delia and I certainly wasn't going to share it with Cameron.

"I'm sorry, Sierra," he said.

"You have no reason to be sorry and I don't want to talk about it anymore. You better eat your dinner before it gets cold. Do you drink alcohol?"

"Yeah." He laughed.

"Let me guess. You're a beer kind of guy."

"A majority of the time, yes. But I do like my hard liquor too."

"Like?"

"Vodka." He smiled.

"Grey Goose?"

"Yep. Grey Goose is great."

I got up from the table and walked over to the cabinet next to the sink. I took out a bottle of Grey Goose and a small glass. I held both up as I walked back over to the table. He flashed me his bright smile and I swear to God I started dripping, and not from my armpits. I poured some vodka in the glass and handed it to him.

"Cheers." I smiled as held up my glass and threw back the tequila.

We started eating the dinner Rosa made for us. Cameron sat across from me and he seemed to really enjoy Rosa's pasta.

"This is so good. I haven't had a home-cooked meal in a very long time."

"You'll get one every night now. Rosa is a superior cook."

He looked across the table at me and smiled. "Can I ask you something?"

"Sure," I said as I put the fork down and wiped my mouth.

"Why did you tell your mom that you hired me as an escort?"

I laughed as I took a sip of my tequila. "Delia and I have a different kind of relationship. I don't like to tell her too much about my life because she likes to put me down."

"Why would she do that?"

"Because she's Delia and she couldn't mold me into the perfect little princess she wanted me to be. It's exactly what she's doing with Ava right now. When my parents got divorced, I lived with my father for two weeks out of the month. He threw me into the corporate world and taught me everything I needed to know. I guess you could say that he molded me into what he wanted me to be and my mother resented him for that. So, when Delia asks me things that are none of her business, I tell her things to shock her."

"I think you really did shock her with the escort introduction." He chuckled. "The look on her face was kind of funny."

"She'll figure it out soon enough why you're really here."

****

Cameron

Dinner was great and, when we finished eating, I asked Sierra if she wanted to go sit on the patio.

"I thought maybe since I'm going to be living here for a while and working on your house all day, maybe we should know a little bit about each other."

"Okay," she said as she grabbed the bottle of tequila, vodka and both our glasses. "Let's go."

I followed her outside and we sat down in the oversized, cushy lounge chairs. "The view is really beautiful, Sierra. I can see why you bought this place."

"Sunset is my favorite time of the day. I like to come out here and watch it set over the hills. So, Mr. Cole, tell me about you. You already know about my crazy mother."

I laughed as I took a drink from my glass. "Well, you know I'm from North Carolina. My dad started the company when he was twenty years old with a hundred dollars in his pocket and a hammer. Now that he's retired, he and my mom opened up a small fruit market down the road from the house. Did I mention that I have five brothers and sisters?"

Sierra nearly choked as she sipped the tequila from the cup. "What?! There are six of you?"

I couldn't help but laugh because she was so cute in the way she said that. "Yep. There's Austin who's eighteen, Jolene, who's twenty, Mark, who's twenty-two, Kelly who's twenty-four, Jaden who's twenty-six, and then me, who will turn the big three-O in a couple of weeks."

"Really? When's your birthday?" she asked.

"July eighteenth" I replied.

She looked at me and cocked her head. "My birthday is July eighteenth and I'll be the dreaded three-O too."

"No way!" I said.

"Yes way!" She laughed. "Wow. Look at that; we have something in common."

"We sure do." I smiled.

I couldn't help but stare at her. Shit. The more we talked, the more I liked her. I didn't want any of this. I couldn't fall for her because I wasn't staying in Los Angeles. From what I gathered by the bits that Delia and Kirsty said, her heart was broken pretty badly and I would never want to hurt her. Los Angeles wasn't my home and, to be honest, I didn't know if it ever could be.

"Are any of your brothers in the building business?" she asked.

"Nah. Austin works for my parents while he goes to school. Mark is a bartender at a bar in town, and Jaden just passed his bar exam. Jolene is still in college. She's studying architectural history and Kelly is a hairdresser who's happily married with a baby."

"I take it you're all really close?"

"Yeah. We're a very close family." I smiled.

"And you like to build things, right?" she asked.

"I do. It all started with Legos when I was a kid."

She laughed and smiled.

"I don't mean to get too personal, but do you have a girlfriend back home?"

"Nope. No girlfriend." I wondered why she was asking. Was she curious for a reason? I decided to throw her question back at her.

"The guy from your office; is he your boyfriend?"

She poured some tequila in her glass and sipped it before answering my question. She wouldn't look at me when she finally decided to answer it.

"No. He's not my boyfriend. He's just a friend. Listen; it's getting pretty late and I have to be up early for work, so I'm going to head up to bed."

"Oh, shit. I forgot to tell you. Is there another room you can sleep in? I still have all the plastic covering everything. Tomorrow, Paolo and I are going to get the wall painted and then, as soon as it dries, I can put up the shelves. Then you'll be able to display all your stylish shoes." I smiled.

"Sure. I can stay in the guest room." She smiled back as she got up. "Sleep well in your new bed, Mr. Cole. I'll see you in the morning," she said as she walked into the house.

I would sleep well if she was in my bed, lying next to me. The thoughts I didn't want to have kept filling my head. How her lips would taste when I pressed mine against them. How soft her skin would be when mine was touching hers. How soft her hair would be while I ran my fingers through it. How beautiful and soft her breasts were and how good it would feel to be inside her. How good would it feel to make love to her all night long and wake up with her body wrapped around mine.

Chapter 13

Sierra

"Holy shit!" I yelled as I rolled over and curled up into a ball. Cramps. Fucking holy hell of all cramps. I picked up my phone from the nightstand and called Rosa. She should be here by now. She was always here at six a.m.

"Why are you calling me from your phone, *senorita*?"

"Pills, Rosa. I need cramp pills. I can't move."

"I'll be right up."

These damn cramps had been getting worse by the month. Every time Kirsty made me a doctor's appointment, I canceled. Why? Because they started to feel better and then I was over it. But today; today was the worst yet. I sent Kirsty a text message.

"Call Dr. Hollis and get me in today. I'm dying."

"You're not dying and if you would have kept your previous doctor appointments, you wouldn't be in so much pain."

"I swear I'm firing you."

"See you soon," she replied.

Rosa walked in the room and handed me two ibuprofen pills and a glass of water. I smelled it first just to make sure she wasn't trying to be funny. I popped the pills in my mouth, washed them down with water, and then curled back up in a ball.

"Thanks, Rosa," I said as I put the pillow over my head.

"You get up now and get ready for work. I'll make you a bagel."

I pulled my hand out from under the covers and motioned at her to go away. She didn't shut the door and, a few moments later, I heard footsteps in the room.

"Rosa, I told you to go away."

"Umm. Good morning," Cameron said.

Shit.

"Are you not going in to work again?" he asked.

"I'm going."

"Are you okay?"

"No, I'm not okay. What's with the thousand questions?" I snapped as I threw the pillow across the room and looked at him in my morning mess. "I have cramps. Really, really bad cramps. Cramps so debilitating that I can't move."

"Oh. Sorry about that. Do you have any chamomile tea?"

I looked at him in irritation. "I don't think so. Who the hell drinks chamomile tea?"

"My sisters used to get horrible cramps and they would drink a cup of tea and they said it really helped."

"Really?"

"Yeah, really." he smiled.

I picked up my phone and dialed Kirsty.

"I'm almost there," she answered.

"I need you to stop and get me chamomile tea."

"For what?"

"Don't question. Just pick some up, please, and hurry!"

"Okay. Okay. I'll be there soon." *Click.*

I pulled the covers over my head. "Okay, you can go now. I don't need you seeing me like this."

Next thing I knew, he pulled the covers down and, when I looked at him, he had a wide smile across his face.

"I don't mind seeing you like this. I think you're kind of cute." He winked and then got up from the bed.

I watched him walk out of the room and I lay there as my panties became moist. Shit. The ibuprofen started to take the edge off the pain, so I crawled out of bed. I walked down the hall to my bedroom. I stepped inside my closet and screamed when I saw Cameron standing there.

"Jesus Christ, you scared me," I squawked.

"You knew I was finishing your closet today."

"I didn't expect you to be creeping out in here."

"Creeping out? What the hell does that mean?"

"Listen, I have to get my clothes. Can you please leave until I shower and get dressed?"

"Yes, boss," he said with an attitude as he walked away.

I rolled my eyes and stepped into the shower. As the hot water streamed down my body, I thought about Cameron and how sweet he was when he was telling me about the tea. But then his attitude when he scared the shit out of me. Like it was my fault. Fuck him. I was in no mood. I got out of the shower and got dressed. I threw some mousse in my hair and let it air dry into waves while I applied my makeup. After putting on my Chanel suit and jewelry, I walked downstairs, only to find James, Cameron, and Kirsty sitting at the table, eating breakfast.

"I made your tea," Rosa said as she handed me the cup.

"Good morning, Sierra," James said.

"Morning."

I took my cup and sat down at the table next to James. Kirsty pulled out her iPad and began to rattle off the events of the day.

"You have back-to-back meetings all day. How the hell am I going to squeeze in a doctor's appointment?" she said as she looked up from her iPad.

"I don't know. Just do it."

"Are you feeling better?" James asked.

"Yeah, I am. Thanks to Cameron for suggesting this tea."

He glanced up from his plate and gave me a small smile. He finished the last of his eggs, took his plate to the sink, and walked upstairs without saying a word.

"What did you do to him?" Kirsty said through gritted teeth.

"I didn't do anything to him!"

"The *senorita* yelled at him," Rosa said.

"I did not."

"You did. I heard you. I was coming up the stairs and I heard you yell at him."

James looked at me and grabbed my hand. "Go apologize, Sierra."

I sighed and left the kitchen. I went to my room and pushed the door open. "Hey, Cameron."

"Yeah," he said without even turning around.

I walked over to where he was standing by the wall. "I'm sorry about earlier. I didn't mean to give you an attitude. I'm on edge, you know, with the cramps and hormones out of whack. I'm a terrible PMS'er."

"Don't worry about it. I get it."

I turned around, and as I started to walk out of the room, I heard him say, "Have a good day, Sierra."

"You too," I replied.

****

"How long have you been having cramps like that?" Dr. Hollis asked as I lay on the table against the scratchy paper wrap with my feet in the stirrups.

"For a couple of years, but they seem to be getting worse."

"Have you ever been on the pill?" he asked as his face stared up my vagina.

"No."

"What do you use for contraception?"

"The sponge and condoms."

He pulled the speculum out of me and I let out a deep breath. I was all for having something up there, but not that thing. This was one doctor's appointment I always tried to avoid. He removed his rubber gloves and washed his hands.

"I'm going to write you a prescription for birth control pills. They'll help the cramps. But if you continue to have them this bad while on the pill, you are to make another appointment. There could be something else going on."

"Like what?"

"You could have some endometriosis, ovarian cysts. The list could go on and on. But, let's try this first. I know how busy you are and you're not exactly good about coming in for regular visits." He smiled as he handed me the script.

"Thank you, Dr. Hollis. I'll give these a try and if things don't get better, I'll come back."

"Sounds good. Take care, Sierra."

He left the room and I got dressed. James was waiting for me out in the waiting room. Yeah, I made my driver come into the office with me.

"Well, what did he say?" James asked as we walked out of the office.

"He put me on the pill. He said it should help. Now, how fast can you get me to the office? Kirsty has been blowing up my phone. I have a meeting in fifteen minutes."

"I'll do my best, but traffic sucks this time of the day," he said.

****

Cameron

Paolo and I stood back and looked at the wall. We had just put the last coat of paint on it and I was getting hungry.

"As soon as it dries, I'll put up the shelves."

"Do you need me to help you?" Paolo asked.

"Nah. I need you to get to the Ross job and help Malcolm put down the tile on her bathroom floor. I can put up the shelves myself. But first, let's go grab some lunch. I'm starving."

We walked downstairs and Rosa was in the kitchen.

"Where are you two going?" she asked.

"We'll be back. We're going to grab some lunch."

"Oh no," she said. "I'll make you lunch right now."

"No, Rosa. I don't want you to go to any trouble."

She stood there with her hand on her hip. "Are you refusing my food again?"

"No. I know you're busy." I smiled.

"The two of you sit down right now," she said as she pushed us over to the table. "I'll make you some sandwiches. It'll only take a few minutes."

Paolo looked at me and smiled. "Shit, man. I could get so used to this," he whispered.

After we ate the nice lunch Rosa made, Paolo left and I went to clean up Sierra's bedroom. I picked up the picture she had sitting on her nightstand of her and who I assumed was her father. As I looked closer, I noticed it was taken right outside the café that was in the painting she just bought. She looked beautiful. There was a happiness about her in that picture that I had yet to see.

I was going over a few things in the guest house when I heard a knock on the door. I opened it and Rosa stood there with a dish in her hand.

"Here's dinner for you. I'm leaving to go home now."

"Rosa, you're too kind. You really are." I smiled.

"It's no trouble. You're a part of this household now and I'm here to make sure you're taken care of, just like Sierra. So, eat up and enjoy. I'll see you in the morning."

"She's not home yet from the office?" I asked.

"No, not yet. Have a good night, Cameron." She smiled.

"Thank you for dinner, Rosa."

She put up her hand and waved at me as she walked back into the house. I set the dish on the table and took off the foil that was covering the top. It looked delicious and I couldn't wait to dig in.

After I ate, I put on my pajama bottoms and sat down on the couch to relax and watch some TV before going to bed. I had put up the shelves in Sierra's closet and, now that one project was done, tomorrow I would start on one of the bathrooms. I saw the light go on in the backyard, so I got up and walked over to the window. I looked at my watch. It was midnight. What the hell was Sierra doing? I watched her as she took off the little sundress she was wearing. I gasped when she stood there, naked, and jumped into the pool. Instantly, I became hard. I sometimes pictured what she would look like completely naked and now I saw. She was even more perfect than I had imagined. Her curves were amazing, as were her perfectly round, large breasts. I felt like a fucking stalker for staring at her in the pool. But I couldn't help it. As hard as I tried not to think about her, I couldn't stop. Sierra Adams was way out of my league, but maybe, just maybe, I could show her that there was more to life than money and Los Angeles. After she swam for a while and I stood there and watched her, I noticed her looking around.

"Shit," I heard her say.

I didn't see her bring out a towel, so I decided to yell from the window.

"Do you need a towel?" I smiled.

She jumped and ducked down so the water came up to her neck.

"Cameron, what the hell!" she yelled.

"Do you need a towel?" I asked again.

"YES!"

I laughed as I grabbed a beach towel from the closet and walked over to the pool.

"This is not funny!" she exclaimed.

"Do you always go skinny dipping at midnight?"

"TURN AROUND!" she said as she grabbed the towel from my hand.

I smiled at her and turned around so she could get out of the pool and cover herself up. "Well? Answer the question."

"Sometimes I do. I thought you were asleep. I didn't see any lights on."

"I was watching TV and I saw the light go on out here, so I peeked out my window and saw you in the pool."

"Did you see anything?" she asked.

"No," I lied.

I didn't want to embarrass her. I could tell she was embarrassed enough.

"Are you sure?" she asked with narrow eyes.

"I swear, Sierra. I saw nothing. I just saw you in the pool and noticed you didn't have a towel. Did you just get home from the office?"

"Yeah. I had a lot of work to do and a lot of problems to deal with. Now, if you'll excuse me, I'm going to bed."

"Me too." I smiled with the thought of her naked body in my head. "Night, Sierra."

"Night, Cameron. Thank you for the towel."

Chapter 14

Sierra

I got out of bed extra early so I could arrange all my pretty shoes on my shelves. Ah, hell, I was up all night, anyway, thinking about Cameron and the pool incident. I texted Kirsty when I woke up and told her about what happened. She didn't text me back, which I thought was odd.

"Hello? Are you in that monstrosity of a closet?" Kirsty yelled.

"Yes," I yelled back.

"Oh wow, look at all those pretty shoes. Cameron did a great job with the wall," she said as she handed me a coffee from Tim Hortons.

"Yeah, he did. My shoes are really happy now that they aren't shoved in those little boxes anymore. Thank you for the coffee."

"Speaking of Cameron, what was up with that text message?"

"I took a little dip in the pool last night around midnight and I forgot to bring out a towel and he asked me through the window of the guest house if I needed one."

"So? That was nice of him."

"My point is, Kirsty, that I think he saw me naked."

"And?"

"What do you mean 'and'?"

"You let your suits see you naked all the time. Why is Cameron different?"

My shoulders dropped and I just stood there and stared at her.

"Yeah, that's what I thought. You don't have an answer. You should be happy if he *did* see you naked. With that body of yours, you probably got him all hot and bothered enough to where he went and jacked off."

"OH MY GOD! I can't believe you just said that."

"Relax, Sierra. I'm hungry. Do you think Rosa fixed breakfast yet?" she asked as she left me standing in my closet.

I shook my head and walked downstairs. Before I entered the kitchen, I peeked around the corner to make sure Cameron wasn't in there. I didn't want to see him after last night. The more I thought about it, I knew he saw me naked. I quietly opened the front door and climbed into the limo.

"Where are you? I'm ready to leave," I texted James.

"On my way, but you never leave this early. What's going on?"

"Just hurry up and get here!"

I sent a text message to Kirsty.

"Get your ass in the limo NOW!"

"But Rosa is making me breakfast."

"We'll stop at a drive thru. GET OUT HERE!"

The door opened and Kirsty climbed inside. James pulled up and opened the door.

"What the hell is going on, Sierra?" he asked as he got behind the wheel.

"I don't want to see Cameron. Let's go!"

"Sierra thinks Cameron saw her naked last night because she went skinny dipping and he brought her out a towel."

"So. You don't seem to care if guys see you naked."

"Right? That's exactly what I said," Kirsty replied.

"I hate you both. Now drive."

****

Later that day, I received a call from Delia.

"Hello," I answered hesitantly.

"Sierra, have you talked to Ava yet?"

Shit. "No, I was going to have James pick her up later and bring her over to my house. I'll talk to her over dinner."

"Very well." *Click.*

I rolled my eyes and sighed as I sent a message to James.

"I need you to pick up Ava before picking me up at the office."

"All right. Does she know I'm coming?"

"Yes."

Actually, she didn't know, but I was going to tell her now and I dialed her number.

"Hello," she answered.

"Hey, Ava. James is going to pick you up in a while and then we're going to hang out at my house, have some dinner, and talk."

"Let me guess. Delia?"

"Yeah, but we haven't really had a chance to talk in a while, so I think it'll be good for us. I'll tell Rosa to order us pizza and salad."

"Okay!" she said with excitement.

****

We could smell the pizza from the driveway. As I said goodbye to James and Kirsty, Ava and I walked into the house and followed the smell to the kitchen.

"Hey," Cameron said.

"Ava, this is Cameron. Cameron, this is my sister, Ava."

"It's nice to meet you, Ava." Cameron smiled as he held out his hand.

"Is this the escort?" she asked.

"How did you know about that?" I asked with a smile.

"I overheard Mom telling my dad about it."

"Cameron is my builder/remodeler. He's redoing some things in the house."

"I figured." She smiled.

"Don't tell Delia, though. Let her think the worst." I winked.

Rosa put the salad in a bowl and set it on the table. We helped ourselves to the pizza, and when we sat down to eat, I started my talk with Ava.

"So tell me about this boy you like."

"He's so amazing, Sierra. I can't wait for you to meet him."

"How old is he?" I asked.

"Sixteen."

Cameron sat there, listening as he ate his pizza. I wasn't sure if he should be present during our talk, but Ava wanted him to stay.

"You're so young, Ava. It's okay to like this boy, but just don't let him deter you from what's going on in your life. Don't give up anything for him."

"I'm not," she said.

"Delia seems to think you are. She doesn't think you're working as hard as you should be."

She shrugged her shoulders as she took a bite of her pizza. "Boys complicate things. They come into your life, make promises, break your heart, and then leave without giving you or your feelings a second thought. You're too young to have to go through that and I don't want to see you get hurt. Listen; just do me a favor. Focus on your competitions first and then on this boy. Because if you don't, Delia will never stop. Deal?" I asked as I held out my hand.

"Deal," she said as we shook hands.

Cameron went back to his house while Ava and I ate some ice cream and continued our girl talk. After James took Ava home, I poured a glass of wine and took it outside on the patio. I curled up on the lounge chair and read a text message I received earlier from Chris. As Kirsty would say, another one of my suits.

"Hey, babe. It's been a while since we went out for drinks. Why don't you give me a call and we'll set something up. I'd like to see you again."

****

Cameron

It was such a beautiful night out that I decided to go for a swim. I grabbed a towel and when I walked out the door, I saw Sierra sitting in the lounge chair, looking at her phone.

"No tequila tonight?" I smiled.

She looked at her glass and then at me. "No, I decided to be bold and go with the red liquid tonight."

"Ah, that is very bold of you," I said. "If you don't mind, I was going to go for a swim."

"Sure, go ahead. Swim away."

I did a few laps and then got out, dried myself off, and sat down in the chair next to Sierra.

"My shoes thank you." She smiled.

"Well, you can tell them that I said welcome and that I was happy to accommodate them."

Sierra took a sip of her wine. "I will."

"Ava seems like a nice girl," I said.

"She is. She just needs to be a kid and not be pushed into growing up so fast."

"You know, not all boys are like you described to her," I said.

"I wouldn't be so sure of that. All men are cut from the same cloth. Have you ever broken a girl's heart?"

"Once. But I didn't disregard her feelings. I talked to her and explained to her why it wouldn't work. She eventually understood. Have you ever broken a man's heart?"

She flashed me her beautiful smile. "No. It was always the other way around. I have a habit of turning men gay."

"What?" I chuckled.

"You laugh, but it's true. I caught two of my ex-boyfriends in bed with another man. That was years ago, but I'll never forget."

"You do realize that it had nothing to do with you, right?" I asked in all seriousness.

"Yeah, I know. But still it hurt."

"What about that Ryan guy?" I asked.

She finished off her glass of wine and looked straight ahead at the beautiful view of the hills. "Nah, he just left me for some whore he met on the internet. Told me he was going on a business trip for work, called me a few days later, and told me that he wasn't coming back. I guess the seven years we spent together didn't mean a fucking thing."

The sadness in her voice became more real to me than before.

"That's the reason I don't get into relationships. Royce, the guy you saw in my office, he's casual sex. No strings, no dating, no commitment. Just sex. In fact, all the suits I date are that way. When you're in the corporate world, you have two types of relationships: the no-strings relationship and the mistress-type of relationship. I prefer the no-strings. I won't date a guy who's in a relationship. I wouldn't do that to another woman. No strings, no hurt."

I sat there and took in everything she said. Was she saying these things to let me know that she wasn't interested? I knew she was interested in me. I could tell by the way she looked at me and I wanted to get to know her better. If she thought she was going to scare me off by saying those things about her suits and relationships, she was wrong; dead wrong. I'd thought about Sierra every day since I first saw her standing in line at Starbucks. She was the last thing on my mind before I fell asleep every night and she was the first thing on my mind when I woke up. I was conflicted because I didn't know how to approach her and tell her that I wanted to take her out. I didn't know how to tell her that I was desperate to kiss her beautiful lips and I didn't know how to tell her that I wanted to hold her hand in mine. But then again, I was also scared because I had no plans of staying in Los Angeles.

Chapter 15

Sierra

I was sitting at my desk when Kirsty came busting through the door.

"What are you doing for your birthday? Wait; don't answer that. I'll tell you what you're doing for your birthday. We are celebrating it at Lure and you can't say no because I already booked it and I had to give a large, non-refundable deposit. The only thing is, since your birthday is on a Sunday, we're doing it on Friday night. Saturday was already booked," she pouted.

"Really? You really want to do this for me?"

"Of course I do." She smiled. "You're my bestie and it's a big birthday for you. So we're doing it and that's all there is to it."

I sighed. She knew damn well I hated big parties like that, but it meant a lot to her to put this together for me, so I agreed.

"Fine."

"Yay!" she exclaimed as she jumped up and down. "You're going to have so much fun!"

I rolled my eyes at her enthusiasm and then told her about Cameron.

"Did you know that Cameron's birthday is the same day as mine and he's also going to be thirty?"

"Shut the fuck up! Are you serious? Wow. What a coincidence, Sierra. I'm inviting him so we can celebrate his birthday too."

"I doubt he'll come. He doesn't seem like the type of guy who gets into those things."

"He'll come. Trust me." She smiled as she walked out the door. A few moments later, she popped her head back in. "Oh, by the way, I signed us up for ballroom dance lessons. James is going to be my partner, so you better find one fast. Lessons start tomorrow."

"What?! I'm not taking ballroom dancing lessons. What the hell is the matter with you?"

"I figured you'd react that way. You really have no choice. Areulia and Co. are looking for a new advertising agency. They're one of the biggest ballroom dance companies in the world. This account means millions. So you're going to brush up on your ballroom dancing skills and know what the hell you're talking about when you meet with them in a month. Word on the street is that they only are interested in those who are as passionate about ballroom dancing as they are."

"So why the hell are *you* taking lessons? Why can't James be my partner?"

"Because I want to dance with him." She winked. "Find someone. Ask one of your suits or, better yet, get Builder Boy to join us."

"I'm firing you!" I yelled as I threw my stress reliever ball at the door.

The day was a big clusterfuck, as usual. I left the office around ten p.m. and, when I got home, I headed straight to the kitchen and pulled out the bottle of tequila and did a shot. I looked out the window at the guesthouse and all the lights were off. *He sure goes to bed early*, I thought to myself. I was startled when Cameron walked into the kitchen, wiping his hands on a cloth.

"Whatcha looking at?"

I put my hand over my heart, as it felt like it was going to jump out of my throat. "My God, you scared me."

"Sorry." He smiled.

"Why are you still here?"

"Why are you just getting home?" he asked.

"Excuse me?" I said.

"I'm still here for the same reason you're just getting home. There were more problems with the tear out in your bathroom than anticipated, so I didn't want to get behind."

"How is that the same reason as mine?"

"Were you at the office?" he asked.

"Yes. It was a big clusterfuck of a day."

"See. Same reason. Your bathroom is one big clusterfuck." He smiled.

I couldn't help but laugh. "Okay. I don't want to know what kind of clusterfuck it is; just rebuild it. Would you like some tequila, since we both had such clusterfucks of a day?" I asked.

"I would love some. Thank you."

I took another glass from the cupboard, poured some tequila in, and handed it to him. "Cheers." I smiled as I held up my glass.

He threw it back and shook his head. "Whew, it's been a while since I had tequila."

"So what are you doing tomorrow night?" I asked.

"Nothing that I know of. Why?"

I put my glass down and shimmied over to him, dancing around him with my arms up in the air.

"Because you're coming with me to take a ballroom dancing class." I smiled.

His head turned from side to side as I danced around him. "Yeah, right. I don't dance."

"But it will be so much fun!" I whined as I continued dancing around him.

"Will you stop that?" he asked.

"Stop what? Dancing around you?"

"Yes. You're driving me nuts." He chuckled.

"Then say yes and I'll stop."

"No, Sierra. I'm not taking ballroom dancing lessons with you."

"I promise to show you my titties if you do." I smiled as I bit down on my bottom lip.

"I already saw them."

I stopped dancing and looked at him. "What do you mean, you already saw them?"

"That night you went skinny dipping. I saw you take your dress off before you dove into the pool."

"I KNEW IT!" I exclaimed as I pointed my finger at him. "You asshole! You lied to me."

"Just a teeny one. I didn't want to embarrass you. If it makes you feel any better, I think you have perfect titties and a perfect body."

"Really?" I asked.

"Yeah, really." He smiled shyly.

"Well, then, it's settled. You'll be attending dancing lessons with me tomorrow night, since you were a perv and you stared at my naked body without me knowing. That classifies you as a peeping Tom."

"I am not a peeping Tom. You can't say that!" he said.

"Hmm. Let's see." I took my phone from the counter and googled "peeping Tom." "Here's the definition: a person who gets sexual pleasure from secretly watching people undressing or engaging in sexual activity. Did you get aroused when you watched me take off my dress and saw my naked body? Well, did you?"

He stood there and looked at me with a smirk on his face. "I am a man, after all, Sierra."

Shit. What Kirsty said was probably true. He probably did jack off that night after seeing me. I wasn't about to ask him.

But he was going to take dancing lessons with me as a punishment.

"Now you shall be punished, Mr. Cole, and your punishment is taking dancing lessons with me."

"Fine. You're right. I shouldn't have stood there and watched you, but you're too damn beautiful not to."

My stomach tied itself in knots and my heart began racing. He just told me that I was too damn beautiful. How was I supposed to react to that? I needed to stay calm and cool, but I really wanted to jump on him and kiss him passionately.

"Thank you for the compliment."

"You're welcome. By the way, why are you taking those lessons?"

I poured us another shot of tequila. "I have a potential client who's one of the biggest ballroom dancing companies in the world. They're looking for a new ad agency, so Kirsty did some research and said that word on the street is they're only interested in those that share the same passion as they do."

"I can understand that. Tomorrow night, you said?"

"Yes. Kirsty and James are taking lessons as well. Kirsty is trying to get into his pants."

Cameron laughed. "So does that mean you're trying to get into mine?" He winked.

"Maybe." I winked back with a smile. "I'm going to bed. I'll see you in the morning," I said as I walked away. He grabbed my hand and pulled me into him.

"Let's see first if we have the chemistry to dance together. Because if we don't, it's not going to work."

I smiled as I put my other hand on his shoulder and we moved back and forth. We stared into each other's eyes as we swayed to nothing but silence. My heart began picking up the pace again and my stomach was still tied in knots. The only difference this time was that I was getting wetter by the second.

"I thought you didn't dance," I said.

"I don't. But the reason is because I haven't had anyone to dance with in a long time." He smiled.

That was it. That damn fucking smile that brightened my life and made my panties wet every day was too much at that moment. I needed to kiss him. I bit down on my bottom lip to prevent myself from smashing my mouth against his. He removed his hand from my hip and pushed a strand of my hair behind my ear.

"You truly are beautiful," he said as he leaned his face closer to mine.

Oh hell. Fuck it. I leaned my face closer to his as our lips softly met each other and introduced themselves. Our soft kiss became more passionate. He broke his lips from mine and looked at me while he slowly shook his head. I wanted him and I wanted him bad. I smiled at him as a signal that it was okay to keep going. He smiled back and pressed his lips against mine, creating such a force that I almost had an orgasm. His fingers took hold of my cami as he lifted it over my head. I reached down and unbuttoned his jeans and shoved my hands down the back of his pants, grabbing his fine ass. He gasped as he unhooked my bra and threw it on the floor.

He sat me up on the counter and spread my legs as his hand went up my thigh and his fingers reached the edge of my panties. There I sat, on top of my kitchen counter, being ravished by a man who was not my type. Or maybe he was my type, but I just never knew it until now. He wanted me just as bad as I wanted him. He pushed my panties to the side and inserted his finger inside of me. I gasped and I began to moan.

"You're so wet, Sierra."

I wrapped my legs around his waist and his finger played around inside of me. As his tongue and lips explored my neck, my hands reached around from his ass to his hard cock. I took in a deep breath when I felt his length. He had received a wonderful gift from God. As I stroked him up and down, his hands cupped my breasts.

"God, Sierra, I want you so bad. I've wanted you since the first day I saw you," he whispered.

"I want you too. Please fuck me, Cameron. I want you to fuck me."

He suddenly stopped and looked at me. "Fuck. I don't have any condoms."

"Oh, I do!" I said as my face lit up. "My purse, right there. Just dump it and grab one."

"You keep condoms in your purse?" he asked as I continued to stroke his cock.

"Aren't you happy I do?"

"Yes, right now, I am," he said breathlessly as he ripped open the package. I took the condom from his hand.

"Let me put it on you." I smiled as I nipped at his lip.

I rolled it down his cock as his mouth engulfed my breast. He cupped his hands under my ass and brought me closer to the edge of the counter. He took down my panties and pushed his cock inside me. We both moaned in sync and our lips locked tightly. As he thrust in and out me, he fisted my hair and tilted my head back so he could have full access to my neck. My breathing became rapid and I was in the moment. I was in the moment with him. Not with George Clooney, but with Cameron Cole.

"God, Sierra, you feel so good."

"So do you, Cameron," I replied with bated breath.

"I don't want to come this way. I want to pick you up and take you over to the couch, but I don't want to stop."

"Just fuck me, Cameron. Keep fucking me because I'm about to come. I promise we can do it again right after on the couch because I'm going to need more from you."

"God, you're so hot," he said as he moved in and out of me at a rapid pace.

The noise coming from my mouth surprised even me. He was by far the best sex I ever had. "Oh my God. Oh my God. I'm coming," I yelled as my legs tightened around him and my body shook.

"Sierra, you feel so good. FUCK!" he yelled as he pushed deeper inside me. "Ah," he said breathlessly as we held each other tight.

He broke our embrace, pulled out of me, and kissed my lips. He stared into my eyes while giving me a small smile and brushing my hair away from my face. I stared back into his green eyes and then softly kissed his chin. The moment we shared was unlike any other I'd shared with anyone before. I was still horny and I prayed to God he was too. He removed the condom and tossed it in the trash can, then turned and looked at me.

"I hope you don't regret what we just did," he said.

"I won't. Now take me over to the couch and fuck me again." I smiled.

"I have a better idea. How about if I carry you upstairs to your bed and make sweet love to you."

"I think I like that idea."

I looked over at the dumped contents of my purse all over the counter. I didn't see another condom. Shit. "I don't have any more condoms."

"Damn it. I don't either," he said as he stroked my breast.

"You can always pull out and come all over me. I think that's really hot." I smiled.

"It would be my pleasure." He smiled back and lifted me from the counter, carrying me upstairs and into the bedroom.

Chapter 16

Cameron

We lay there together, just like I had imagined, her body tangled with mine. The sheets half off the bed and my arms tightly wrapped around her while her head rested on my chest. We had completed another round of sex and it was amazing.

"Kirsty had the brilliant idea of booking Lure for my birthday party and you're coming," she said.

"I am?"

"Yes, and we're going to celebrate your birthday too. Invite all your friends. It's next Friday night."

"Clubs really aren't my scene."

"I usually don't go to clubs either, but it means a lot to her to do this, so I'm just going to go with it."

"I'm leaving on Saturday," I said. "And I want you to come with me."

She lifted her head from my chest and looked at me. "Where are you going?"

"Back home for my birthday. My whole family will be there and I want you to come."

"Back to that lake place?" she asked.

"Yes, and it's called Lake Santeetlah."

"To meet your family?"

"Well, my family will be there, so you'd have to meet them."

"Are you only asking me because we just had sex? Because it's only sex, Cameron; that's it."

My heart kind of ached when she said that. But I knew that she was scared of any type of relationship, so I decided to play it cool and go with the flow. If sex was all she wanted for now, then so be it.

"You're right, Sierra. It is only sex. But I would like for you to go with me because you've never been there and I would like to show you nature."

"I hate nature. I hate small towns and I hate lakes."

I laughed at her response, even though I knew she was dead serious. "Listen, I'm taking ballroom dancing lessons with you and I'm going to your birthday party at a club. That's two things right there that I'm not comfortable with, but I'm doing it anyway. So, you can do me this one favor and come to North Carolina with me."

"When are you leaving?"

"Saturday. The day after your party. I was going to stay until Tuesday and then get back here and continue working on your house."

"I'll only go if we fly first class and you let me buy the tickets. Consider it your birthday gift."

"I've never flown first class," I said.

"It's the only way I fly."

I wasn't going to argue with her. If she felt more comfortable flying first class, then that was what we'd do. She was already going to be in shock once we arrived in Robbinsville.

"Okay. First class it is, then."

"Good. I'll have Kirsty book our flight in the morning." She smiled as she reached up and kissed my lips.

I closed my eyes as I held her and drifted off into a deep sleep.

****

Sierra

"OH MY GOD! What is going on here?" Kirsty yelled as she saw Cameron and me in bed.

My eyes flew open and I saw her standing over me. "Get out of here," I said as I waved my arm.

"Morning, Kirsty," Cameron said.

"What time is it?" I asked.

"It's seven o'clock. You're supposed to be up and ready! Morning, Cameron."

"Wild night." I smiled. "You should try it some time."

"Rub it in, why don't you? I'll be downstairs waiting," she said as she walked out of the room.

Cameron chuckled as he rolled me over and climbed on top of me. "Good morning."

"Good morning." I smiled as he leaned down and kissed my lips.

"We better get up or she'll have Rosa up here, beating us out of bed."

"Yeah. I can't believe I slept this late. Shit."

"Go get ready for work and I'll do the same. I'll meet you in the kitchen for coffee." He winked.

I climbed out of bed and stepped into the bathroom to take a shower. When I got out, there was a cup of coffee sitting on the bathroom counter with a note that read: *"I thought you would like this now."* I smiled as I took a sip. It was sex. Only sex. Just like with my suits. In fact, it was amazing sex, great sex, the ultimate sex. Once I finished getting ready, I headed to the kitchen, where all eyes fell upon me when I entered.

"What?"

"Nothing," Kirsty and James said at the same time as they looked down and continued eating their breakfast.

"So you had sex last night with Builder Boy, eh?" Rosa said.

"So what if I did? My sex life is nobody's business. This is my house and I'll have sex in it. In fact, we had sex right here on this very counter," I said as I put my finger on it.

"Good lord," Rosa snapped as she took out the bleach and a rag.

Cameron walked through the door and all eyes turned to him. "Oh for God's sake, we had sex! It was only sex. Now get over it and move on!" I snapped.

Cameron laughed as he sat at the table and Rosa set his plate of eggs in front of him.

"Kirsty, James; let's go."

I looked at Cameron and he winked at me. I bit down on my bottom lip as I smiled at him and then turned around and headed to the limo.

"Okay; spill it, Adams."

"Spill what?"

"You know what! I want details. How was he? How big is his cock?"

I looked up at James and he was shaking his head from the front seat. I lightly kicked Kirsty and she got the hint.

"Not that size matters. I just wondered. It really doesn't matter."

"He was amazing and, to answer your question, yes, his cock is quite large and the best I think I've ever had. Now, with that being said, I need you to book two tickets to Robbinsville, NC for next Saturday."

"Huh?" she asked with a weird look on her face.

"Cameron asked me to go home with him for his birthday."

"Oh, so does this mean you're in a relationship now?" she asked with a smile.

"Umm, no. There is no relationship, but a casual sexual relationship. We talked about it and he agrees. He said that since he's doing me the favor of being my partner for these damn ballroom dancing lessons you signed me up for, the least

I could do is just travel with him back home. It's only for three days, so clear my schedule for Monday and Tuesday."

"Oh, okay then. I'll get right on it as soon as we get to the office."

"Thank you, friend." I smiled.

She rolled her eyes and mumbled under her breath, "No relationship, my ass."

****

Cameron

We were repairing some of the drywall that got damaged when I told Paolo about my ballroom dancing lessons.

"Dude, are you seeing her or something? Why would you agree to that?"

"We're friends and friends do things for each other. She's going home with me for my birthday. Oh, which reminds me; she's having a birthday party at Lure on Friday night, so I want you to come and tell all the guys."

"Wait. I'm confused, man. She's giving you a birthday party?"

"No." I laughed. "I guess I didn't tell you that her birthday is the same day as mine."

"Ah, I see. Okay, we'll all be there. So the two of you aren't dating?"

"No. We're friends."

I didn't want to tell Paolo about last night. It wasn't something I liked to talk about with the guys. I was more of a private person and it was my and Sierra's business, even though I'm sure Kirsty told the world. Paolo left to go check on another job for me and I sent a text message to Sierra. I was really missing her bad.

"Hey, beautiful. Do you have time on your lunch to go to the store and pick out your fixtures for your bathroom?"

"Hey. Shit. I forgot about that. Yes. I have time. Will you come with me?"

"I already planned on it. I'll pick you up at your office."

"Thank you. See you soon."

As I walked through the kitchen to go to the guest house, Rosa stopped me.

"Excuse me, Mr. Cole."

"Yes, Rosa."

"I like you and I know you have feelings for Sierra. Don't hurt her. Okay? That poor girl has been through enough with her ex and her mother. It got worse after her father passed. They were very close."

"Do you know what happened with that ex of hers?"

"He left and never came back. He broke her and her self-esteem. He told her that she was lousy in bed and that there were hotter girls in the world. He also told her that there was no way she would survive in the corporate world and to give it up. Then he told her that she wasn't good enough for him and that he could do better and he had with the whore he met over the internet. Seven years with that bastard and he says all that to her. She needs to be brought back to life. Sierra doesn't know happiness anymore. But I think you may be the one to help her. Don't let her and her stubborn, stuck-up ways fool you. She's built up a wall so high and so tough that it's going to take a miracle to knock them down. I think you're that miracle," she said as she placed her hand on my cheek.

"Thanks, Rosa. We'll see what happens." I smiled.

I washed up, changed out of my dirty work clothes, and headed to Sierra's office. When I pulled up to the curb, she was just walking out of the building.

"Hey, stranger." She smiled.

"Hey, beautiful. Are you ready to pick out some tubs and toilets?"

"I guess." She laughed. "Don't forget about our first dance lesson tonight. The class starts at six o'clock, so James will be by to pick us up around five-thirty. I brought my stuff with me, so we can just go back to my house after we shop."

"What am I supposed to wear to this class?"

She looked at me and twisted her face. "Shit. I don't know. I better call Kirsty and ask her."

She dialed Kirsty and, after a few expletive words, she hung up and looked at me. "Well, I guess we need to stop at the dance store and pick up some shoes."

"Shoes? What kind of shoes?"

"Dance shoes. I'm swear I'm firing her."

I put my hand on her knee and told her to relax. "Do you know where the nearest dance store is?" I asked.

She called her secretary, Sasha, and told her to find one. Sasha texted her the address and it ended up being about five miles from where we were.

"I guess we're going to get some dance shoes," I said as I raised one eyebrow.

Chapter 17

Sierra

The little bell that hung above the entrance made its cute little ringing noise the minute we opened the door. A tall and very thin woman walked over with a smile.

"Hello. How can I help you today?"

"We need shoes for ballroom dancing," I said.

"Okie dokie. We have our men's selection on this wall and our women's on this wall over here. For you, I would recommend this one." She smiled as she handed me the little-heeled shoe. "And for the gentleman over there, I would recommend this shoe."

Did she really just say "okie dokie"? She brought us our sizes and I tried them on. They were kind of cute. I looked over at poor Cameron and he stood there, looking down at his feet.

"Aw, look at you. You look like a professional dancer." I smiled.

"You'll pay for this." He pointed.

"Excuse me, miss. What kind of clothing do we wear for ballroom lessons?"

She glanced over at Cameron. "Do you have black dress pants and a black t-shirt?"

"Yes," he replied.

"Then you're all set. As for you," she said as she looked me up and down. "I have the perfect outfit for you. If you're going to dance, you might as well do it in style, right?"

"Of course. I like the way you think." I smiled.

Cameron rolled his eyes.

"Then you must try this on!" she said as she handed me a light pink body suit with a sheer skirt attached to it.

I took it from her and looked it over. I took it in the dressing room and tried it on. When I walked out to show Cameron, he whistled.

"I'll take it." I smiled.

Once we were finished at the dance store, we went to look at bathroom stuff. I really should have hired an interior designer to do all this. When we arrived at the store, I was overwhelmed at first until Cameron helped me. Over an hour later, I picked everything I needed for both bathrooms and we headed home.

"You have extremely expensive taste," Cameron said.

"I can't help it. It's in my blood." I smiled.

As we were on our way home, Cameron pulled into the parking lot of a drugstore. "Why are we stopping here?"

He looked over at me and smiled. "I need to pick up something."

"Oh, so do I."

We walked in together. Even though we went opposite ways, we ended up in the same aisle, in front of the boxes of condoms. We looked at each other and smiled.

"I see we had the same idea," he said.

"Great minds think alike."

"Would you like to pick which ones?" he asked as he waved his hand over the choices.

"You pick. Wait," I said as I grabbed a box from the hook. "Look at these: ultra-thin and warming pleasure. I like warming pleasure." I smiled.

He closed his eyes for a moment and put his hand in his pocket. "Can we try them out later? Please. Because being in the aisle with you, looking at condoms, is unbearable."

I laughed. "Of course we can try them out later. I'm excited to feel that warming pleasure." I winked.

"I need to get out of this aisle. Are you ready?" he asked.

We took the box up to the counter and the cashier looked at us and smiled.

"Have you ever used these?" I asked.

I thought Cameron was going to die.

"I haven't personally used them, but let me ask Matt. "Hey, Matt," she yelled across to the next register. "Have you ever tried this one?" she asked as she held up the box.

Cameron put his hand over his eyes and shook his head. "What?" I asked.

"Yeah, I have. My girlfriend loves them. Good choice, dude." He smiled as he looked at Cameron.

"I don't need a bag." I smiled as I put the box in my purse and paid the cashier.

We hopped into Cameron's truck and he looked over at me. "I don't think I've ever been so embarrassed in my life."

"What? Why? I wanted to know if they were any good. They say on the box they're new. So, isn't it better to get someone's opinion on them first?"

He just shook his head pretty much the whole way home.

****

"Where are you? We have to leave!" Kirsty spoke as she busted through my bedroom door.

"I'm ready." I smiled as I came from the bathroom in my new dance outfit, twirling around.

"Ugh. Where did you get that? I love it. Now I feel like a slob," she whined.

"You look great in your cropped yoga pants and tank top."

We walked downstairs and James and Cameron were waiting for us in the foyer. I took one look at Cameron all in black and just about had a major orgasm. He had one hell of a body.

"Look at you, all dolled up like a princess." James smiled.

"You mean a queen." I winked.

"After you, my queen," James said as he opened the door.

We climbed in the limo and Cameron looked around. "This is nice."

"You've never been in a limo before?" I asked.

"Nope. This is my first time."

"How does one get to be thirty years old and has never been in a limo?"

"It's called the simple life, Sierra. You should try it some time." He smiled.

"Uh, no thanks. I like my limo."

He looked at me with those green eyes and there was something in them that made me feel like he was going to show me the simple life in North Carolina.

****

Cameron

She looked amazing in her cute pink dance outfit. I couldn't wait until tonight. All I wanted to do was to make love to her again and hold her in my arms. The way we fell asleep last night was bliss. Our bodies fit perfectly together like the right two pieces of a puzzle.

We arrived at the dance studio and as soon as we walked through the door, the instructor clapped his hands and told us we were late. The rest of the class stared at us.

"So sorry." Sierra said to him.

He told us where our places were as he proceeded to teach us the box step. "1.2.3.4." He clapped as he repeated it over and over again. We practiced individually first and then after about twenty times, he told us to grab our partners and practice as a couple. I smiled as I held out my hand to Sierra. She placed her hand on my shoulder and we began to do the box step.

"Oh, sorry," she said as she stepped on me.

"It's okay." I smiled.

I looked over at James and Kirsty and they seemed like naturals. Even the instructor commented on how well they were doing. After what seemed like several minutes, the instructor showed us how to apply the box step to the waltz. I couldn't stop laughing because once we started that, Sierra was all over the place.

"Stop laughing."

"I can't help it. You're funny."

"I hate this kind of dancing. It makes me feel really old."

"You can show me how you rock and roll later." I winked.

Class was finally over and we climbed in the limo.

"That was so much fun!" Kirsty exclaimed.

"I don't like it. I would rather learn belly dancing or something fun," Sierra said.

"When we get a belly dancing client, then you can take belly dancing classes."

When we arrived at Sierra's house, I overheard James ask Kirsty if she wanted to have a drink before he took her home. Her face lit up and I thought she was going to pass out. I followed Sierra inside and she set her purse on the counter. I walked over to her and placed my hands on her hips. I wanted to make love to her.

"Are you ready to try out those new condoms?" I asked.

"I sure am." She smiled as she leaned in and kissed my lips. "Let's rip and roll, baby!" she said.

"Did you really just say that?" I chuckled.

"Yep. Come on; rip and roll!"

She took the condoms from her purse and tore open the box. She pulled out the shiny silver package and held it up. "This better provide the warming pleasure it says it does."

"Don't you worry about it," I said as I took down the straps to her leotard. "If it doesn't, I promise to provide you with all the warming pleasure you want."

"Okay, let's go. Up the stairs now! I can't wait any longer," she said as she grabbed my hand and we went up to the bedroom.

We had enjoyed a shitload of foreplay. Probably the best foreplay I'd ever had or done. She was begging me to fuck her, which turned me on even more, so I grabbed the condom from the nightstand and ripped open the package. I placed it on the tip of my dick and as I began to roll it down, it ripped. I looked at Sierra and laughed.

"Wow. This isn't good," I said.

"No, it's not. Let's try another one," she said as she took another condom from the box.

I once again ripped the package and began to roll it down my dick. When I got halfway down, it started to rip. "What the hell!" I yelled.

"Take that off," Sierra said as she took another condom from the box. "Let me do it. Maybe you're using too much force."

"Too much force? If it's doing that by my hand putting it on, what's it going to do when I'm fucking you?"

"Shush," she said as she took hold of me and began to slowly roll the condom down my hard cock.

"What the fuck!" she said as it tore. "This must be a bad batch or something."

"Now what?" I asked with desperation.

"Oh no. I'll be right back," she said as she flew from the bed and into the bathroom.

"What's wrong?"

She walked out of the bathroom with a sad look on her face. "I just started my period."

I put my hands up in the air. "Of course you did."

"Would you like to see?" she asked.

"No. Of course not. I believe you. It's just the timing sucks."

She walked over to me and placed her hand on my chest. "I know, but there's a bright side."

"What's that?" I said as I put my hands on her hips.

"By the time my period is over, we won't have to use condoms anymore. I'm on the pill."

I looked at her in confusion. "Then why were we using them?" I asked.

"Because I just got on it for my cramps. That day that I went to the doctor, he gave me a prescription for them. So I should be good to go and condom free in about a week!"

"But if you started your period, then you can't get pregnant." I smiled.

"True, but I don't have sex while I'm on my period. That's just gross."

She sat down on the bed and looked up at me and smiled as I stood in front of her, naked.

"Let me make it up to you." She smiled before wrapping her lips around my cock.

Chapter 18

Sierra

Over the next few days, I worked extra hard to make sure I didn't have to worry about anything while I was in North Carolina. Cameron and I didn't see each other very much because I worked really late and he was gone by time I got home. I would see him in the morning for coffee, but that was about it. I found that I missed him and our little talks. Work was really getting to me and I sort of looked forward to this trip with him. I just wished it was somewhere like Belize, Aruba, Hawaii. You get my point. I was far from a small-town girl and I was used to my comforts. I hoped that I was going to be able to handle it. Kirsty was running around like a maniac, trying to get things ready for my party. My period seemed to be over and I wanted nothing more than to have sex with Cameron. I missed his big cock. Royce and a few other gentlemen kept calling me and asking me to "visit" them, but I always came up with an excuse not to. I liked having Cameron around and that was what scared me. I was in my bedroom, trying to pack my suitcase, and unsure of what to bring, so I sent Cameron a text message.

"Can you come up to my room? I have a packing question."

"Sure, I'll be up in a minute."

I pulled out three pairs of Jimmy Choos and a couple of my Chanel dresses. A few moments later, Cameron walked in.

"What's up?" he asked with a smile.

146

"I don't know what to bring to Lake whatever."

He chuckled. "Comfort clothes, Sierra," he said as he looked on the bed and saw my Jimmy Choos. "No heels, especially those. Bring some shorts and tank tops. Maybe a pair of jeans and a couple of t-shirts. And one dress, just in case we go somewhere nice."

"Like one of my Chanel dresses?" I asked.

"Umm. No. Like one of your long dresses. What are those things called?"

"You mean a maxi dress?"

"Yes." He smiled. "We need to talk about something," he said as he sat on the bed.

"Why do you sound so serious?" I asked nervously.

He took in a deep breath. "I need you to do me a favor."

"What is it?"

"Don't get mad."

"I'll try. Just tell me what the favor is."

"Can you please dress very casual when we're in North Carolina and try not to look like a CEO/millionaire type of girl?"

I narrowed my eyes at him.

"Listen, Sierra. I come from a small town and everyone there isn't like you."

"What's wrong with me?" I asked.

"Nothing's wrong with you. Absolutely nothing." He smiled as he took hold of both my hands. "It's just you'll stick out and I don't want you to be uncomfortable. So no Jimmy Choos, designer dresses, or expensive purses. Just simple."

"But I don't have 'simple' clothing and I'm not a simple girl. I'm from Los Angeles. I run one of the largest advertising agencies in the world. This is who I am and how dare you try to change me."

"I'm not trying to change you. I swear I'm not. I just want you to be comfortable and I don't want you to ruin your expensive clothes."

Was this worth the argument that I was getting ready to have with him? I was suddenly having flashbacks of Ryan. He used to tell me that he wished that I would dress sexier. One night, we were going out and I bought the sexiest dress I could find. When I put it on and showed him, he told me that I looked like a whore and not to embarrass him in public by wearing it. That was a couple of months before he left Los Angeles. God, he was an asshole. An asshole with a small dick. I looked at Cameron and told him not to worry and that I'd pack simple.

He pulled me down on top of him as he fell back on the bed. His lips pressed against the flesh of my neck and I could feel him getting hard beneath me.

"I'm still on my period," I said.

"Still?"

"Yeah," I lied. "Sometimes, I can have it for ten days. It just depends on the month." I was a little ticked off at him and I didn't want to have sex with him.

"Okay," he sighed.

"I better go shopping for simple clothes," I said as I got up.

"Make sure to pick up a pair of hiking shoes. There are some amazing hiking trails I want to take you on."

I smiled at him as he walked out of my room. Fuck my life. *How the hell did I agree to this?* I grabbed my phone and sent Kirsty a text message.

"We need to go shopping, now."

"I can't. I'm getting things ready for tonight."

"Ugh. Fine. I'll just take James."

"Oh, I'm jealous, but I can't. I have too much to do still. Don't forget I'm doing this for you."

I rolled my eyes and called James.

"Hello, Sierra. How can I assist you?" he answered.

"You know I hate when you answer the phone like that. I need to go shopping and I need to leave like now."

"I can be there in ten."

"Thanks, James." *Click.*

I could always count on James. After all, I knew he was one of the highest paid drivers in LA. He told me all the drivers gathered, like a pack of wolves, and talked about what they liked and didn't like about their employers while they played cards. They shared secrets and sometimes James would give me the dirt on some of L.A.'s finest socialites. He would stun me. No. Not really. I knew these bitches and I wasn't surprised. I stepped into the kitchen as Rosa was cleaning up.

"I have to go shopping for simple clothes," I said to her.

"What?" she asked.

"For my trip to Lake whatever with Cameron. He wants me to dress simple and not look like a CEO/millionaire type of girl."

"You are going to a small town, so it would probably be in your best interest to dress like everyone else there."

"Thanks for taking his side, Rosa."

"No sides, *senorita*. I'm just telling the truth. You'll want to be comfortable while you're there and you won't be in your fancy clothes."

"Fine. James is here. I have to go."

"Have fun."

****

"Rodeo Drive?" James asked as I climbed in the back of the limo.

"I wish. Unfortunately, we need to go to less expensive stores and I also need hiking shoes."

He laughed. "Right. Sierra Adams is going hiking?"

"I guess I am, according to Cameron."

"I want videos of this trip." He smiled. "I think Old Navy would suit you."

"Really?" I said.

"Yep and I know where one is and there's a sporting goods store next to it, so you can buy your hiking shoes." He laughed.

"Stop laughing and let's go."

He pulled up to the curb of Old Navy and got out and opened the door for me. "What are you doing?" I asked.

"Uh, letting you out."

"No...no...no, dear James. You are coming in with me." I smiled.

"Come on, Sierra. I was going to sit in that deli right over there and have a sandwich."

"Your sandwich can wait. I need your help."

"Are you that incapable of picking out your own clothes?"

"NO! But I need your opinion. So park this baby and let's go."

We walked in the store and I looked around. I picked up a pair of jean shorts they had sitting on the table.

"Those are nice," James said.

I looked at the price tag and then did a double take. "Twenty dollars. That's it. I'm sure they'll fall apart after one wash."

"Try them on, Sierra. Here; look at how cute this tank top is to go with it."

I took it from his hands and examined it. I looked at the price tag. It was twelve dollars. I was in shock at the prices of these clothes. I usually paid about a hundred dollars for my shorts and my tops, depending on what style, usually ran about the same, if not more.

"These prices are insane," I said.

I tried on four pairs of shorts, five tops, and a cute little black floral chiffon skirt. Everything fit perfect. As I was in the dressing room, James handed me a pair of short boots over the door.

"Here, try these with that skirt. I think you'll look adorable."

I tried them on and then snapped a selfie and sent it to Kirsty. She sent me back a bunch of laughing faces. I bought everything I tried on, including a pair of jeans.

"Off to get those hiking boots." James laughed.

"Shut it!"

We stepped into Dick's Sporting Goods and James found the display of boots. The hot-looking salesman asked if he could help me. I wanted to tell him in more ways than one! He talked to me about the different boots and then suggested the pair I should try on. He brought out my size, and when I tried them on, James smiled.

"What?"

"Nothing. I'm just used to seeing you in heels. This is a different look for you."

"Yeah, well, they'll be donated after this trip."

****

Cameron

"Hey, Sierra. Are you ready?" I said as I lightly knocked on her bedroom door.

"Yeah. Come on in."

I opened the door and gasped when she walked out from her closet in a sexy, short, black dress.

"Well?" she asked as she spun around.

"Wow! You look amazing."

The dress was strapless and fit her body like a glove. She wore her hair pinned up and she had on high-heeled silver shoes that made her legs look even sexier than they already were.

"Thank you. You look quite handsome yourself." She smiled.

All I could think about was throwing her across the bed, spreading her legs, and making love to her all night. Things with her were getting out of control, as far as I was concerned. I was falling in love with her and, as much as I tried to fight it, I couldn't. The one thing I was not looking forward to was seeing all the guys she knew at the party. I was going to have to keep my cool if they touched her because she wasn't mine, and not because I didn't want her to be, but because she refused to get into a relationship. I was taking her on this trip, hoping that by the time we came home, she'd be mine and I'd be hers. We could work out the details of me leaving Los Angeles later. But as long as I was here, I wanted nothing more than to be with her.

"It's time to go." I smiled.

She grabbed her clutch and I started walking towards my truck. Since James was a guest at the party, I told her that I'd drive us.

"Where are you going?" she asked.

"To the truck. Why aren't you following?"

"We aren't taking your truck," she said.

"What are we taking?"

She smiled as she began to walk down the driveway. "This."

My eyes felt like they popped out of my head. "That's a Porsche 911. Where did you get that?"

"I rented it. It's yours for the night." She smiled.

I ran to it like a kid on Christmas day and opened the door for her. I climbed in on the driver's side and started that baby up. The revving of the engine was amazing. I was in my full glory, getting to drive around Los Angeles in this. When we arrived at Lure, I pulled up and handed the keys over to the valet. I placed my hand on the small of Sierra's back and we walked inside. Kirsty was at the door and immediately grabbed hold her hand and led us to where the party was.

Chapter 19

Sierra

I rolled over and, instantly, I felt like I was going to be sick. Cameron had his arm wrapped around me, and I picked it up and ran to the bathroom.

"Are you okay?" he asked as he stood in the doorway in his boxers.

"I'll be fine as soon as soon as I quit throwing up."

He walked over and took hold of my hair while I vomited.

"Thanks, but you don't need to be in here while I'm puking my guts out."

"Someone has to make sure you don't fall face first in the toilet." He chuckled.

"Very funny," I said as I proceeded to throw up more.

"Our flight leaves in four hours and we need to leave here in two. Are you going to be okay?"

"I'll be okay. Don't worry."

I finally finished and Cameron handed me a towel. I wished I remembered last night. I didn't even remember fucking him. I stood up and he wrapped his arms around me.

"Come on; go lie down for a few minutes."

"Will you hate me if I tell you that I don't remember us having sex last night?"

He laughed. "I didn't think you'd remember. You were so wasted. I had to carry you in the house. You couldn't even walk."

"So, you took advantage of me while I was drunk?"

"Umm, no. You took advantage of me. I was bringing you upstairs to bed and you grabbed me and undid my pants. I told you that we weren't having sex because you were too drunk, but you begged. In fact, at one point, you started crying and saying things like I didn't find you attractive."

"Oh. Sorry." I pouted.

"Trust me. There's no need to apologize. You were one wild ride last night, Sierra Adams."

I smiled at him and buried my face in his chest. I was slightly embarrassed. Oh shit. I told him earlier in the day I was still on my period.

"There was no mess, right?" I asked.

"No. None at all." He smiled.

****

I rolled my two suitcases down the hall and stopped at the top of the stairs when my phone began to ring. I looked at it, only to see that Delia was calling. Cameron started up the steps as I answered it.

"Hello, Mother."

"Hello, darling. Don't make plans for tomorrow. Clive, Ava, and I are taking you to dinner for your birthday."

"Sorry. No can do. I'm actually on my way to the airport. I'm flying to North Carolina. I won't be back until Tuesday night."

"Why on earth are you going to North Carolina?"

This was going to be good. "Remember the escort I rented? You know, the one you met at my house? Well, it turns out that the escort service he works for is based in North Carolina and since I was so impressed with their services and their men, I thought that maybe it would be a great business opportunity to take them on as a client for Adams Advertising. My team came up with the best slogan."

"That's not a good way to spend your birthday, Sierra. Especially your thirtieth."

"Then maybe you shouldn't have waited until the day before my birthday to make plans. Goodbye, Mother. I'll call you when I get back and we can set something up."

"Fine, Sierra. Enjoy your trip," she said with an attitude.

I hung up and, before I could grab my suitcase, Cameron already had it in his hand. "How do you come up with that shit so fast?"

"It's a talent, baby. A God-given talent."

"Is it also a God-given talent to pack two large suitcases for a three-day trip?"

"Please. One suitcase is for clothes and the other suitcase is for all my makeup. You never know what you might be in the mood to wear, so it's always best to be prepared."

He laughed as he shook his head and took my suitcases downstairs. When I reached the last step, Kirsty and James came through the door. Neither one of them would look at me and they headed straight to the kitchen.

"STOP!" I yelled.

They both stopped in their tracks and slowly turned around. Cameron stopped in the middle of the foyer and looked at me.

"A simple hello would be nice. Also, why are you here, Kirsty?"

"Oh, I just wanted to go to the airport and say goodbye to you since tomorrow is your birthday and I won't see you," she said with a slight nervous tone.

"I'm calling bullshit."

"No, Sierra. You can't."

"I can and I am. The truth is the two of you hooked up last night. Didn't you?"

Kirsty looked down in shame while James looked straight at me. "Yes. Yes we did hook up and it was fantastic! There, it's out in the open now. We had sex and, to quote you, Miss Adams, 'now get over it and move on,'" he said.

"Well said, James. Glad it's out in the open now. Can we please get a move on? Cameron and I have a plane to catch."

James smiled at me as he and Cameron grabbed the suitcases and put them in the limo.

"That was amazing!" Kirsty smiled as she high-fived me.

"Not awkward at all. I'm happy for you. Are you two spending the weekend together?"

"Yeah. We're going to lock ourselves in my apartment, watch movies, and have lots of sex."

I put my arm around her and gave her a squeeze.

Cameron and I had an hour before our flight took off, so we decided to grab something to eat at California Pizza Kitchen. We ordered one pizza, half with pineapple and ham and the other with pepperoni and mushrooms. Take one guess which half was mine. As he sipped on his water, Cameron stared across the table at me.

"How did you know?"

"Know what?" I asked.

"That James and Kirsty hooked up last night."

"Easy. She told me about it via text messages last night, which I didn't read until this morning. So, when I got out of the shower, I called her and we put together a plan."

"You're sneaky. By the way, I like your dress." He smiled.

"Really?"

"Yeah. It looks very nice on you."

"Thank you. It's one of my less expensive maxi dresses."

I looked at my phone. Our plane was going to start boarding any minute. "Come on; we better get to our gate."

We boarded the plane and Cameron smiled when he sat down in his seat and the flight attendant offered him an alcoholic beverage.

"Welcome to first class, Mr. Cole." I smiled.

I pulled out my iPad and turned it on. Cameron looked over and commented. "I thought you weren't bringing any work with you."

"I'm just checking a couple of emails. Relax."

"I'm sorry. I just want you to forget about Adams Advertising for a couple of days. I want you to have fun and just forget about the corporate world."

He wants. He wants. He wants. That was the problem with guys that weren't in my corporate world. They didn't understand that my job was pretty much 24/7. My dad built that company up from the ground and turned it into something huge. It was his life and now it was mine. I needed to keep it that way because there was no other way of life for me. Maybe at one time, there could have been, but not anymore. I looked over at him as he stared straight ahead. I closed the cover to my iPad and put it away in my bag. Why? I wasn't sure. I just knew it was the right thing to do.

Chapter 20

Cameron

We stepped off the plane and I grabbed her hand. Once we were in the airport, she looked around as if she was in a foreign country; unsure and skeptical.

"Welcome to North Carolina, Sierra."

"It looks nice." She smiled.

"It's the airport." I laughed.

She sighed because she knew she wasn't fooling me. She was out of her comfort zone and out of her own world. But I had hoped to change all that for her during our trip.

"How far is it to your house?"

"About a two-hour drive. I rented a car. We need to go and pick it up."

"A limo?" She smiled.

"No, babe. A regular car."

"Did you just call me 'babe'?"

"Yeah, I did. Sorry about that. It just kind of slipped out."

She arched her eyebrow at me, but I didn't care. I could tell she secretly liked it. We stepped up to the desk of the Enterprise Rent-A-Car and I handed the clerk my driver's license. She keyed in all the necessary information and handed it back to me along with the keys to a Toyota Prius. I opened the door for Sierra, and she looked at me.

"Really? It's so small." She hesitated.

"I guess it's all they had. Get in and put on your seatbelt. You're going to fall in love with the scenery. It's a really beautiful drive. There's no smog or tall buildings."

"I like the smog and tall buildings."

I rolled my eyes. "Trust me, you'll like this scenery too. It's very peaceful. It's not a chaotic mess like Los Angeles is."

"I like the chaotic mess." She smiled.

"Okay. I'm done trying to convince you. You'll just have to make your own judgments."

She rubbed her thumb across my cheek. "You're so cute when you're irritated."

We finally reached my parents' house and, when we pulled up the graveled driveway, Sierra squinted her eyes and leaned closer to the windshield.

"Your house is a log cabin?" she asked.

I chuckled. "It's a house made out of logs. It's not a cabin. Pretty cool, huh?"

"Sure," she said hesitantly.

I could already tell this may not have been such a good idea.

****

Sierra

The house was cute from the outside. I'd never actually seen a house made out of logs. It actually looked quite cozy. As I was taking in the surrounding area, a man and woman, who I presumed were Cameron's dad and mom, came from the house.

"Cameron." She smiled with her arms out.

"Hi, Mom." He hugged her tight.

"How's it going, son?"

"Hi, Dad." They lightly hugged.

"Mom, Dad, I would like you to meet my friend, Sierra Adams."

"Hello." I smiled as I stuck out my hand. "It's nice to meet you."

"It's nice to meet you too. Please call us Jerry and Luanne."

Good boy, introducing me as his friend. I stood there with a smile plastered on my face, waiting for the obvious question of the day. One. Two and three. Go.

"So, how did you two meet again?" Luanne asked.

And there it was.

"We met at Starbucks and now I'm doing work for her on her house," Cameron said.

His dad took my suitcases and Cameron took his.

"So, you work at Starbucks making the coffee drinks that everyone seems to be obsessed over?" Luanne asked.

Really? Did I look like a barista chick?

"Yes. She's the barista at Starbucks and she can make one hell of a cup of coffee." Cameron smiled.

"So are the two of you having sex?" Jerry blurted out as we entered the house.

I gasped. "Ah, no, Dad. We're just friends. When I told her I was coming here for my birthday, she asked if she could come because she'd never been to North Carolina. Sierra's birthday is tomorrow too."

"Well, I'll be damned," Jerry said. "Do you have a boyfriend?" he asked.

I narrowed my eyebrows and then looked at Cameron. "No, I don't have a boyfriend." I looked to the right, behind me, and then to the left. I leaned in closer to his parents and softly spoke.

"I'm a lesbian."

Jerry's and Luanne's eyes widened. "But you're too hot to be a lesbian," Jerry said as he looked me up and down.

Cameron put his hand on the small of my back and squeezed a little too tight. I took in a deep breath and tried to wiggle my way away from him.

"Come on, Sierra. I'll show you to your room."

"Aren't we sharing a room?" I whispered as we walked up the stairs.

"No. My mom has a strict rule. If you're not married, then you aren't allowed to share a room. But now that you told them you are a lesbian, I'm sure they won't care!"

"That's a dumb rule. How are we supposed to have sex?"

He laughed. "You'll be sharing a room with Jolene and we'll have to sneak around."

"You started it," I said as we stepped into Jolene's room.

He set my bags on the bed across from Jolene's. "*I* started it? You started it when you told your mother that I was the escort you hired!"

Okay, so I started it. Whatever. He didn't have to go and tell them that I was a barista.

"Okay, fine. But a barista, Cameron?"

He laughed, and as he stepped closer to wrap his arms around me, his sister walked through the door.

"Cam, you're here!" Jolene said as she ran in and hugged him.

"Hey, sis. I want you to meet Sierra."

"Hi," she said with a big smile. "I'm happy to share my room with you."

She was cute girl with her brown side braid and green eyes. "Nice to meet you."

Luanne called up the stairs for us to come down because the rest of the family had arrived, except Kelly, and dinner was almost ready. I followed behind Cameron and Jolene and met the rest of the family. Austin, the eighteen-year-old, looked just like Cameron. The only difference was he wasn't as tall.

I took my seat at the table next to Cameron. Luanne had made a nice dinner that consisted of a rather large pot roast, mashed potatoes with gravy, creamed corn, a tossed salad, and biscuits. The feeling of awkwardness settled in as the whole Cole family took turns staring at me. Cameron poured me a glass of wine and smiled as he sat down. He leaned over and whispered in my ear, "Sorry, there's no tequila."

"This is fine. Thank you."

Mark, Cameron's bartender brother, kept looking at me in a way that told me he may have liked me. "So, are you and Cam shacking up?"

"I didn't think anyone said that anymore. It must be a southern thing." I smiled.

"No, Mark, they aren't shacking up. Sierra is a lesbian."

Mark was in the middle of taking a drink of water and he inadvertently spit it out.

"Are you serious? You're really a lesbian?" he asked.

I slowly nodded my head as I tore into a biscuit. "Yep. One hundred percent pure lesbian."

Cameron wrapped his foot around my ankle and lightly tapped it. I looked at him and smiled.

The whole family took turns talking about their jobs and lives and, as I sat there and listened to them talk, I sort of wished I had grown up in a family like this. Once dinner was finished and I helped clear the table, Cameron took me down by the lake.

"I don't think your mom likes me."

"Why would you say that?"

"Have you seen the way she keeps looking at me? She must hate lesbians." I smiled as I nudged him.

"She's staring at you because you're beautiful. You're the most beautiful girl I've ever brought home."

"And the only lesbian you ever brought home."

"Will you knock it off with the lesbian shit?" He smiled as he brought his hand up to my cheek. "So, what do you think of it out here?"

"It's nice," I replied as I smacked my arm to kill the mosquito that had landed on it.

"Nice? Is that all you can say?"

"I told you that I'm a big city girl. The country life doesn't really do it for me."

I could see the look of disappointment cross his face as he stared straight ahead at the lake. I took hold of his hand and gently squeezed it.

"Thank you for saying that I'm beautiful."

"You're welcome and don't ever let anyone tell you different."

My heart was pounding and my palm was starting to sweat. Shit. My whole body was sweating in this swamp-like heat.

"So you're okay with our relationship as is? Just friends with benefits?"

He looked over at me with the corners of his mouth slightly curved up. "Yeah. I'm okay with it."

"Why? Why would you be?"

There was a moment of silence between us before he turned his head and looked in the other direction.

"Because if being friends means that I get to spend any time with you at all, then I'm okay with that. I like spending time with you and I like doing things with you. Like when we went shopping for bathroom fixtures and dance shoes. I don't want to do anything to compromise that. So, yeah, I'm okay with it."

That had to be the sweetest thing anyone had ever said to me. Why the hell did my heart have to hurt so bad thinking about relationships and being with someone? Cameron was a sweet guy. The sweetest and nicest guy I'd ever met and he deserved so much more than me.

"My dad is taking all of us out tomorrow night for dinner and then Mark wants us to come to the bar after. So, what would you like to do tomorrow during the day?"

I could have thought of a million things to do. Shop on Rodeo Drive, get a facial and massage at the spa. Maybe fly to New York for a Broadway play or even spend the day on a yacht, soaking up the sun and drinking lots of tequila.

"Oh, I don't know. You pick. It's your birthday too."

"I would love to go out on the boat." He smiled.

Now he was talking! "I would love to go out on the boat."

"Great. Then we'll spend the day on the boat and then go to dinner and the bar at night."

"Damn it!" I yelled as I smacked the side of my leg. "These bugs are driving me crazy. Can we go inside?"

Cameron put his arm around me and kissed the side of my head. I ducked out from under his arm and waved my finger at him.

"No. No. I'm a lesbian, remember?" I laughed as I ran ahead of him.

"A damn hot and sexy one," he said as he grabbed me, picked me up, and carried me around to the side of the house. He took my face in his hands and pressed his lips against mine. His tongue slid through my parted lips and met with mine.

We heard footsteps and he immediately broke our kiss. "And this over here is where—Hey, Mark," Cameron said with a small wave.

"Hey. Mom wanted me to come find you. It's time to start game night."

Game night? Was he serious?

"Okay, we'll be there in a sec."

"Games?" I said.

"Yeah. Whenever the whole family is together, we have game night."

"What kind of games do you play?"

"You'll see." He smiled as I followed him into the house.

When we walked through the door, there were two games set up. One game was Monopoly and the other was the game of LIFE.

"Everyone take a seat at a game board," Luanne said.

"Which game do you want to play first?" Cameron asked.

I seriously couldn't believe that I was going to sit here and play a board game with this family. "Since I'm already playing the game of life, I guess I'll play Monopoly."

"I was hoping you'd say that. I always win." He smiled.

Since there was an odd number of us, Cameron, Jolene, Mark, Austin, and I sat down at the Monopoly table. The rest of the family sat at the game of LIFE.

"You need to watch out for Cam. He likes to cheat." Austin smiled.

Cameron looked at me with those piercing green eyes and smiled. "I do not cheat. I'm just good at this game."

"We'll see." I smiled back.

Chapter 21

Cameron

I sat there in disbelief as Sierra bankrupted all of us and owned every piece of property on the board. My dad walked over and shook his head.

"Maybe you should be in the corporate business, little lady."

She looked over at me and winked. It was the first time in a long time that I lost. She drank the last bit of wine that was in her glass and said that she was heading up to bed. Jolene jumped up and said she was heading up to bed too. She seemed really excited to have a roommate.

I took off my pants and shirt and tossed them on the dresser. As I climbed into bed, I took my phone and sent a text message to Sierra.

"Can you come to my room?"

"Already there."

She slowly opened the door and stepped inside, making sure to close it quietly behind her. I lifted up the covers and she climbed in, sitting up with her back against the headboard.

"You totally rocked that game."

"You need to remember where I come from."

"I let you win." I smiled.

"You did not. It was all perfectly strategized on my part. Can we have sex?" she blurted out.

"I don't know. With you being a lesbian and all."

She laughed as I grabbed her hands when she went to smack me.

"Take off that nightshirt and get down here." I smiled.

She quickly lifted her nightshirt over her head and tossed it on the floor. She positioned her body perfectly against mine so we were spooning. The more her naked flesh pressed against mine, the harder I became.

"Feel that?" I asked as I pressed my erection against her bare ass. "If you want this, then you have to be quiet."

"I'm always quiet." She giggled.

"I beg to differ," I whispered as I cupped her beautiful breasts in my hands and pushed myself until I was deep inside her.

Once we were finished, she sat up, put on her nightshirt, and kissed my lips. "Thanks for the booty call and Happy Birthday." She winked.

"Anytime, babe. Happy Birthday to you." I winked back.

She quietly left the room and, as I lay there, I couldn't help but think about how much I wanted her every day and how much I wanted her to need me. She was becoming an addiction and that was something I didn't ask for.

****

Sierra

I couldn't sleep. Not only did I feel like an egg sizzling on the sidewalk in the damn heat, but the loud snore that came from little Jolene was obnoxious. I took my phone from the nightstand and looked at it. Not one single happy birthday text. *Are you fucking kidding me?* As I looked closer, I noticed I had no service, zero, zilch. Damn country. I looked at the time. It was five forty-five. I got out of bed and went downstairs to the kitchen. I popped a k-cup in the Keurig and, once it brewed, I took it outside on the patio. I jumped when I saw Cameron sitting in one of the chairs.

"Shit!" I quietly yelled as some coffee spilled from the cup. "I didn't know anyone was out here."

He got up and handed me a napkin. "Are you okay?"

"I'm fine. You just startled me."

"Happy Birthday." He smiled as his lips brushed against mine.

"Thank you. Happy Birthday to you. Why are you up so early?"

"Why are you?"

"I'll tell you why. Your sister saws logs all night and it's as hot as a camel standing in the middle of a desert."

"Huh?" he said.

I gave him a wave of my hand and sat down in the chair next to him.

"Why are you up and out here so early?"

"I love being out here with my coffee and watching the morning fog rise off the lake. It's so peaceful and it's enough to make you really think about life."

Suddenly, my phone started blowing up. Service must have finally kicked in. I had over a hundred text messages from everyone wishing me a happy birthday, including one from Ava with a picture of us from last year's birthday celebration. Cameron smiled as he took the phone out of my hand and set it down on the table.

"Enjoy this view while it lasts."

I didn't want to enjoy the view. I wanted to read all my text messages and emails. The service was sketchy up here and I didn't know when I'd get it back. There was a text message that came through and caught my attention. It was from Ryan.

"Happy Birthday, Sierra. I just thought I'd let you know that I've moved back to Los Angeles. Maybe we can catch up some time."

I needed to take in a deep breath because I couldn't believe the nerve of that asshole. How dare he fucking text me. HOW. DARE. HE.

****

Cameron drove us to the marina. I looked around and was really confused because this marina didn't look like the marinas back in Los Angeles. Where were the big, exciting boats? I started to worry. Cameron took my hand and led me to the dock where a boat was sitting. He climbed on and turned around and looked at me when I stopped.

"What's wrong? Climb in."

"What's this?" I asked with a smile.

"It's a fishing boat. We're going fishing."

I was confused because he never said a word about fishing. "No, we're not. We're going to spend the day on a boat. A real boat."

"Sierra, this is a real boat and we are spending the day on it. We're going to fish. I'm teaching you how to fish!" He smiled.

The fake smile that was plastered to my face stayed. "I don't fish. I hate fish. I won't even eat fish. When you said we were spending the day on the boat, I thought you meant, like, drinking and basking in the sun."

"This is a lake. A beautiful, peaceful lake. Not an ocean. This lake is meant to enjoy fishing and that's what we're going to do. Now get your sweet ass in here so we can go." He smiled.

"No," I said as I folded my arms.

"No? Really, Sierra?"

He stepped out of the boat like he was mad and walked over to me, picked me up, and carried me onto the boat.

"No. This was not my idea of a boat trip," I said, kicking.

"Yeah, well, it wasn't my idea to take ballroom dancing lessons and wear those stupid shoes. But I did it anyway for you. So you will do this for me and you will like it!"

I sat down on the seat and looked at him. He was really hot when he was being authoritative. I was getting turned on, but I didn't let him know that. I was mad at him, no matter how sexy he was.

"Here," he said as he handed me a brown paper bag.

I grabbed it out of his hand, opened it, and pulled out a bottle of tequila and a plastic glass.

"I figured you would need and want that," he said as he untied the boat and we began to take off across the lake.

"Thank you, but I'm still mad."

"That's okay, Sierra. You can be mad all you want. In fact, sit there in silence if you wish. I'm going to do some fishing. It's been a long time since I was out here and I miss it. Maybe, just maybe, if you opened your eyes to the other side of life, instead of being so caught up in your material world, you'd appreciate life a little more and you'd see the beauty in things you never knew existed."

I rolled my eyes. How dare him. What the hell was the matter with these guys? Whatever. I was just going to get my tequila on and soak up the sun. My phone chimed with a text message from Royce.

"Happy Birthday, sexy. If you're around, I'd love to give you your birthday gift. It's about ten orgasms wrapped up in a new toy I acquired. How about it?"

Right now, that sounded good. I could go for George giving me ten orgasms. Oh yeah. I forgot. I was in the middle of a lake, being held captive, and forced to look at slimy fish.

"Sorry, Royce. I'm in North Carolina on a fishing boat. Go me!"

"Sounds dreadful. I'm sorry you got yourself into that situation. We'll fuck when you get back. Call me and Happy Birthday."

Cameron got out his fishing rod and lures. He stopped the boat in the middle of the lake and cast his reel out into the water. I stood up and took off the sun dress I was wearing, revealing the bikini I had on underneath. I sipped on my tequila and closed my eyes, taking in the hot rays of the sun. I was startled and grabbed the side of the boat as Cameron jumped up and started to reel in his rod.

"Look at that beauty!" He smiled as he dangled his rod with the fish he caught in front of me.

"Get that thing away from me!" I said as I fell onto the floor.

He laughed. "Come on, Sierra. It's only a fish."

"I HATE FISH! I already told you that. They creep me out."

He took the fish off the hook and threw it back into the water, then he held out his hand and helped me up.

"I'm sorry." He chuckled.

"It just tickles me pink that you find my fears so amusing."

He cocked his head as his eyes traveled from my head down to my toes. "You look extra sexy in that bikini."

"Save it for the fish." I scowled.

Cameron sighed and went back to fishing while I went back to drinking my tequila, trying to forget how miserable this birthday was becoming.

Chapter 22

Cameron

I looked behind me and saw that Sierra was sprawled out over the bench with her eyes closed. I couldn't help but stare at how beautiful her body was. She had me hard from the minute she took off that dress. I didn't dare let her know. She was already pissed off at me for taking her fishing. What I wouldn't give to make love to her on the boat, in the middle of the lake. I was starting to get hungry as I looked at the cooler I brought with us.

"Hey, Sierra."

She opened one eye and, if looks could kill, I'd be dead right about now.

"What?"

"Could you hold the rod for me while I eat a sandwich? I'm hungry."

She sat up and took the rod from my hand. "Do you want one?" I asked.

"No, thank you."

"Just hold it still. Don't move it, mess with it, nothing."

I grabbed a sandwich and a coke from the cooler and sat down on the bench. I was enjoying my sandwich until Sierra began to scream.

"Cameron, I think we caught something!" she exclaimed as she pulled up the rod.

I jumped up from my seat and stood behind her while I told her what to do.

"Reel it in and pull. Oh my God, this baby is huge. Pull back and reel it in. You can do it."

She struggled, but I was there to guide her. She finally reeled in the line and there was a beautiful big fish hanging from the end of it.

"Look!" She smiled.

"Congratulations, babe. You just caught your very first fish."

"Yay, me! Just go ahead and keep it over there while you unhook him."

At that moment, a part of Sierra had been opened up to a whole new world. As much as she hated to admit it, I could tell how excited she was when she reeled that fish out of the water.

"So, do you have another reel?"

"Really? You want to fish now?" I asked.

"Yeah, that was kind of fun." She smiled.

I grabbed the other rod and taught her how to tie the lure on. We spent the next three hours catching fish and making fun of each other. Before we headed back, I laid Sierra down on the floor and made love to her under a blanket. We almost got caught. Almost.

****

Sierra

"So, what's it like?" Jolene asked as she sat on her bed and watched me do my hair.

"What is what like?"

"Being a lesbian?"

Oh, for fuck sake. *Did she really just ask me that?* "Umm. It's fine, I guess. Why are you asking?"

"I don't know. I kissed a girl last year. A random girl in a bar and it kind of stayed with me."

I shuddered. "Do you have a boyfriend?" I asked.

"No. I've never had a boyfriend. I've just never really been interested in guys."

Oh boy. I thought Cameron's little sister was trying to tell me she might be a lesbian.

"I find girls more attractive," she said.

I stopped brushing my hair and turned around to face her. "Then go with your feelings. Never hide who you are."

Before I knew it, Jolene jumped up from the bed and smashed her mouth against mine. It was only for a second and I was completely caught off guard.

"What the hell is going on?" Cameron yelled as he walked in the room.

"Nothing. I was just testing something," she said as she walked out.

I stood there, my eyes as wide as they could get and in shock.

"Would you like to tell me what the hell just happened?"

"I think Jolene is a lesbian and she may have just confirmed it with me."

"What? My sister is not a lesbian."

"Yeah, Cam. I think she is," I said with a twisted face.

He shook his head and told me that it was time to leave for dinner. "By the way, you look really nice," he said before walking out of the room.

I smiled as I set the brush down on the dresser and took one last look at myself. My cute little floral print skirt that I bought from Old Navy and my ankle boots looked nice. This was an interesting birthday and one I wouldn't be forgetting any time soon.

"Look at you. You look adorable." Luanne smiled as I walked down the steps. "Kelly and her husband Jeff are going to meet us at the restaurant. You'll get to meet our grandbaby, Savannah." She giggled.

Great. I could hardly wait. Cameron and I climbed into the rental car and Mark and Jaden got in the back.

"Hey, do either of you know anything about Jolene liking girls?" Cameron asked.

"I wouldn't be surprised," Jaden said. "She's never been on a date with a guy."

"Sierra," Mark spoke from the back seat. "How long has it been since you've been out of the closet?"

Cameron looked at me and chuckled.

"Oh, it feels like it was only yesterday," I replied with an eye roll and a wave of my hand.

We pulled up to the restaurant and, when we walked inside, the Cole family was already sitting at a table, waiting for us. I met Kelly, her baby, Savannah, and her husband, Jeff. Like any dinner with a one-year-old, it was eventful. Lots of whining and crying when she didn't get her way. If I wanted to hear all that, I could have stayed in Los Angeles with Kirsty. After we finished eating, the waitress brought out a birthday cake and everyone sang "Happy Birthday" to me and Cameron. As I sat and watched Cameron and his family, I could feel the love that poured out of all of them. The conversations they had were funny but heart-warming. A dinner with my mother, Clive, and Ava could never be like that. Our dinners always revolved around complaining about the latest designer or who didn't get invited to certain social events.

"You guys coming to the bar?" Mark asked.

"Yep. You ready?" Cameron replied.

Kelly handed Savannah over to Luanne and Jerry because they were the designated babysitters while Kelly and Jeff went to the bar with us. We pulled up in the gravel parking lot and I stared straight ahead at the wood-sided building that sat far back in what seemed like the middle of the woods. To me, this was as creepy as shit. Like something out of a horror movie.

"Did they film a horror movie using this bar? I swear I've seen it in a horror flick."

"Stop being ridiculous, Sierra." Cameron laughed.

He thought I was being funny. I was being serious. We walked inside and, surprisingly, it was bigger than it looked from the outside. The bar had a cabin feel to it. Everything, right down to the floor, was wood. Mark walked behind the bar to grab us some drinks. The rest of us sat in the only round booth in the joint. It had a white *"Reserved"* sign sitting in the middle of it. There was a band that was setting up in one corner. A couple of pool tables sat across the other side of the bar. Mark set the tray of drinks on the table.

"Here's to Cameron's and Sierra's thirtieth birthdays!" Jaden yelled as he held up his glass.

"And to a newfound friendship." Cameron smiled as he stared into my eyes.

I reached over and pressed my lips against his cheek. "Happy Birthday."

"Woo hoo," everyone cheered as we threw back our drinks.

Everyone walked over to the other side of the bar to play pool. I really didn't feel like playing, so I told Cameron that I'd stay back at the table for a while and I'd join them later. He nodded and walked away just as Mark brought me another glass of tequila. He slid in the seat across from me and took a drink of his beer.

"So, what's going on with you and my brother?" he asked.

I narrowed my eyes at him.

"I know you're not a lesbian, Sierra. But I don't think you two are in a relationship. So what's the deal?"

"I am a lesbian, Mark."

"No, you're not."

"Yes, I am."

He laughed. "I can see why my brother looks at you the way he does. You're fucking adorable."

I smiled and laughed at the same time. "Fine. I'm not a lesbian, but don't you go spreading that around. Got it?"

He nodded his head as he leaned back and folded his arms. "So why pretend?"

"It's a long story and one I'd rather not get into at the moment. Cameron and I have a special relationship. We like each other very much."

"You mean you're fuck buddies. No strings attached, right?"

"How did you know?"

"First off, I knew you weren't a lesbian by the way he looks at you and the way his face lights up when you walk into the room. I haven't seen my brother this happy in a very long time."

"Unfortunately, sex and friendship are all I can give him. I can't be in a relationship."

"You can't or you won't? Bad experience?" he asked.

"Something like that."

"Well, your secret is safe with me. Just don't hurt him. Please. He's a good guy."

How could I hurt him when we both fully understand the nature of our relationship? I flashed him my "don't worry, but I can't make any promises" smile and finished off my tequila.

"Hey, Sierra," I heard Cameron yell across the bar. "Come on. You're playing."

I took in a deep breath and I got up and walked over to Cameron.

"Here." He smiled as he handed me the pool stick. "Do you know how to play?"

I looked at the pool table, ran my tongue across my bottom lip, and looked at Cameron. "It can't be that hard, right? I just hit the balls with this stick?" I asked.

"Yep." He smiled.

It was me and him. Everyone else stood back and watched. Cameron let me break. I leaned over the table and positioned the stick.

"Wait a second. You're holding the stick wrong." He laughed.

He came up behind me and repositioned the stick so I was holding it correctly. He also gave me a little tutorial on how to hit the ball. The first time I went to strike the ball, I missed.

"It's okay. It just takes some practice." Cameron smiled.

He was good. Really good. A good pool player. My balls wouldn't go in the pockets; his did. He kept making little comments about it being okay and don't worry, not everyone can play pool. When it was my turn again, I looked at Mark.

"Before I take my turn, do you think you can get me a double shot of tequila?"

"Coming right up." He smiled.

"Sierra. Are you taking your turn or what?" Cameron asked.

"Hold your horses, boy. Give me a second. You're kicking my ass and I need a drink."

He shook his head and smiled as Mark handed me the shot glass. I threw it back like it was water and handed it back to him.

"Let's get this party started." I smiled as I hit every one of my balls into the pockets. "Black ball, corner left pocket." I grinned as I hit it and in it went.

"What the fuck! You're a scam!" Cameron playfully shouted as he grabbed the sides of his head and did a little spin.

I began laughing as I did my little dance around him. He grabbed me, set me up on the pool table, and whispered in my ear.

"Do you know how bad I want to fuck you on this pool table?"

"Probably as bad as I want you to. It's obvious you have never been in my basement." I winked as I jumped down.

Everyone was staring at us except Jolene. *Where was Jolene?* My eyes scanned the bar and stopped as they saw her talking to, or possibly flirting with, some chick at a table in the corner. I silently smiled to myself, not wanting to draw attention to her with the rest of the family.

"Cool. Real cool, Sierra." Mark winked.

Chapter 23

Cameron

I couldn't believe her. She was playing me the whole time. As I looked at her and shook my head, she flashed me that smile. A smile like the one I saw in the picture of her and her father. A happy smile. The band announced that they wanted everyone on the dance floor to shake it to Luke Bryan's "Country Girl (Shake it for Me)" line dance. I turned to Sierra, grabbed her hand, and led her to the dance floor.

"Oh my God, no!" she exclaimed. "I don't know how to do it."

"Just follow me." I smiled.

My brothers and sisters howled as they ran to the dance floor and the music began to play. We started the line dance and Sierra watched me intently, trying to follow the dance moves.

"I thought you don't dance," she said.

"I'm more comfortable in my own element. Besides, I ballroom dance, don't I?"

She was moving with us, stumbling a few times, but keeping up. She was shaking her ass, and what a fine ass it was in that short skirt. She didn't take her eyes off of me and the smile never left her face. It was happening. She was opening up to the other side of life. When the music stopped, she grabbed my hand and led me outside the bar.

"What's wrong?" I asked.

"It's really hot in there. I just needed some fresh air."

We took a seat at a wooden picnic table that sat next to the bar. The parking lot was full and people were still coming. I sat across from her and stared at her as she tried to catch her breath.

"You did good on the dance floor."

"Thanks. It was fun." She smiled.

"You never told me you could play pool." I smirked.

"I didn't know that I should have. Is it just something a girl tells a guy out of the clear blue? 'Hey, guess what? I can play pool and I can probably kick your ass at it.'"

I chuckled as I pulled my phone from my pocket. "Do you want a drink?" I asked.

"Yeah. I'll have a beer." She smiled.

I smiled back and sent a text message to Mark, asking him to bring us out two bottles of beer.

"So, where did you learn to play pool like that?"

She looked down at the table as she ran her finger across the rough wood. "My dad taught me. Pool was his way to unwind after a long and stressful day at the office. He'd come home, ask me if I did my homework, and then take me downstairs to play. Sometimes, he'd have a group of friends over and he'd show off what he taught me. He used to say, 'Sierra, you are the pool cue and the ball is your life. Once you have both lined up with precision, you hit hard in the direction you want to roll.'"

"Wow. He sounds like he was a great father."

"He was and I wouldn't be where I am today if it wasn't for him. I miss him so much."

My heart ached for her. I could tell that her relationship with her father was nothing like the one she had with her mother. I reached across the table and placed my fingers on hers. She looked up at me and smiled softly.

"I think I drank too much," she spoke.

"Would you like to go back to my house?"

"No. I want to go to a fucking hotel where we can fuck all night long without your family around."

She already had me rock hard and I was more than committed to making her wish come true.

"I think I can arrange that. But first, we need to go back to my house and get our things for our hike tomorrow."

"Then let's go." She flashed a smile.

We got up from the picnic table and walked inside the bar. I had to let everyone know we were leaving in case they needed a ride back. Mark and Jaden said they all could catch a ride with Kelly and Jeff. We climbed in the car and drove back to the house.

"What hotel are we staying at?" Sierra asked as she turned on the radio.

"You'll see. I'm just hoping they have a room for us."

"What kind of hotel is it?" she asked with concern.

"You'll see." I turned to her and smiled.

We pulled up to the house and I could see from the driveway that my parents were sitting in the living room. Sierra got out of the car and we walked into the house. Or should I say, she stumbled into the house.

"Hello, you two," my mom said as she gave Savannah her bottle.

"Hey, Mom. Sierra and I are going to grab a couple things and get a couple rooms at the bed and breakfast. I want to get on the trails early tomorrow."

"Have fun, you two."

I went to my room and gathered what I needed and then I walked to Sierra's room to find her sleeping on the bed.

"Sierra, wake up!" I said as I gently shook her.

"I'm not sleeping. I'm just trying to make the room stop spinning."

I chuckled and shook my head. "I'll run downstairs and make you a coffee to go. Get your stuff ready. We have to leave."

A few moments later, Sierra walked into the kitchen. I took her bag and handed her a cup of coffee. We walked out the door and drove off to the place where I prayed they had a room available.

Chapter 24

Sierra

"What's this?" I asked as Cameron pulled up in front of what looked like another house.

"It's a bed and breakfast. It's the closest to the trails. Keep your fingers crossed they have a room for us. I'll be right back."

Keeping my fingers crossed, not! I rolled down the window and stared at the wooden house with the long, wooden porch. I craved a plush hotel. The Trump would be nice right about now. Cameron emerged from the house and opened my door.

"I got us the last room!" He smiled as he held the key up in front of my face.

"An actual key? That you put into a lock? Who does that anymore?" I asked.

He sighed with a heavy breath as he grabbed both our bags and led me inside the bed and breakfast and up the stairs to our room. He inserted the key into the lock and twisted the knob to open the door. He reached to the left and flipped on the light switch. I approached with caution. Before stepping inside the incredibly small room, I examined it from the hallway. The entire room was wood, from the ceiling to the walls and right down to the floor. It was too much country for my taste.

"Are you coming in or staying in the hallway?" Cameron asked.

I stepped in and looked at the bed. "Why is this bed so small?" I asked as I stared at it.

"Because it's a queen-sized bed. It's all they had."

I placed the tips of my fingers on top of the quilt that was spread over the bed. I pushed down. The bed squeaked. I looked at Cameron and he shrugged his shoulders.

"Really? How are we supposed to have sex on a squeaky bed?"

"We'll figure it out. Now get undressed and get that sweet ass of yours in here." He smiled as he stripped out of his clothes and climbed under the covers.

I didn't waste any time doing what he asked and we spent an hour making the bed squeak. The way I saw it, it was the owner's fault for not replacing the bed. So if people complained, then that was the story I was sticking to.

****

"Sierra, wake up."

I felt his hot breath blow across my skin and his warm lips pressed against my shoulder.

"What time is it?" I asked as I tried to shoo him away.

"It's six a.m. We need to get ready and hit the trails."

"Are you crazy? This is supposed to be a vacation. Who gets up at six o'clock in the morning on their vacation? Go away. I'll meet you on the trails. Just leave me the address."

I heard him chuckle. "Stop being silly and get up," he said as he started to tickle me.

I jumped. The one thing I hated most was being tickled. I lost control of my bladder every time.

"No." I jumped up and scooted to the other side of the bed. "Listen, buddy," I said with a sleepy voice. "No tickling, ever! Ugh. Damn you, Cole."

He stood there with a smile on his face until I climbed out of bed. As I made my way to the tiny bathroom that barely fit one person, I turned and looked at him.

"You're weird. I just want you to know that."

He laughed and shook his head as he sat down on the bed and put on his shoes. "We're eating breakfast first, so hurry it up. I'll meet you downstairs in the dining room."

"Okay," I yelled from the bathroom. "I know it won't be too hard to find you in this place."

I looked at myself in the mirror as I brushed my teeth. The bags under my eyes told the whole story of last night. I threw my hair up in a ponytail, put on my khaki short shorts and a white tank top. As I dabbed some concealer under my eyes, I heard the faint sound of my phone ringing. I took two steps out of the bathroom and raced to the nightstand where my phone sat. It was Kirsty.

"Hello," I said. Nothing. "HELLO."

"Hey. Can you hear me?" Kirsty asked.

"The service is shit up here. How are you?"

All I could hear was the breaking sound of Kirsty's voice as she kept saying my name.

"I'll call you when I have better service," I said and then the call was gone.

I stared at my phone, feeling isolated from the outside world. I put on my new hiking boots and packed a shitload of Band-Aids in case I needed them. As I walked down the stairs and into the dining room, I saw Cameron sitting at a square table with four chairs, taking a sip of coffee.

"Look at you." He smiled as I sat down across from him.

"Yeah. Yeah," I said as I grabbed his cup and took a sip of coffee from it.

"You can have your own," he said.

"I know. But I need it now."

An older woman walked over to our table and set a cup of coffee in front of me and then proceeded to take our order. I pulled out my phone and held it up in the air, trying to get some sort of fucking signal.

"What are you doing?" Cameron asked.

"Trying to get a signal in this damn place. Kirsty called me and we couldn't talk because she kept breaking up and then the call dropped. I can't get any of my emails and God knows how many text messages I have waiting for me floating out in text-land until they're allowed to come through. It's like they're being held hostage and I don't like it. My text messages are gold to me and they need to be treated with TLC, which they are not getting up in these damn mountains!"

He sat there with a perplexed look on his face. "You're crazy. You are totally off your rocker."

I flashed him my cute smile. "I know. You can blame Delia for my mental condition."

"We'll be back to civilization tomorrow and you can spend the entire plane ride home catching up on everything."

I pouted as I took a bite of my toast. The waitress walked by and I held out my hand to grab her attention.

"Can I get a mimosa, please?" I asked with a pretty smile.

"Oh, I'm sorry, darling. We don't have that here."

"Of course you don't," I said as I looked away.

Cameron let out a soft laugh as he continued to eat his breakfast. "I'm glad you think it's funny."

"You'll be fine, Sierra." He smiled.

"I know I will be because we're stopping at the liquor store and I'm buying those little travel bottles of tequila."

"No, we're not."

"Yes, we are," I said as I took a sip of coffee.

"The closest liquor store is ten miles away. We are hitting the trails that are right here. So hurry up and finish eating. We need to go or else we won't make it back before nightfall."

My mouth dropped when he said that. "Nightfall? We aren't going to be gone that long, are we? Are you trying to kill me?"

"Would you rather stop along the way and set up camp?" he asked.

"Set up camp? As in a-tent-on-the-dirty-ground camp?"

He chuckled. "Yes, that kind of camp."

I lifted my hand and signaled for the waitress. "Can we have our bill please? We're in a bit of a hurry."

"That's what I thought." Cameron smiled.

****

Cameron

We started our hike. I was going to go easy on Sierra because she'd never been hiking before. I grew up hiking. My brothers and I went on five-day hikes and explored what nature had to offer. It was beautiful and there was nothing more refreshing and renewing of the soul than hiking. I planned on taking her on a twelve-mile hike. For Sierra, that might have been rough, so I did have an alternate plan. I wanted her at least to get up one mountain so she could view the world from the top. A small mountain, so don't worry.

We were two miles into our hike and she was already huffing and puffing. She followed behind me and all I kept hearing her say was "I hate you." I couldn't help but laugh because I knew once we reached my planned destination, she was going to love it. I looked behind at her and she kept holding her cell phone up in the air, mumbling expletives. This girl was under my skin, but in a good way. I was falling for her more and more every single day and I knew I was headed for trouble once we went back to L.A. and she was back in her world.

"My feet hurt and my legs feel like they're going to collapse right out from under me. I need to stop for a minute," she whined.

I turned around. She was sitting down on a large rock. I took a bottle of water from my back pack and handed it to her.

"You're doing great, Sierra. You made it a whole two miles already."

She brought the bottle up to her lips. She drank from it and flipped me off at the same time. Suddenly, she jumped when she heard her phone beep.

"OH MY GOD! Yes!" she exclaimed as she looked at her phone. Her smile instantly turned into a frown.

"What's wrong?" I asked.

"Doesn't it figure that the only text message that comes through when there is zero service is one from Delia?"

"What did she say?" I laughed.

"She wants to take me to dinner tomorrow night when we get home for my birthday. I'm not even going to try and respond. I'll just tell her that I never got her message."

"Have you hydrated? Can we get a move on now?"

"Yep. Let's continue this wonderful journey," she said as she rolled her eyes.

"Trust me. You're going to love it once we get there."

She walked next to me for the next ten miles. Okay, we had to stop every mile and she wasn't quiet about it, but she was there and I was happy. Once we reached the spot I wanted to show her, I walked ahead and held out my hand.

"What?" she asked.

"We're going up there." I pointed to the top of the moderate mountain.

"The hell I am. I'm not climbing that thing. Are you crazy?"

"If I didn't think you could do it, I wouldn't have brought you here. Now give me your hand so I can help you get started. This is nothing, Sierra. Little kids can climb this."

"Have I told you today how much I hate you?" she said as she put her hand in mine.

"Yes. About a thousand times."

I held her hand as long as I could until I had to let go and she had to finish on her own.

"Just be careful, Sierra. One step at a time."

"Easy for you to say," she growled.

I made my way to the top with ease and Sierra followed behind. I held out my hand and helped her up.

"Oh wow," she said as she stood there and looked at the view.

"Beautiful, isn't it?"

"This is what you wanted to show me?"

"Yes. Do you like it? Wait. Don't answer that. Just stand here for a few minutes and take in all the beauty."

She looped her arm around mine. The breeze was a little cool, but it felt good as we both stared out into the distance. The glorious view of the mountains was like none other.

"The sky looks so blue up here. I feel like I can almost reach it." Sierra smiled.

"Are you ready?" I asked.

"What? Already? We just got up here. What the hell's the matter with you?" she asked as she smacked my arm. "I didn't hike all those hours and miles and climb up this thing to get a second's look and then have you tear me away from it."

"Did you just hear yourself? Miles and hours. We can't hike back in the dark. Unless you'd rather stay up here all night and we can take turns sleeping because one of us will have to be on watch to make sure some stranger doesn't kill us or rob us."

The look of horror on her face was priceless. She walked a little closer to the edge, put her hands on her hips, and looked around. She took out her phone and took a picture.

"Come here," she said. "We're going to take a selfie."

I walked over to her and put my arm around her as she held her phone up in front of us and we both smiled.

"Okay. That was nice, but it's time to go," she said.

I laughed as I climbed down first and then helped her down. We weren't too far into our hike back when Sierra stopped behind me.

"Give me your back_pack," she said.

"Why?"

"You'll see. Just hand it over."

I removed the back pack and gave it to her. She put it on her back and then jumped on mine and wrapped her legs tightly around my waist.

"My feet and legs hurt. You need to carry me."

I sighed but I didn't mind. I loved having her on me. Whether it be on top, bottom, or on my back.

Chapter 25

Sierra

I scooted down the stairs because it was impossible for me to walk. My legs had used muscles I didn't even know existed.

"What are you doing?" Cameron asked with a smile as he stood at the bottom of the staircase.

"I can't move. I'm dying, Cameron."

"Come on," he said as he helped me up and carried me to the kitchen. He reached in the cabinet and took out a bottle of Motrin. He shook two orange pills into his hand and then handed them to me.

"Take these. You'll feel a little better," he said as he handed me a glass of water.

He went upstairs and grabbed our bags and took them to the car. I walked outside on the patio and took one last look at the lake. It was truly beautiful and peaceful. Jolene came running down the stairs at the speed of light to say goodbye. She threw her arms around me and I almost fell over.

"It was so great sharing a room with you. Thank you," she whispered in my ear.

I wasn't quite sure what the thank you was for. I suspected it something had to do with her finally accepting she was a lesbian. I felt bad for lying to her, but I'd probably never see them again anyway, so what the hell.

"Always be you and nobody else." I smiled at her.

"Do you have a girlfriend?" she asked just as Cameron walked up to say goodbye.

"Yeah. Her name is Kirsty and she's hot!" I pulled out my phone and showed her a picture of the two of us from my birthday party.

"You two are a beautiful couple."

Cameron looked at me and shook his head. I shrugged my shoulders. He hugged his little sister goodbye and we walked out to the car where Luanne and Jerry were waiting for us.

"It was so nice to meet you," Luanne said as she hugged me. "I wish Cameron would meet someone just like you. Well, except the lesbian part." She laughed.

I gave my fake-as-hell laugh and hugged Jerry goodbye. "So long, sugar. You keep making people happy by making that awesome coffee."

"I'll try." I smiled as I climbed in the car.

I pulled out my phone and looked at it. Nothing.

"I need service!" I exclaimed as I shook my phone.

"Relax, sugar. You'll have service soon." Cameron smiled as he looked over at me.

I held up my finger. "No. No. Don't you ever call me that again."

He chuckled and placed his hand on my thigh. "You don't like it when we southerners call you 'sugar'?"

"Very funny." Then it happened. *Ding. Ding. Ding. Ding.* The beautiful and glorious sound of text messages and emails came through loud and clear.

"See. Are you happy now?" he asked.

"Yes! Yes! Yes!"

"You're not having an orgasm, are you?"

"YES! I think I am!" I smiled.

"I'll leave you alone so you and your phone can get reacquainted." Cameron smirked.

"Thank you very much, Mr. Cole. We appreciate it."

I scoured through my text messages. Nothing of real importance. Just a few from James and Kirsty pretty much making fun of me. Another one from Delia asking why I didn't text her back. One from Royce asking for sex the minute I got back and one from Bradly, another suit, wanting me to attend a corporate gala with him at the Ritz-Carlton. The rest were just minor business ones.

"I'm alive!"

"Thank God. I missed your sorry ass."

"Thanks, Kirsty. Remind me to fire you when I get home."

"There's something you should know."

"What?"

"Ryan moved back to Los Angeles."

My stomach started doing sick flips because I had forgotten that text message he sent me.

"He sent me a text message and told me. I actually forgot about it until you just mentioned it. Why did he move back?"

"I don't know. He came by the office and said he needed to talk to you. I face palmed him after calling him a few choice names and told him never to come around again. I think he got the message."

I swore I felt a single tear rise up in my eye. But I wasn't going to let him do that to me again. Enough tears had been shed over his small cock and I refused to go back to that place.

"Good for him. He's my past and the ex-files are staying closed."

"Good girl, but you aren't fooling me. I'll talk to you when you get home. Have a safe flight."

I set my phone down on my lap and looked out the window. *Why was I letting this affect me?*

"Are you okay?" Cameron asked.

"Yeah. I'm just really sore still. Oh, and that reminds me," I said as I sent a text message to Kirsty.

"Book us both massages tomorrow during lunch."

"Awesome. I love massages."

We reached the airport and turned over the rental car keys. We slowly walked to our gate, which was on the other side of the airport, since the goddamn tram was down. Of course it was.

"I can get you a wheelchair if you want," Cameron said as he walked next to me.

"Ha ha. That actually sounds nice. Or how about one of those scooter things?" I smiled.

We got to our gate and they had just started to board the plane. Cameron and I took our seats in first class and I immediately ordered a glass of white wine, then two and three.

"Don't you think you should slow down?"

"Don't you think that you should not pay attention?"

The truth was that I was trying to forget about the fact that Ryan had moved back to Los Angeles and the chances of running into him were greater than ever.

"I'm not carrying you off this plane," he said.

As I sat there and looked at him, I couldn't help but smile on the inside. My whole body felt alive when I was with him.

"You won't have to." I smiled. "Do you mind if I lay my head on your shoulder and close my eyes?"

"Not at all," he said as he kissed the top of my head.

****

Cameron

I couldn't help but stare at her as she slept on my shoulder. I had a great time and I couldn't have asked for a better birthday. I still wasn't sure what she really thought of my hometown. I got the impression that she still pretty much hated it, even when we left. But I'd never forget the look on her face when she got to the top of that mountain and saw the view. Just like I'd never forget the look on her face when she caught her first fish. She probably would never admit it, but I thought she had a great time. Soon, we'd be back in Los

Angeles, back in her world and, to be honest, it scared me a little. I didn't know where this was going or even what this was. Was it more than just sex for her?

****

Sierra

I opened my eyes and let out a long yawn. As I lifted my head from Cameron's shoulder, I cringed from the pain in my neck.

"Oh my God," I said and I took my fingers and rubbed the cramped area.

"What's wrong?"

"My neck has a cramp in it."

He smiled as he told me to turn my head and he massaged the back of my neck with his strong builder hands. I couldn't help it, but I felt turned on. Soon my panties were going to be in need of changing.

"Okay. Stop! Sorry, but you're turning me on."

"Is that a bad thing?" He laughed.

"Right now, yes."

"How much longer until we land?" I asked in anticipation of finally being able to touch the ground of Los Angeles.

"We have another hour."

I held up my hand and summoned for the flight attendant. "Can I please get another glass of white wine?"

"Sure," she said with a friendly smile.

Just as I was about to say something to Cameron, I saw Lowen walking up the aisle. I gasped.

"Sierra Adams." He smiled as he stopped in front of my row.

Shit. Shit. Shit.

"Long time no see, doll. Where have you been playing?" he asked.

"Lowen, it's nice to see you again. I didn't know you were on this plane."

"I saw you earlier and I was going to say hi, but you were sleeping. I didn't want to wake a sleeping beauty."

Lowen was a freak. He was a suit that I fucked a few times but stopped returning his calls because he just got way too freaky. He wanted to do things that I didn't even know existed. One night, I went to his penthouse on Park Avenue and, when I walked in, he was standing in the middle of the living room, completely naked, with a pair of handcuffs around his balls and penis. *What the fuck was that?* I instantly sent a text to Kirsty, telling her to call me immediately. I told Lowen I had a family emergency and I high-tailed it out of there really fast, never to look back. And now, on this plane back to L.A., I looked back and I didn't like it.

"That's very kind of you, Lowen." I wanted him to go away. I didn't want him saying anything in front of Cameron.

"Who's this?" Lowen asked.

It's none of your fucking business, I thought to myself. "This is my friend, Cameron."

"Boyfriend?" he asked.

The nerve of this perv. "Did you hear the word 'boy' in front of 'friend'?"

He sighed. "Still a smart ass. That's what I love most about you, Sierra. You haven't returned my calls since that night you had a family emergency. I hope everything was all right," he said as he looked at me from his black-rimmed glasses.

"Oh yeah. Delia just had a nervous breakdown and I had to commit her to a mental hospital," I said with the wave of my hand.

"Oh. Sorry to hear that. Well, let's hook up when we get to L.A."

"Didn't you know?" Cameron interrupted.

"Know what?" Lowen asked.

"Sierra's a lesbian now."

The look on his face was priceless and I know for damn sure it would have gotten at least a million hits on YouTube.

"For real, Sierra?"

I looked over at Cameron, who was smiling at me.

"Yeah, I'm dabbling in the lesbian ways now. Dick just wasn't doing it for me anymore."

"Well, then. It was nice seeing you. I'm just going to go back to my seat," he said nervously.

"Bye. Bye, Lowen." I waved. "You're good." I smiled at Cameron.

"I didn't like him and I could tell by the look on your face you didn't either."

"You're very observant, Mr. Cole. I may just keep you around." I winked.

"Are you going to tell me about him?"

"No. Trust me, you don't want to know."

He shook his head and laughed as the flight attendant handed me my glass of wine. I wasted no time finishing it off and, before I knew it, we were back in the land of the living.

Chapter 26
Sierra

I walked through the LAX airport with a huge grin on my face. I couldn't help it. I was happy to be home. Cameron and I went to baggage claim and I saw James and Kirsty waiting there for us. Kirsty squealed when she saw me and hugged me tightly.

"So glad you're home," she said.

"Me too. It's good to be back."

James smiled as he hugged me and then shook Cameron's hand. James and Cameron walked over and waited for our suitcases to come around while Kirsty and I talked.

"So, how was it?" she asked.

"Let's just say I'm happy to be home where I have unlimited phone service. That was brutal."

"You look great. Why are you walking funny? Did you and Cameron have too much sex?"

"Umm. No. He made me go hiking with him and climb a small mountain."

"Yeah, right." She laughed.

"I'm serious. My body is screaming in pain and my muscles are asking me why I had to do this to them. I really feel bad for my poor aching muscles."

"That's why you had me book the massage tomorrow. Well, you look great."

"Thanks. I don't think I'll fire you today." I smiled.

Cameron and James walked over to us with our bags and we headed to the limo. While we were driving home, Kirsty asked to see pictures. I pulled out my phone and showed her a few that I had taken of the lake, the mountain view, and me and Cameron.

"Wow, that place looks really pretty."

"It's beautiful. Isn't it, Sierra?" Cameron asked.

I didn't know what to say about it. "Sure. It's pretty there. Just as long as you know what you're getting when you get there. Like no phone service and no internet."

"But you survived, right?"

"I don't know. Did I?" I asked. "I seemed to complain a lot."

"Yes. Yes you did complain a lot, but I think, overall, you enjoyed it."

I didn't say a word because I didn't want to hurt his feelings, so I just smiled.

"Sierra knew someone on the plane. Some guy named Lowen," Cameron said to Kirsty.

"Oh my God. Isn't that the guy who had the handcuffs around his dick?"

Thank you, Kirsty.

Cameron's eyebrow arched as he turned and looked at me.

"Forget she said that. I told you that you didn't want to know. Anyway, Cameron told him I was a lesbian."

"Huh? Why?"

"It's a long story. One I don't want to discuss right now, but Cameron's sister, Jolene seems to think me and you are a hot-looking couple." I winked.

"Huh?" she asked again in confusion and James smiled at me through the rearview mirror.

"Sierra, I don't think I'll ever be able to live without being a part of your crazy life," he said.

We pulled up to the house and I headed straight to my room and fell back on my plush, king-sized bed. I ran my hand over the comforter, taking in the softness and beauty of being back home.

"Oh, how I've missed you," I said to it.

"You talk to your bed?" Cameron asked as he walked in the room with my suitcase.

"I sure do. This bed never fails me and I'm happy to be lying on it."

"You're weird." He smiled.

"I know. But somehow, I think you like my weirdness."

"I do. I don't know why, but I do. Don't forget to call Delia."

"Why did you have to ruin my moment?" I pouted.

"She's your mom and she wants to celebrate your birthday. So call her now!" he commanded.

"Wow. Who put you in charge?"

He laughed and winked at me just as Rosa came into the room.

"Welcome home, senorita."

"Thanks, Rosa. It's good to be home."

Cameron said he was going to go to the guest house and that he'd get back to work on my bathroom first thing in the morning. I watched him as he walked out of the room and Rosa looked at me.

"You better have been nice to him," she said.

"I'm always nice, Rosa. What the hell are you talking about?"

"I know exactly where you were and it's a small place. Not much going on, like here. I could just see you swearing up a storm and complaining about every little thing."

I looked away from her. Damn it. I hated when people knew me too well.

"It was different, but sort of pretty, and I kept the complaints to a minimum," I said as I tried to get up from the bed. "Help me, Rosa."

"What's the matter with you?" she asked as she took hold of my arm.

"I went hiking and it was brutal. Now, I can't move."

"You? Hiking?" She laughed.

"Spare me, Rosa. I'm hungry. Will you make me something? I'm going to go in the hot tub. Maybe that will help my aching body."

"I guess. Should I make Builder Boy something?"

"I don't know. Go ask him."

I changed into my bikini and walked downstairs and to the hot tub. I climbed in and sighed as my body took in the amazing feel of the warm water and relaxing jets. I closed my eyes and relaxed. This was living. I couldn't stay in here long. As much as I didn't want to, I had to go into the office and play catch up.

"What's going on out here?" I heard Cameron's voice say.

I opened one eye and looked up as the sun shined down upon him. "I'm trying to soothe my aching body. Would you like to soothe yours too?"

"Nah. Mine doesn't need soothing. I'm going for a swim."

"Okay. Swim away."

"You don't want to join me?" he asked.

"What part of I'm trying to soothe my aching body do you not understand? I can barely walk, let alone swim."

He laughed. I'd noticed that he laughed at me a lot. "Okay, you stay here and relax. I'm going to do some laps."

"You go ahead and do that," I said.

As soon as I heard him jump in the pool, I opened my eyes and watched as he did the breast stroke across the pool. Damn him. *Why doesn't he hurt?* He looked so strong swimming, and sexy too.

"Your food is ready. Come and eat," Rosa said.

Oh God, don't make me get out of here, I thought. I was too relaxed and the thought of having to move from this spot nauseated me.

"Give me your hand and I'll help you out," Cameron said as he stood there, soaking wet with a warm smile.

I extended my hand to his and slowly stepped out of the hot tub. "I suppose this means no sex later?" he whispered in my ear.

"Considering I can barely spread my legs, probably not."

"There are more ways than one and you are fully aware of that." He winked.

I smiled but rolled my eyes. "Is that all you ever think about? Oh, wait. Yes it is, because you're a man."

"Not fair. You're stereotyping."

"And you, my darling, are proving me right."

We sat down at the patio table and ate what Rosa prepared for us. "Rosa," I yelled. "I need some water, please."

She walked out with a glass and shot me a look of disapproval as she set it down in front of me.

"Don't judge," I said.

"I've judged a long time ago, *senorita*."

"Have you called Delia yet?" Cameron asked.

Oh shit. I was so consumed with my aching body that I forgot. "I'm calling her right now."

I picked up my phone and prayed she didn't answer.

"Well, it's about time," she answered.

Shit.

"Hello, Mother. I'm back," I said as I put her on speaker and gulped my tequila.

"How was your trip? Wait. We can talk about that tomorrow at dinner. I've already made reservations at the Beverly Hills Country Club for us tomorrow night at seven."

"I hope you made reservations for five because I'm bringing Cameron," I said as I looked at him and winked.

"Who's Cameron?" she asked.

"The escort I rented."

"I thought that was only for a week. He's still around?" she asked with irritation.

"He was so good at his job, I just had to go and hire him for another week."

"Sierra, I don't like this at all. What has gotten into you?"

Cameron began to laugh. "We'll be there promptly at seven. Now I have to go because another call is coming through. Bye."

I hit end and looked at Cameron. "If I have to go, then so do you!"

"But it's a country club," he whined. "I don't do country clubs."

"And I don't do fishing or hiking."

"But you complained the whole time," he said.

"Just to be fair, you can complain about it because, lord knows, I'll be doing it too. And since we're going to the country club, you'll need a tuxedo. I'll have Kirsty hook you up."

"Tuxedo? I don't wear tuxedos."

"And I don't wear hiking clothes or those dreaded boots, but I did."

"You sure looked sexy in those clothes." He smiled.

"And you'll look sexy in a tux. I have no doubt. Now I have to get to the office and try to catch up on all the madness."

I had difficulty getting up from my chair, but somehow managed while Cameron sat there and laughed.

"This is all your fault," I said.

"Please. Maybe your body's telling you that you're out of shape."

My jaw dropped. "You'll pay for that remark, Mr. Cole," I said as I walked away and pointed at him.

"I'm looking forward to it, Miss Adams."

Chapter 27

Cameron

I took my and Sierra's plates into the kitchen and put them in the dishwasher for Rosa.

"No need to do that, Builder Boy. I can clean up."

"It's no problem, Rosa. My mom always taught us kids to clean up after yourself because it's nobody's mess but your own."

"She's a smart woman. So tell me how bad the senorita complained on your hiking trip."

I smiled and threw in a light chuckle. "She complained the entire time about everything. Do you want to know what the best part was? I told my parents that she was a barista at Starbucks."

"No! I would have given anything to see the look on her face," Rosa said with a wide grin.

"Do you know what her comeback was?"

"What?" she asked with anticipation.

"She told my parents that she's a lesbian."

Rosa's mouth dropped as she put her hand over it. "She did no such thing."

"Yes, she did, and my parents still think she's a lesbian barista." I laughed.

Rosa was in hysterics. She was a great woman and I'd become very fond of her.

"Okay, I'm going to go do some work on the bathroom. I told Sierra I would start up again tomorrow, but since I'm here, I should work on it."

As soon as I stepped into the bathroom, my phone rang and it was Sierra.

"Hello," I answered.

"It's me. You need to meet Kirsty at Elite Tuxedo on Westwood Blvd. She's waiting for you. Have James drive you. He's on his way back to the house."

"I can drive myself, Sierra. I know where it's at."

"Okay. Have fun. I'll see you later."

I hung up and sighed. Tuxedos weren't my thing. In fact, I'd never worn a tuxedo. Not even for Kelly's wedding. I hopped into my truck and drove to Elite Tuxedo. As soon as I stepped through the door, Kirsty ran over to me and grabbed my hand.

"This is Cameron. Cameron, this is Raul. He's going to handle your tuxedo while we wait."

I smiled and nodded at Raul and then turned to Kirsty. "What do you mean 'while we wait'?"

"Sierra gave strict instructions that he is to alter your tuxedo here in the store and we are to take it with us. She wasn't taking any chances that it won't be ready tomorrow."

"How long is this going to take?"

"Are you in some kind of hurry?" She frowned.

"Well, I was going to do some work on the bathroom."

"Forget the bathroom. You can do that tomorrow. You have to look like the escort the Madame hired you to be." She winked.

Raul took out his tape measure and took my measurements. A few moments later, he emerged with a black tuxedo hanging nicely on a hanger. He walked over to a shelf and grabbed a white dress shirt.

"Go try this on and we'll work from there."

I stepped into the dressing room and pulled the curtain close. I stripped down to my boxers and then slid into the pants. Suddenly, Kirsty's head appeared in the mirror.

"What the hell?"

"Oh, please. It's not like you have something I've never seen before. But you do have one hell of a six pack. Or is that an eight pack? Turn around."

"Will you get out of here and let me finish getting dressed?"

"Whatever. Hurry it up," she said as she rolled her eyes and closed the curtain.

I put on the dress shirt and then the jacket. When I walked out of the dressing room, Raul was standing there with the black bow tie. I stood there while he pinned a couple areas.

"This is almost a perfect fit. You can tell Miss Adams that she's lucky and it won't cost her as much as I thought it would."

Kirsty pulled out her phone and dialed Sierra, then proceeded to put her on speaker.

"What's up?" she answered.

"Raul says the tux is almost a perfect fit, so it won't cost you as much, and I have you on speaker."

"Hi, Raul. Thank you," Sierra yelled through the phone.

"You're welcome, Miss Adams. Her father bought all his tuxedos from me," he said as I stood there with my arms spread. "Such a shame what that Ryan boy did to her. She's such a nice person. He was in here the other day. I accidentally poked him with a pin. Okay, maybe not by accident. But he deserved it."

"Wait a minute? Ryan's here in Los Angeles?" I asked.

"Yes, sir. He moved back just a few days ago."

I couldn't believe it. I wondered if Sierra knew. But if she did, she would have told me. I looked at Kirsty. If anyone would know, it would be her.

"Kirsty," I called.

"Yeah."

"Did you know that Sierra's ex moved back to L.A.?"

"How did you know that?"

"Raul just said he did."

"Raul, you idiot."

"I didn't know it was a secret," he said.

"So you did know and, if you knew, then that means Sierra knows and she didn't tell me."

"Relax, Cam. She hates him and wants nothing to do with him. She just found out."

"But still, she knew and didn't tell me."

I was a little pissed off at her for not mentioning it to me.

"You can't be mad at her. I'm sure she was going to tell you."

"Well, she didn't. Please don't tell her that I know."

Raul told me to go change back into my clothes. When I finished, I met Kirsty at the cash register.

"Here you go, Mr. Cole. I hope you get many years of wear out of it."

"Excuse me? This is only a rental. Don't I have to return it tomorrow?"

"No. No. Miss Adams bought you the tuxedo. She didn't rent it."

"Well, I can't."

Kirsty grabbed it from my hand and began to walk away. "Don't question it; accept it and let's go."

"No. I won't accept that."

"You have no choice, Cam," she said as she set the tuxedo bag around the hook in the back of the truck.

She patted me on the chest. "Please don't piss her off. I have to deal with her for a full day tomorrow and she's already going to be in a foul mood because of dinner."

She walked away, got in her car, and left. I was mad at Sierra for buying me the tuxedo. That was a lot of money to waste on something that I'd never wear again. When I got home. I went straight to the guest house. Screw the bathroom. I'd start on it tomorrow. I just needed to be by myself tonight and think.

About three hours later, my phone beeped with a text message from Sierra.

"Hey, I'm lying in bed, sore as hell, if you want to come up and sleep with me tonight."

"Nah, I'm already in bed. I'm really tired."

"Did you like the tuxedo?"

"Sure. It's nice. Thank you."

"Are you sure you don't want to come up? I kind of don't want to sleep alone."

"Sorry, Sierra, but I just don't feel like getting out of bed."

"Okay then. Good night."

"Good night."

****

Sierra

What the hell is his problem? I thought as I read his last message. I couldn't believe that he wouldn't come and lie with me. After spending the last four days with him, practically glued to his side, I kind of found myself missing him when he wasn't around. Damn him. I couldn't and I wouldn't do this again. Especially now that Douchebag was back in town. What would I do if I saw him? I'd probably claw out his eyes. No, wait. I'd grab his small balls and squeeze them so he couldn't breathe. Hell, I'd probably just look at him and become a fumbled mess. I cringed as I rolled onto my side and closed my eyes. I prayed that the pain would lessen up by morning. I still couldn't believe Cameron wouldn't come up here. Men. They were as hormonal as women at times.

I slammed my hand down on the button to turn the annoying-as-hell alarm off. I stretched slowly and my legs still ached. But not as bad as yesterday. I stepped into the shower and when I walked out from the bathroom with a towel wrapped around me, I saw Cameron going up the spiral staircase.

"Good morning," I yelled.

"Morning," I heard him say.

I kept the towel wrapped tight as I climbed up the staircase and saw Cameron with his tool box.

"I thought you were doing the bathroom today?"

"Paolo is going to finish up the one that's almost done and I've hired two other guys to start the tear out in the other bathroom. While they're doing that, I'll start your office. Things will get done a lot quicker that way or else I'll be here forever."

Forever didn't sound too bad to me. I liked having him around. He was a fun friend.

"Oh, okay. Are you all right? You seem off."

"I'm good, Sierra. Now if you'll excuse me, I have a lot of work to do," he said as he walked by me and down the stairs.

I didn't know how to feel at that moment. He was pissed off about something. I could tell. I stepped into my closet and pulled out my light pink Prada suit. As I was changing, Kirsty walked in.

"Where are you? Rosa said you hadn't been downstairs yet."

"In my closet. I'm getting dressed," I said as I walked out.

"Wow, is that new?" Kirsty asked.

"Sort of. I just haven't worn it yet."

"I love the short skirt with the longer jacket. You look hot, girlfriend."

I gave her a small smile as I slipped my feet into my Prada platform pumps.

"What's wrong? You look majorly bummed."

"I'm just thinking about this dinner with the clan tonight. Do me a favor and book a mani/pedi for later."

"Already did. Did you think I was going to let you go the country club when your feet were shoved in hiking boots and your hands were roughing it on rocks?"

"I knew firing you wasn't a good idea." I smiled. "Also, call Neiman Marcus and have them send some cocktail dresses to the house around three o'clock."

"You have a shit load of dresses in there," she said as she pointed to my closet. "And I'm pretty sure more than half of them still have the tags on."

"I'm in the mood for something new. So do as you're told and call Paul. Tell him that I'm going to the country club with Delia for dinner and he'll know exactly what to send over."

"If you say so, boss."

Cameron was sitting at the table, eating pancakes. He looked up at me, looked down, and then looked at me again. I think he liked my suit.

"Good morning, all," Paolo said as he walked in.

Everyone said good morning and Rosa handed him a plate of pancakes. As he was on his way to the table, he stopped and looked at my shoes.

"Nice Pradas." He smiled.

"Thank you, Paolo."

As soon as he sat down, Cameron looked at him and shook his head. "I don't even want to know how you know her shoes are Prada."

I took a sip of my coffee and my phone beeped with a text message from Royce.

"Hey, baby. I hope you're wearing something extra sexy for after our meeting. I think your desk is calling for some action."

Shit. Fuck. Shit. I looked at Kirsty, who was sitting next to James and staring at him as he ate.

"Do I have a meeting with Royce today?"

"Yes."

"Why?"

"He called the other day and said he needed to go over some figures with you, and he wanted to meet ASAP."

I rolled my eyes. "I'll take care of this."

I pulled up my contacts and scrolled until I found Royce. I hit the call button and waited patiently for him to answer.

"Hello, gorgeous," he answered.

"Royce, darling. I'm sending Wayne over to your office for the meeting. I have a doctor's appointment today and I won't be able to attend."

"Are you all right?"

"I don't know. I'm on my period and I'm bleeding all over the place. Ugh. It's such a mess. Tampons aren't plugging it up and pads aren't absorbing like they're supposed to. It's a disaster area down there. Oh, and the odor is unbelievable. Poor Kirsty can't stand to be within a few feet of me. It's utterly embarrassing, so I need to have it checked out. But no worries. Wayne is the expert and he'll report back to me. Have a good day, Royce."

There was a moment of what I assumed was speechlessness on the other end.

"You too. Good luck with your problem."

"Thank you. We'll talk soon." *Click.*

I looked over at the table. Kirsty was hysterically laughing, James was shaking his head, Cameron just stared at me in disbelief, and Paolo was smiling and saying how much he loved me.

"Sorry if I offended anyone, but he had it coming."

"Ha ha. He thought he was going to be *coming,* all right!" Kirsty laughed.

Chapter 28

Cameron

Paolo needed my help with some wiring in the bathroom before I went up and started working on Sierra's office.

"Dude, I noticed at breakfast you were acting weird with Sierra. What's going on?"

"Nothing."

"Something is, man. I'm not dumb and I know when a guy is giving a girl the cold shoulder and that's exactly what it looked like to me."

"I don't know what the fuck I'm doing. I really like her and she didn't tell me something and now I'm pissed off."

I didn't know if I should tell him or not, but I felt like I needed to talk to someone about it.

"What didn't she tell you?"

"That her ex moved back to L.A."

"Why does it matter if she told you or not? Are the two of you in a relationship? Because the last time I heard, it was a friends-with-benefits-type of arrangement."

"It matters because we're friends. Don't you think that's something she should have mentioned?"

"I don't know. If you were in a serious relationship, yes. But you're not, so drop it."

"Thanks, Paolo. I appreciate these little talks we have. Now, if you're done needing my help, I'm going up to the office."

"Sorry, man. Sometimes the truth hurts," he said as I walked away.

I walked down the hall and entered her bedroom to get up to her soon-to-be office. Maybe Paolo was right; it wasn't my business about her ex. I stood in front of the window and looked out over the hills. It was beautiful, especially this early in the morning. As I was taking in the view and thinking, I heard Rosa's voice behind me.

"Excuse me, Builder Boy, but I overheard you and Builder Boy Two talking. One thing you should know about me is that I make everything my business. So as long as you're in this house, get used to it."

I smiled at her as she stood next to me. "I don't want to talk about it, Rosa."

"I have a few things to say on the matter and you're going to listen. You don't have to talk about it, but I am. Kirsty told me that pompous ass moved back here and, believe me, I'm not happy about it. It took a lot for Sierra to come back from what he did and I'm not even sure if she's completely back yet. I worked for her father for years and I watched Sierra grow. Seven years of her life she gave to that man, if that's what you want to call him. I prefer to call him a dick wad."

I chuckled because coming from Rosa and hearing her say that in her accent was funny.

"I watched her shut down more and more every day. So, forgive her for not telling you that he's back. If she were to tell you, it would be admitting something that she's not ready for, or thinks she's not ready for. I like you and I like you and Sierra together. You fit nicely together."

"We're total opposites, Rosa. I'm not sure we fit at all."

"You do. Trust me. Don't hold her not telling you about Dick Wad against her. She needs you more than ever for tonight. You've met Delia. You've heard the things Delia says. Don't let Sierra down, not tonight. Now, I have to get back to cleaning. We'll talk later," she said as she patted me on the back. "Oh. You're strong." She smiled.

Rosa was right; Sierra was damaged in more than one way. I know if I had a mother like Delia, I'd be emancipating myself.

****

Sierra

I sat in my chair and faced the window as I looked out over the city of Los Angeles. Between thinking about how weird Cameron was acting and having dinner with Delia, I was about to go insane. I got up from my chair and walked over to my bar area. I grabbed the bottle of Kahlua and poured it in my empty coffee cup. Oops, I forgot the coffee. Oh well. As I was sipping it, Sasha came through on the intercom to let me know that Don was here to see me. What the hell was he doing here? I went to my desk and looked at my appointments. He wasn't on the schedule.

"Tell Don that I'm busy at the moment and he doesn't have an appointment."

Suddenly, my office door opened and he came barreling through it. I sighed and cocked my head as I sat down behind my desk.

"What's going on, Don? How dare you just waltz in here like you own the place!"

"I need to talk to you."

"Then talk," I said as I looked at the time on my phone. "You have about fifteen minutes. I have a massage scheduled and I'll be damned if I'm going to miss it."

"I can massage you," he said.

"Fourteen minutes."

"Okay. Okay. Marta Clareheart is blackmailing me."

"Why the hell would she do that?"

"Because I didn't tell her about Milania and now she's out for revenge. Apparently, she's in love with me."

Why the hell would she do something stupid like that?

"She told me that I better sign over all my accounts to her advertising firm or she's going public with our little affair we had going on. I hope you're not jealous."

Jesus Christ, he makes me laugh.

"If I am jealous, Don. I'll get over it. Trust me. If you hand over all your accounts to her, then we wouldn't be servicing you anymore, which would mean a great loss of money for this agency."

The lesser of two evils. Decisions. Decisions.

"Let me ask you this. Why would you fuck her?"

He leaned back in his chair and brought his ankle up to his thigh. "Because she's hot as fuck and I wanted to sample her. Then the samples became appetizers, and the appetizers became full course meals."

"Spare me the details," I said as I waved my hands in front of my face.

"Please, Sierra. I know you're young, but you have that fire that your dad had, and I know you can help me on this."

"What makes you think that she'd listen to me?"

"You're scary sometimes."

Oh, I liked that he thought of me as scary. I gently smiled at him. "What's in it for me?"

"I knew you'd ask that. Well, for one, you'd get to keep my accounts and all the money I pay your agency."

"Keep going," I said.

"I would never bother you sexually again. You would have my word on that. Even if it does kill me to say it."

"Are you sure?"

"Yes. Please, Sierra. I know you can do this. She's competition and you're bigger than her. You can crush her. In fact, you can buy her agency."

"You'll never text me inappropriate things again? You'll never say sexually harassing things to me either?"

"I promise. You have my word. And when the king gives his word, it's solid."

"You better keep that promise or else I'll crush your little world, Don."

"Thank you, Sierra. I knew I could count on you."

"Yeah. Yeah. Now get out of here. I have a massage to get to."

"Please, just one kiss on the cheek to seal the deal."

I sighed as I pointed to my cheek and he softly kissed it one last time forever.

"Thanks, Sierra. You really are a good friend."

****

Kirsty and I walked down the street to the spa where our massages were scheduled. I'd been going to Nathan for a couple of years. His hands were a work of God and he was the best at his job. Kirsty and I lay on our tables, which were side by side, in nothing but towels covering us.

"Hey, Sierra," Nathan said as he and Nolan walked into the room. "Any concerns?"

"I went hiking. That's concern enough."

I heard him laugh. "You went hiking? Why?"

"Long story. Now work your magic and heal my poor aching body."

As we were basking in the glory of strong hands upon our flesh, Kirsty looked over at me.

"Cameron knows about Ryan."

"What? How?"

"Raul mentioned it yesterday during the tuxedo fitting. Apparently, Ryan was in the shop earlier this week and told him that he moved back."

"Shit."

"I think it upset him that you knew and didn't tell him."

"Ah. So that's why he was acting strange last night and today."

"Why wouldn't you tell him?"

"Why would I? We aren't in a relationship and it doesn't concern him. I wouldn't care if his ex-girlfriend moved here. I wouldn't expect him to tell me."

"Bullshit, Sierra. You care about Cameron more than you're willing to admit."

"No, I don't. That's not how I operate; you know that."

"I know you. And I knew you before Ryan. So I do know how you operate."

"I don't want to talk about this. I have enough on my mind with this dinner tonight. I don't need you telling me what I should or shouldn't do."

"Okay. I'll wait until tomorrow." She smiled.

"Then tomorrow is the day that I fire you."

She rolled her eyes and turned her head the other way. I lay there as Nathan worked his magical hands over my body and I thought way too much about Cameron.

After our massage, we headed for our manicures and pedicures. Instead of talking, Kirsty was doing business, heading off messages that weren't important to me. I looked at the clock on the wall. It was almost time for my dresses to be delivered. We climbed in the limo and headed back to the house. I didn't ask Kirsty about her and James because it was awkward for me. Two of my employees fucking each other. They didn't act like they were in some type of relationship during work hours, but they were seeing each other at night. As I walked into the house, the Neiman Marcus truck pulled up in the driveway. A big smile spread across my face. It was time to shop.

"Good to see you, Sierra," Paul said as he kissed both my cheeks. I brought you some goodies." He smiled.

"You can set up shop in the living room. I'll be there in a minute. There's something I need to take care of."

I followed the banging sound up the stairs, into my bedroom, and then up the spiral staircase. Cameron was pounding away at some two by fours he put up.

"Hey," I said nervously as I stood in the doorway.

"Hey," he replied as he turned around.

"Can I talk to you for a minute?"

"Yeah. What's up?" he asked as he continued hammering away.

"Do you think you could stop doing that for a minute?"

He stopped pounding and turned around and looked at me. "Okay."

"I know you know that Ryan moved back to Los Angeles, and I should have told you when I found out and I didn't and I'm sorry."

"It's none of my business, Sierra."

"But you're mad. I can tell because you've had an attitude with me since yesterday."

"Nah, you're imagining things. I don't have an attitude with you."

"Yes, you do. Just admit it," I snapped.

"Okay, fine. Yeah, I am pissed off that you didn't tell me. It obviously upset you and I thought you trusted me enough to open up to me. We're friends, Sierra, and I'm here for you."

At that moment, I felt like a complete bitch. I had hurt his feelings because I didn't talk about mine. I walked over to him and took the hammer out of his hand and set it down. I took hold of both his hands and looked into his green eyes.

"I'm sorry. I just wanted to erase the fact that he's back. If I talked about it, then it would make it real to me. I don't want it to be real. So if I don't talk about it, then it's not. You can thank Delia for giving me that trait."

"Come here," he said as he wrapped his arms around me and pulled me into him. "I understand. I really do and I'm sorry that I gave you an attitude. I had no right," he said as he kissed the top of my head.

"Are we good?" I asked as my arms tightened around his muscular back.

"We're good." He smiled as he broke our embrace and kissed my lips.

"I have to some shopping to do downstairs."

"Huh?"

"Paul from Neiman Marcus brought over some dresses for me to look at for tonight. Would you like to come down and help me pick something?"

"Surprise me." He smiled.

I went downstairs and then I examined all the dresses Paul brought. Kirsty was in heaven and James was sitting on the couch, watching her. Rosa emerged from the kitchen with lemonade for everyone and sat down next to James while I decided which dress to buy.

"They're all amazing."

"Well, I have one more that I haven't shown you yet," Paul said with excitement.

He unzipped the ivory garment bag and took out a Valentino sleeveless, side-draped dress in red. My eyes just about popped out of their sockets. I held it up to me and looked in the full-length mirror that he had brought with him.

"I love it!" I smiled.

"It's perfect." Cameron winked as he walked through the room and headed towards the kitchen.

"I'll take it."

"Excellent choice. It was made for you, Sierra." Paul smiled.

"Great choice, Sierra. You're going to look fab in it!" Kirsty said.

As soon as Paul and his men packed up and left, it was time for me to start getting ready for the dreaded night ahead. Kirsty and James left, but he assured me that he'd be back promptly at six thirty to pick us up. Rosa told me to behave myself and went home for the evening. I went to my room and stripped out of my business suit. I slipped on my short, silk robe and walked up the spiral staircase. I cleared my throat and Cameron turned around.

"Excuse me, but I have something that needs pounding." I smiled as I undid my robe and let it fall to the floor.

He smiled as he set down his hammer and unbuckled his belt. "Is that so? How hard does it need it?"

"Very hard," I said as I stood with my back against the wall.

Cameron took in a sharp breath as he stripped down to nothing. His cock was standing tall and at full force before he even reached me. He placed his hands on the wall on each side of my head as his mouth crashed forcefully into mine. My hands instantly gravitated to his hard cock as my fingers wrapped around him. A deep moan rumbled in his chest as his fingers slid down to the area that was aching for his touch. I arched my back as he plunged two fingers in me and worked my insides. My heart was racing and my skin was on fire.

"Wrap your legs around my waist," he commanded breathlessly.

He placed his hands on my ass and held me as my legs wrapped around him.

"Are you ready for some pounding?"

"Yes," I whispered.

He thrust inside me with such force that I gasped. He felt amazing and I didn't want it to end. He moved in and out of me at a rapid pace as our moans were in sync with each other. His fingers squeezed my ass as he pounded into me, sending me right over the edge and into a beautiful orgasm.

"That's it, babe. Come for me. I love it when I make you come. You're so amazing."

My legs tightened and my body shook as a whirlpool of pleasure overtook me.

"Oh my God, Sierra, you're making me come," he yelled as he pushed deep inside and spilled every last drop of his magical semen inside me and stared into my eyes.

I softly kissed his lips as he finished off. I grabbed the sides of his face. "Now I feel like I can face the night." I smiled.

"I was happy to oblige." He laughed.

"I need to go get ready and so do you."

He let go of me as I unwrapped my legs and stood on the ground. I bent down, picked up my silk robe and slipped it on. "I need to go shower. I'll see you promptly at six thirty."

"I'll be waiting." He smiled.

Chapter 29

Cameron

I stepped out of the shower and, as I wiped the steam from the mirror, I looked at myself. Sierra felt bad for not telling me about Ryan and that was a step in the right direction. I was in love with her. There. I admitted it. I was in love with Sierra Adams, the girl who was way out of my league. I knew deep down, somewhere in that beautiful soul of hers, she wanted more than just sex from me. I had already started bringing her into my world and now that she was halfway in, I was going to make it my mission to completely break down her walls and make her admit that she loved me. There was something about that pretty little head of hers that told me she was falling.

I dressed in my tuxedo and walked over to the main house. As soon as I entered the foyer, I became breathless as Sierra slowly walked down the steps.

"You look beautiful." I smiled.

"Thank you. You look very handsome in that tuxedo." She smiled back as she straightened my bow tie.

Sierra ran her hand across my cheek and went to the kitchen. I followed behind and watched her as she took the bottle of tequila, opened it, and drank from it.

"Starting early?"

"It's never too early, especially when Delia's involved."

I heard the front door open and James found us in the kitchen.

"How did I know you'd be hitting the bottle already?" He smiled.

She took one last swig and put the bottle away. "Okay. Now we can leave," she said as she grabbed her handbag from the table and headed out the door.

****

Sierra

I climbed into the limo and Cameron climbed in next to me. I pulled my phone from my purse and told him I had to make a quick phone call. I pulled my contact list up and scrolled until I found Marta's name. I hit call.

"Sierra Adams. Long time no talk," she answered.

"Marta, it's been way too long. How are you?"

The fakeness between us was always a good one.

"I'm great, and how may you be?"

"I'm good. To be honest, the word on the street is that you're blackmailing Don. Is that true? I know it couldn't be."

She laughed lightly before answering my question. "Oh, Sierra, always sticking her nose where it doesn't belong."

This was going to get good, so I put her on speaker. I held up my finger to Cameron and gave him a wink.

"Just answer the question, Marta? Would you do something like that?"

"Don and I have a special relationship. He broke my trust and he's not going to get away with it."

"Don is a slime ball, Marta. You of all people are smart enough to see that. Why the interest in him? He's a liar and, to be honest, he's Don."

"You'll never understand, Sierra."

"You're right, I never will, and I can't believe I'm doing this, but you are to back the fuck off and you are to stop blackmailing him."

"Don't be silly. You will not tell me what to do. I'm going to forget that we had this conversation and you can go back to playing CEO."

OH NO SHE DIDN'T. There was a moment of silence on my part due to the fact that I had to compose myself.

"Oh, Marta." I laughed lightly. "Listen to me, you wanna-be-a-successful-corporate bitch. Now it's my turn. You are to stop your sick little blackmail scheme or a certain person over at the IRS may be getting a phone call about your company's unethical financial decisions, if you get my drift. It would such a shame if your firm was to be audited."

"You wouldn't dare," she said with a nervous voice.

"Oh yes, I would. Did you really think that since my father died, all would be forgotten? Silly girl. Never underestimate me and the things my father passed on to me. Are we clear?" I snapped.

"Very."

"Have a nice night, Marta. It was good speaking to you. We should do lunch some time. I'll have Sasha call Belinda and set something up. Ta ta."

As I went to put my phone back in my purse, Cameron reached over, grabbed my hand, and stared at me in disbelief.

"Sorry you had to hear that. I didn't think she was going to act like that." I smiled.

He just kept staring at me, not saying a word. "What? Why do you keep looking at me like that?"

"You just—I—you—"

"I just put her in her place. I know. I was trying to be nice about it. But you heard her, right? I had no choice. Plus, she told me to go and play CEO. When I heard those—"

"Stop babbling." He smiled as he smashed his mouth against mine.

Before I knew it, the limo stopped and we arrived at the Beverly Hills Country Club. I broke our kiss and double checked my lips. I licked my thumb and wiped off some of my lipstick from the corner of Cameron's mouth.

"That's gross. I can't believe you just used your spit on my face."

"Really? Because you don't seem to mind my spit when it's all over your dick."

"Did you just really go there?"

"I did."

"Not fair. It's totally different."

"Spit is spit no matter where it is on the body."

"Can the two of you get out of the limo?" James smiled.

We walked into the restaurant and were immediately taken to our table. My stomach started flipping out when I saw Delia and Clive sitting down. Fake smile. Check.

"Sierra, happy belated birthday, darling," Delia said as she stood up and hugged me.

"Thank you, Mother."

"Happy Birthday, Sierra," Clive said as he kissed my cheek.

"Mother, you remember Cameron, my escort?"

"I'm sorry. Say that again," Clive said. I swear the man needs a hearing aid.

"This is Cameron; he's the escort I hired for the week. Cameron, this is Clive, my step-daddy."

I sat down next to Ava and gave her a hug. She smiled at Cameron and the two of them fist-pumped.

I needed a drink and I needed it now. This was no time for a waitress to be slacking on the job. A tall brunette carrying a tray of drinks stopped at our table and set down a cosmopolitan in front of me.

"I took the liberty of ordering that for you," Delia said.

That works.

"How's Adams Advertising, Sierra?" Clive asked.

"It's great. I have no complaints. How was your trip?" I asked.

"It was good. I closed a lot of business deals."

I bet you did.

"I saw Ryan the other day. Did you know he moved back?"

Delia smacked Clive on the arm. "I told you not to mention that."

"Yes, I know he did."

I handed Cameron a menu and his eyes widened as he opened it and saw the prices. "It's a country club," I whispered.

After the waitress took our order, I asked her to bring me two, not one, but two more cosmopolitans.

"I ordered your birthday present from Italy. So it should be arriving to your house within the week," Delia said.

"Thanks, Mother. You shouldn't have."

Ava handed me a square box that was wrapped in pretty paper with little pink flowers all over it. I scrunched my nose at her as I unwrapped it. I carefully removed the lid, and inside the box sat a beautiful silver bracelet with a dangling heart that said "sister" on it.

"Ava, it's beautiful," I said as I took it from the box and slipped it on.

"I'm happy you like it. I have the matching one." She smiled as she held out her wrist.

I reached over and gave her a big hug. "Thank you," I whispered as I kissed her head.

"Sierra, I found a remodeler for you. Remind me before we leave to give you his number. He comes highly recommended."

I looked over at Cameron and saw that he was about to burst into laughter. I gently kicked him under the table.

The waitress set my cosmos down and then our dinner came shortly after. As we were eating, I almost choked to death on my chicken when Delia told me she wanted to set me up on a date.

"I have someone I want you to meet."

"No thanks, Mother. I'm way too busy to date."

"If you dated properly, you wouldn't need to hire men like him," she said as she looked at Cameron.

He smiled awkwardly and continued eating.

"In fact, he's here tonight," she said as she looked around. "He graduated from Harvard and he runs his father's property management company."

"I don't care if he was the King of England. I'm not interested," I said as I consumed my drink.

"Oh, look; there he is. Davison, over here!" she yelled.

"Just fucking kill me right now," I whispered to Cameron.

He had the audacity to laugh.

"Davison, this is my daughter, Sierra. Sierra, this is Davison, the gentleman I was telling you about."

He was cute. He wasn't hot. He wasn't muscular. He was your average Harvard boy. His hair was a little too blonde for my liking and my gaydar was off the charts.

He. Was. Gay.

"It's nice to meet you, Sierra. Is that a Valentino?"

"Yes. It is. Do you like?"

"I love. I wish I could stay and chat, but my friend is waiting for me. Let's meet for coffee one morning. I'd love to discuss that dress."

"Sounds great."

He walked away and before Delia could say anything, I looked at her and smiled.

"He's gay."

"He most certainly is not. He went to Harvard."

I gulped the second cosmo and the effects were starting to set in. "Are you saying that only straight people go to Harvard?"

"No."

"I think you are."

"I am not, Sierra."

I turned to Ava and asked her how things were going. As we were conversing, Delia insisted that Clive dance with her. Cameron took hold of my hand as he got up from his seat.

"What are you doing?"

"I think this would be the perfect opportunity to practice our ballroom dancing skills. Don't we have a class tomorrow night?"

"Ugh. That's right," I said as I got up from my chair.

He led me to the dance floor and we began practicing what we had learned in our one class we attended.

"We're going to look like fools out here in front of all these old people that have been doing this for centuries."

He laughed. "Just follow my lead, Sierra. I'll stop you from looking like a fool."

We were pretty good together and I was ignoring the evil looks that Delia was shooting my way.

"I need some tequila." I smiled as I looked into his green eyes.

"No, you don't. I think you've had enough to drink."

"Who put you in charge of my life?"

"You did when you hired me to be your escort." He winked.

"One more drink after this dance and we'll call it a night."

"Promise only one more," he said.

"Promise on my Prada bag." I smiled.

The song was over and so was our dance. As we were walking back to our table, my heart instantly stopped and I lost all breath.

"Hello, Sierra," Ryan said.

I couldn't move. I couldn't breathe and I couldn't think. All normal functions went out the window when I heard his voice. I took in what little breath I had and mustered up one word.

"Fuck."

"You look amazing, Sierra."

Then, *snap*! I was back in reality.

"I know. I always do, don't I? But then again, there are hotter girls out there for you."

"Do you think maybe we could go outside and talk?"

"You lost the right to talk to me when you left me a voicemail saying that you weren't coming back. So the answer to your idiotic question is no."

"I see you're still pissed."

"Goodbye, Ryan." I smiled as Cameron and I walked away.

I sat in my seat and all eyes from my family were on me. Ava grabbed my hand and held it.

"Are you—"

"I'm fine," I interrupted.

I called for the waitress that was walking by and told her to bring me two double shots of tequila. She gave me a look and nodded her head. Shots in a country club was very unclassy. I pulled out my phone and sent a text message to James.

"COME NOW! RYAN'S HERE."

"Oh, boy. I'm on my way."

"Sierra, I swear I didn't know he was going to be here," Delia said.

"It doesn't matter. It was only a matter of time before we ran into each other."

Where were those fucking shots?

The waitress walked over and set the shot glasses in front of me.

"It's about time." I scowled.

Delia got up from the table and gave me a hug before I could drink my shots.

"We have to get going now. Clive has an early flight in the morning. We'll talk soon, darling."

"Thank you for dinner." I smiled as I hugged Clive and Ava goodbye.

As soon as they left, I downed both shots like water.

"Feel better now?" Cameron asked.

"A little." I smiled.

My phone beeped with a text message from Kirsty.

"James and I are here. Are you okay?"

Cameron and I left the country club and met them out front. Kirsty came running over to me. "Are you okay, sweetie?" she asked as she pulled me into an embrace.

"I'm fine. Let's get the hell out of here," I slurred.

As I was about to get in the limo, I looked over and saw Ryan standing on the grass. His back was turned and it looked like he was on the phone. At that moment, something inside of me snapped. I guess it was the last three years of self-pity and no answers that did it. My heart began to pick up the pace as I stood there and watched him casually talk on the phone. I took off my shoes.

"Sierra, what are you doing?" Cameron asked.

I threw them down on the cement, as well as my purse, and started speed-walking towards Ryan.

"Sierra, don't," I heard Cameron say in the distance.

"You never put a Prada on the cement," Kirsty yelled as she ran after me.

Some sort of possession took over me as a strange growl erupted from my chest and out of my mouth as I ran and tackled him to the ground.

"You fucking piece of shit!" I yelled as I pounded on him. "What happened to your little whore? You know, the one that was hotter than me and better in bed, you stupid little fuck!"

"Sierra, oh my God, stop it!" he yelled back as he tried to grab my wrists.

Cameron pulled me off of him and held me back by my arms. I tried to wiggle free, but no luck. He was strong.

Ryan sat there on the ground in disbelief as he stared at me with wide eyes.

"You fucked up my life. *You* did. Seven lousy years with you and you did nothing but belittle me. You said horrible and mean things that affected me in a bad way. Let me tell you something, you sorry piece of shit. You're no man. You're a coward because you couldn't face me. You and your little girly balls couldn't face me. YOU'RE A FUCKING COWARD."

"Sierra, I'm sorry," he said as he wiped a spot of blood from his lip.

"SORRY. YOU'RE SORRY!" I screamed. "I'm sorry too. I'm sorry for the day I ever met you. You, Ryan, never existed in my life. Yep, that's right. So from now on, when we see each other on the streets, we're total strangers. Strangers who never met and never will. Do you understand me?"

He nodded his head as he stood up and stared at me.

"Good. Let's go," I said as I yanked my arm away from Cameron, grabbed my Prada bag from Kirsty, and walked back to the limo.

We climbed in and I immediately put up my hands. "I had a temporary moment of insanity and now it's over. I don't want to talk about it ever again."

Chapter 30
Cameron

I lightly brushed the strands of blonde hair away from her face as she slept. I was still in shock that Sierra did what she did. She took tough to a whole new level as far as I was concerned. I had hoped now that she saw him and got out all her pent-up anger that she would start to see things more clearly where relationships were concerned. She opened her eyes and looked at me as my finger traveled down her cheek.

"Morning."

"Morning. What time is it?"

"It's almost six o'clock. Your alarm will be going off in a few minutes."

"Why are you up already?" she asked with a sleepy voice.

"I couldn't sleep. I kept thinking about you and what you did last night." I smiled.

"Ugh," she said as she rolled over and hit the button of her alarm. "We better get up. I have to get to the office," she said as she kissed my lips.

I lay there and watched as her naked body climbed out of bed and strolled to the bathroom. Today was going to be the day I started to win her over.

"Sierra, I'm going down to my place to get ready. I'll see you at breakfast."

"Okay," she said.

I went downstairs and Rosa was just coming in. "Morning, Rosa." I smiled.

"Good morning, Builder Boy. Is she up?"

"Yes. She's in the shower."

"Good. Breakfast will be ready soon."

"Thanks, Rosa."

****

Sierra

"Congratulations. You made the front page of the newspaper. What the hell happened last night?" Rosa asked as she handed me a cup of coffee.

"Great. Just fucking great."

A few moments later, Cameron walked in. "You have that look. What's wrong?"

"Senorita made the front page. Here, see for yourself," Rosa said.

Cameron took the paper from her and followed me to the table. He began to laugh as he was reading.

"What's so funny?" I asked.

"This picture. Look at you. You were pissed as hell."

Of all the pictures for the paper to print, they had to pick the one where I was on top of Ryan and looking like the daughter of Satan.

"Oh my God," Kirsty said as she stormed into the kitchen. "Did you see this?"

"Yes," I said as I waved my hand.

"I'm going to have to do damage control. Our clients aren't going to want a firm that beats other people up representing them. We're going to have to say it was joke. A publicity stunt or something."

"We aren't saying anything. It'll blow over."

"How scandalous is this?" James smiled.

I rolled my eyes. "He deserved it. I don't have any regrets and I'm certainly not going to apologize to anyone."

"I would have given anything to see that," Rosa said as she set a plate of French toast on the table.

"Aren't you going to eat?" Cameron asked as I got up from my chair.

"No. I'm going to take two aspirin and go change handbags. It's a Michael Kors kind of day."

When I walked into my room, my phone was ringing. It was Delia. I hit ignore because I wasn't in the mood to deal with her. I was sure she saw the newspaper. I changed handbags and fetched Kirsty and James to start the dreaded day that I knew was coming my way.

I walked into the building of Adams Advertising and, just as I expected, all eyes were on me. People were trying not to stare, but I could see them out of the corner of my eye. As I walked through the lobby and to the elevator, I stopped, turned around, and put out my arms.

"What? He deserved it. Seven years and he deserved it," I said as Kirsty pushed me into the elevator.

"Stop that. Don't feed into it."

Sasha was waiting for me, like she always did every morning, holding a cup of coffee in her hand. Today, she had a huge grin on her face.

"I put a little something extra in there for you. I figured you'd need it."

"Thank you, Sasha." I smiled as I took the cup from her.

I pulled my ringing phone from my purse. It was Don calling.

"Hello, Don."

"Sierra, I love you. Don't take that in a sexual way; it's meant as the love of friendship. Whatever you said to Marta, it worked. I am forever indebted to you."

"You're welcome, Don. Remember our little agreement."

"I do and I will. I saw you in the newspaper. Good for you. I always knew you had a wild side, girl. Have a good day. We'll talk soon."

I hit end as my mouth curved up into a small smile. Kirsty went to her office and Sasha came in with some news.

"Excuse me, Sierra. The Board of Directors called a meeting for tomorrow morning at nine o'clock."

"Of course they did, the sexist pigs. It's fine. I'm sure they want to discuss my actions of last night. I'll be prepared to fight back." I smiled. "Send Kirsty in here, please."

Just as I turned on my computer, Kirsty came through the door. "What's up?"

"The board called a meeting for tomorrow morning."

"Uh oh," she said.

"I want you and Sasha to spend the day digging up everything recent on every board member. I want to know what they've spent their money on and where they went."

"Sierra, you're playing with fire."

"No, Kirsty. They're the ones playing with fire. This is my company and they've had it out for me since my father died. Well, now they're the ones who are going to get burned."

"Okay. If you say so," she sighed as she walked out.

I went over to my wall safe and put in the combination. As I opened the door, I pulled out a black book with a leather cover that my father gave me right before he passed away. I sat back in my chair and recalled the day he handed it over.

"I want you to keep this in a very safe place. This book is yours now and it's filled with information on every board member. Information they never want anyone to know. I already know they aren't going to be happy about you taking over the company, so this is your firing weapon if you should need it. Use the knowledge that I gave you over the last many years, Sierra. Use what I taught you to your advantage."

A few hours later, and as I was studying the pages in the book, my phone rang and, when I looked at it, Cameron was calling.

"Hey you," I answered.

"Are you hungry?"

"For food or sex?" I replied.

"Both sound good to me. But I was referring to food."

"Yeah, I am kind of hungry. I didn't eat breakfast, remember?"

"I do remember."

I heard my office door open and, when I looked up, Cameron was standing there, holding up a brown bag from the deli down the street. I smiled as I hung up and he walked in, closing the door behind him.

"I bring you food. Solid food, not liquid food."

"What a nice surprise. Thank you. Shouldn't you be at my house, working on my office?"

"I should and I was, but I got hungry and I remembered you didn't eat, so I called Kirsty and asked her what I should get you."

"That was sweet, thank you. Have a seat."

I cleared off my desk as he took the sandwiches out of the bag.

"It looks like you were reading."

"More like studying."

"Studying?" he asked.

"The Board of Directors called a meeting for tomorrow morning. They're going to scold me for last night. So, I'm preparing to fight back."

"I have no doubt you'll win. From what I can tell, your father taught you very well."

****

Cameron

I drove back to the house and when I walked through the door, Rosa noticed my smile.

"What's going on with you, Builder Boy?" she asked as she stopped dusting.

"I'm happy, Rosa. I just had lunch with Sierra. Can you keep a secret?"

"Of course, but it's no secret to me that you're in love with her."

"That's right. I am in love with her and today was day one of doing something special for her. Rosa, I want Sierra to fall in love with me. I want us to have a real relationship." I smiled.

She walked over to me and put her hand on my face. "You are a good man and she'd be crazy not to love you. I'm on your side."

"Thanks, Rosa," I said as I kissed her cheek. "If you'll excuse me, I have an office to build."

After a few hours, I heard footsteps coming up the stairs. I turned around and Sierra was standing there, staring at the room.

"It's looking good in here, Mr. Cole."

"Thanks. It's coming along."

"Don't forget we have our dance lesson in about an hour. I sure hope you're going to shower. I don't want to have a stinky partner or I may have to pawn you off on Kirsty and take James." She smiled.

"I was just finishing this piece and then I was going to get myself cleaned up."

"Okay. Then I'll meet you downstairs."

"I'll be waiting." I smiled.

We met Kirsty and James at the dance studio. During our dance lesson, Sierra seemed off. She seemed sad and I hated that something was bothering her.

"How about we go for a swim when we get back," I said as I drove us home.

"Sure. We can do that," she said with a small smile.

We finally reached Sierra's house and I told her that I'd meet her in the pool. I went and changed into my swim trunks, grabbed a towel, and jumped in. After doing a couple of laps, I wiped the water from my eyes and looked up to see Sierra staring down at me. She was holding a bottle of wine and two glasses.

"You in?" she asked.

"I'm in."

She poured the wine and handed me a glass before stepping into the pool.

"What's wrong, Sierra? And don't you dare say 'nothing,' because I can tell something's bothering you."

"I'm just a little pissed off and worried about tomorrow's meeting. When my father was sick, they tried to talk him out of leaving me the company. They said that I was too young, a woman on the mend of a broken heart, and a pushover to be running one of the largest advertising agencies in the world. They never had faith in me."

"But you proved them wrong. Look at you. You're fierce. You have fire and passion for your company and I think you do a damn good job."

She smiled as she took a sip from her glass. "I am fierce, aren't I?"

"The fiercest woman I've ever met."

"I know I've asked you this before, but why don't you have a girlfriend?"

I chuckled. "I guess I haven't found anyone that I want to spend my time with."

"Well, when you do, she'll be very lucky to have you." She smiled as she poured more wine in our glasses.

I hoped and prayed that she'd be the one who felt lucky when the time came.

Chapter 31

Sierra

I scoured the bar and couldn't find any Baileys. Shit. Shit. Shit. I went through each bottle and even all the travel-size bottles were gone. Damn it. I drank too much. I walked over to the door, opened it, and looked at Sasha.

"Can you come in here for a minute?"

"Sure," she said as she got up from her seat. "Is something wrong?"

"If you consider my coffee liquor gone, something being wrong, then yes. Your number one job working for me is to make sure my bar is stocked at all times."

"Sierra, I just stocked it last week. There's no way you went through that already."

"Oh," I said as I twisted up my face and looked up.

"Hold on," she said as she left the office.

A few moments later, she came back in with a pint of Kahlua. "This is the emergency stash I keep hidden away."

"I love you and you're getting a raise." I smiled as I took it from her and poured half coffee and half Kahlua in my travel mug.

"Good luck with the board," she said.

"You should be wishing them luck." I winked as I walked out and over to the boardroom.

Kirsty was placing the booklets I had her make yesterday at each member's place. As I walked in, my phone beeped with a text from Cameron.

"Fierce. Good luck."

"Thank you. Would you like their numbers so you can wish them luck?"

"That's my girl."

I read that last text and a funny feeling erupted in my stomach. Then it got worse as the board members strolled in one by one. Walking proud, holding their Styrofoam cups in their hands and file folders under their arms. Preparing themselves to launch their attack on me and the integrity of my company.

"Good morning, gentlemen," I said as I took a long sip of my coffee. "Please have a seat."

I took my seat at the head of the table and Kirsty took hers to the left of me. I pushed the intercom button on the phone and asked Sasha to join us with her notepad and pen.

"Sierra," William spoke. "The reason we called this meeting is because we're concerned about your—" He cleared this throat. "Your mental stability and how it's going to affect this company."

As I sat there, I stared at him with a smile plastered across my face and my hands folded neatly and resting on the table.

"We weren't happy seeing your picture all over the front page of the newspaper. You attacked that man."

"And that's not how a CEO represents their company," Julian spoke.

I looked down along the table at the twelve men that sat before me. I studied them as they all agreed with each other, nodding their heads like a bunch of Boy Scouts playing Follow the Leader.

"We're concerned that your reputation is going to become the downfall of this company and we can't have that. We want to make a suggestion to you," Bill spoke.

I picked up my cup and took the last sip of coffee. "What's your suggestion, gentlemen?" I asked in a polite manner.

"We think you should take some time off and go seek some help. Maybe go to one of those Zen retreats or something," Doug said. "We can appoint an interim CEO until you get back. We were thinking maybe a six-month hiatus would be good for you."

THE. NERVE. OF. THESE. FUCKERS. I looked over at Kirsty and she smiled at me. Not her bright and cute smile, but her evil smile. The show was about to start.

I smiled as I got up from my seat and walked around the table in a complete circle before I singled out each member personally.

"Gentlemen, first of all, he's no man. He's a mere boy. A boy with tiny little balls. A boy on whom I took out my three years of anger because, after a seven-year relationship, he called me on the phone from wherever the hell he was and said he was never coming back. So, excuse me if I was feeling a little hurt. Did I mention he did it through a voicemail?"

Once I reached my seat, I took the pile of file folders from Kirsty. "Before I go over these files, I would like you all to take a look at the numbers and profits for the last quarter. Numbers are up over sixty percent. It must be my inner crazy that did that." I smiled.

"Sierra, this doesn't—"

"Ah, William," I interrupted. "Your file just happens to be the first on top," I said as I threw it down in front of him and leaned in closer. "How's your son doing at Yale?"

"Have you been drinking? I swear I smell alcohol on your breath," he said.

"Of course not. I barely drink at all. I really can't stand the taste of alcohol. What you're smelling is the Kahlua-flavored coffee that Sasha just bought down the street at The Beanery. She can make you a cup if you'd like."

"No, that's all right."

"Now, back to your son. How does he like Yale?"

"He loves it and he's doing well. Why are you asking?"

I walked around to the other side of the table. "Is he doing well, William? Because word on the street is he's struggling. I wonder why that would be. You have to be uber smart even to be considered a potential candidate for Yale, and your son is uber smart, right? I mean with his 4.0 average, which really was a 3.1 until you had his transcripts doctored, along with his ACT scores. I wonder how Yale would feel about that," I said with a twisted face.

His face was turning red as he opened the file and saw the proof sitting in front of him. "You can have that file. I have a few more copies." I smiled.

The room was dead silent. You could hear a pin drop on the carpet if you listened close enough. Next, it was Julian's turn. I walked over and threw his file folder in front of him.

"How's your wife, Julian? Does she know anything about the hundreds of thousands of dollars you owe in back taxes? How's that sporty little red Porsche of yours? Still hiding it in that storage facility so she won't find out about it? Oh, and how's that friend of yours doing? What's her name?" I asked as I brought my finger to my lip.

"Alyssa," Kirsty replied.

"Ah, yes. Alyssa. She's how old again?"

"Eighteen," Kirsty said.

"Yes, that's right. I bet little eighteen-year-old Alyssa loves that red Porsche. In fact, I do believe there's a picture of the two of you kissing in it."

"Damn you, Sierra. That's enough," Julian yelled as he slammed his fists down on the table.

"Calm yourself, Julian. That's the only warning you're going to get. Now, moving on to you, Bill." I smiled as I put down his folder. "How's your divorce going? Does your wife know about the several accounts you have hiding over in the Caymans?"

"How do you know about those?" he asked with such a nervousness that I thought he was going to pass out.

"I know everything." I smiled. "The question here is: does she know? I'm sure her attorney would love to know about those accounts and think of the life your wife could live having half of that money she's, by law, entitled to."

I walked around and threw the folders down in front of the rest of the members. "Let's see, Doug. You said that I should go seek some help. How's that sex addiction working for you? Have you looked into therapy for that?"

A look of horror swept over his face as he took off his glasses and rubbed the bridge of his nose. "Normally, I wouldn't give a damn who you sleep with, but I think, correct me if I'm wrong, that hiring a prostitute is illegal in our good old state of California. I'm really shocked because your wife is absolutely gorgeous. But, an illness is an illness and you really should go and get help for yours, Doug."

When I made it back around to my chair, I took a seat and opened the bottle of water that was sitting in front of me. I took a drink before I said my final words.

"Bottom line, gentlemen. You sit there on your high horses, pointing your crooked little fingers at me because I'm a woman who you think doesn't deserve to be the CEO of a company her father spent his whole life building. This is my company and how dare you come in here and talk about my behavior. In fact, I should ask each and every one of you in here for your resignation right now. But I'm not going to do that. Ask me why? Come on, ask me why," I said as I lifted my hands.

"Why, Sierra?" they all said in unison.

"Because, believe it or not, you all do a damn good job, regardless of your personal issues. Just like I do. Profits are at an all-time high. We secured ten new clients in the past three months and we're growing more and more every day. This company is in my blood and I'll be damned if I let you fuckers try and take it from me. Are we clear?" I asked as I pointed to William first.

"Yes," he replied.

I went down the table and pointed to each member as they all had the same answer: yes.

"Now get the hell out of here. But remember this, don't play with fire because you will always get burned. Oh, and by the way, my attorney has a copy of each of your files. Have a great day, gentlemen." I winked.

They got up from their chairs and walked out of the room, but not before giving me the evil eye. Sasha got up from her chair and hugged me.

"You were amazing. I'm so proud to call you my boss."

"Thanks, Sasha. Now you better get back to work."

Once the boardroom was clear, Kirsty reached over and gave me a hug. "I think that was the best show I've ever seen. Did you see the looks on their faces? I think they all shit their pants when you put their files in front of them."

"I couldn't have done it without you, Kirsty. Thank you."

"We make a great team." She smiled.

"We always have," I replied.

I went back to my office and sat in my comfy oversized leather chair. I pulled up Cameron's number and hit call.

"Hey, I was just thinking about you," he answered. "How did it go?"

"It went well, very well. I think they've had a change of heart about me, especially when I threatened to remove them all from the board."

"Good girl. I never doubted you for a second."

All I could hear was banging. "What is going on?"

"Your office. That's what's going on. I'm taking you to dinner tonight to celebrate. In fact, ask Kirsty and James to join us."

"You don't have to do that, Cameron."

"I know I don't, Sierra. But I want to. Now, I have to go. There's work that needs to be done."

"Bye, Cameron."

"Bye, Sierra."

As the day went on and one problem after another arose, Sasha walked into the office, carrying a dozen yellow roses in a beautiful glass vase.

"Look what just arrived for you."

"They're beautiful. Who are they from?" I asked.

"I don't know; read the card that came with them." She smiled as she handed me the small, sealed envelope.

I picked up my letter opener from the desk and ran it across the top of the envelope. I pulled out the card inside that read:

Then You Happened

Congratulations.

Your father would be very proud of you.

I know I am.

Love, Cameron

"Well, who are they from?"

"Cameron. He just congratulated me for a successful meeting today."

"I like him. I think he's a great guy. Very normal and down to earth. Unlike some of the others you date."

"He is a great guy, isn't he?"

Sasha left and I sat at my desk and stared at the beautiful roses. I picked up my phone and sent Cameron a text message.

"Thank you for the beautiful roses. You shouldn't have done that."

"You're welcome and I wanted to. You deserved them."

"Thank you, Cameron. You're a good friend."

"So are you, Sierra. I'll see you later."

As I was in deep thought, Kirsty strolled in.

"Whoa, which suit sent you those beauties?" she asked.

"They aren't from a suit. They're from Cameron. He sent them as a congratulations for a successful meeting."

"I think he's in love with you, Sierra."

"He better not be. He knows the rules. Sex only."

"Pish posh. Are you going to sit there and tell me that you're not falling for him?"

"Yes, I am. He's a good friend who is great to have sex with. Nothing more, Kirsty."

"You're a fool," she said as she bent over and took a whiff of the roses.

"Actually, I'm not. I'll never be a fool again. Life is good the way it is. I don't need any complications. Oh, by the way, if you have plans for tonight, cancel them. Cameron is taking us and James to dinner."

Chapter 32

Cameron

I stepped into the shower and washed away all the dirt and dust from work today. I put on a pair of jeans and a t-shirt and headed back to Sierra's house. This dinner was probably going to be the most casual dinner she'd ever had. When I walked in, I found her standing in the kitchen with a bottle of water. She was dressed in a pretty and simple designer dress with a pair of designer heels on her feet. I couldn't help but laugh.

"What's so funny?" she asked.

"You're going to want to change into something more casual, like jeans and t-shirt."

"Are you serious?" she asked.

"Yeah, Sierra. I'm serious."

"Where are you taking us?"

"It's a surprise. But trust me, you'll be more comfortable in jeans."

"But I look pretty in my dress," she pouted.

"Indeed you do. Tonight's dinner is very casual."

"Great," she said as she gave me a look and walked upstairs.

As I waited for her, Rosa came in to say goodbye. "Why is Sierra upstairs complaining?" she asked.

"Because I told her she had to change out of her pretty dress and into jeans for dinner."

Rosa burst into laughter. "Where are you taking her?"

"Danny's Tacos."

Her eyes suddenly widened when she heard the name. "That is my favorite place, or truck, I should say. Make sure to have your camera ready. I want to see the look on her face when you take her there. You do know she's going to be pissed, right?"

"She'll get over it and she'll love it. It won't hurt her not to go to an expensive, fancy restaurant for once."

"No, it won't hurt her, but she may just hurt you. You better wear some protection." She laughed.

Kirsty and James walked in and both were dressed in jeans and t-shirt. I had called them during the day and told them where we were going, so they were on alert.

"Where's Sierra?" Kirsty asked.

"Upstairs, changing out of her designer dress. I made her put on jeans."

"Way to go, Cam. I think you just ruined our night." She smiled.

A few moments later, Sierra came down and a wide smile graced my face when I saw her in her jeans and a Bebe t-shirt. Then I looked down at her feet and began to shake my head.

"What now?" she asked with irritation.

"No heels. We're doing a lot of walking, so you need comfortable shoes."

"I thought we were going to dinner?"

"We are. It just involves a lot of walking."

"You're really starting to get on my nerves, Cole," she said as she stomped out of the kitchen.

I chuckled along with James. Another moment passed and she came down the stairs in her black flats.

"Better, your majesty?"

"Yes. Way better." I smiled as I kissed her cheek.

I was nervous but excited to introduce her to the best tacos in Los Angeles. When I lived in my apartment, I frequently visited Danny's Tacos on my way home from work and grabbed a carryout. The four of us hopped in my truck and we headed to eat.

****

Sierra

I sat there, looking out the window, confused, and trying my damnedest to figure out where he was taking me to dinner. We were in Santa Monica now and he parallel parked outside of a dry cleaners.

"We're having dinner at a dry cleaners?" I asked.

Cameron walked around and opened the door for me. I stepped out and he grabbed my hand. James and Kirsty followed behind.

"Seriously, where are we eating?"

"Why? Are you worried or something?" He smiled.

"A little bit."

We walked up and stood in a line that was in front of a white food truck. "This is where we're eating."

I looked at him in confusion as I looked around. James and Kirsty were behind us, laughing.

"Where? Is this a joke or something?"

I looked straight ahead at the truck and it said *Danny's Tacos* across the top of it. I started to laugh.

"Okay. You guys are hilarious. Come on now; let's go the restaurant," I said as I grabbed Cameron's hand and began to walk away.

"This is no joke. You are going to love the food here. I promise." He smiled.

"You're fucking crazy if you think that I'm eating food from a truck. Oh my God, why would you do this to me?"

"Relax, Sierra. I'm sure it's good," Kirsty said.

Cameron leaned over and whispered in my ear. "Trust me. That's all I ask."

Trust him. Those were the last words a spineless, no-balls boy said to me over the phone before he left. I could recall the conversation as if it happened yesterday.

"So you'll be home when I get back from my trip?" I asked Ryan.

"Yeah, I'll be waiting for you. Just have a good trip with Kirsty, Sierra, and don't worry about anything."

I recalled something in his voice sounded really off.

"Okay, if you say so."

"Trust me."

The sad part was that even though I had a bad feeling, I did trust him. Shame on me and I wouldn't make that mistake again. I didn't say another word about Danny's Tacos and it was finally our turn to order. Cameron asked what everyone wanted. What he didn't know was that I wasn't eating it. There was no way in hell I was eating food from a truck.

"I'll have two chicken tacos," I said. "Do you have any tequila?" I asked with a smile.

"Just beer, ma'am."

"Beer? You're a Mexican truck. Tequila is your specialty."

"Sorry, just beer."

"Fine, give me a beer," I said.

Cameron chuckled at me and I didn't think it was very funny. "Beer and tacos. Way to go, Cameron."

He put his arm around me. "Stop bitching or I'm going to leave your rich ass here."

"I'll fire you."

"Go ahead. Good luck trying to find someone else who will give you great sex and remodel your house for cheap." He winked.

I sighed. I hated when he was right, and I hated that he was starting to sound like Kirsty.

When Danny handed us our beers and bags, we walked over to a nearby park and sat down at a wooden table. Cameron and James opened the bags and handed each of us our food. I took a swig of my beer and set it down.

"Aren't you going to eat?" Cameron asked.

"In a minute," I replied with uncertainty.

I looked down at the tacos wrapped in white paper and slowly unwrapped them. I looked at Kirsty, who was chowing down on her *carnita* bowl.

"Sierra, this is absolutely the best," she said.

"The best," James said as he tore into his burrito.

I picked up my taco and, against my better judgment, I took a bite. HOLY SHIT. I wasn't going to admit it, but it was the best taco I'd ever had. I took another bite and then another. Cameron nudged my shoulder.

"You like it, don't you?" He smiled.

"Maybe."

"Come on, Sierra." He playfully nudged me again. "Admit it."

"Okay, fine. It's fucking fantastic. Who would've thought that tacos from a truck would be so damn good?"

"Do you want to try my burrito?" he asked as he held it out to me.

I wrapped my hands around his as he held it up to my mouth and I took a bite. "I want one," I said.

"Seriously?" He smiled.

"Yes. That is one fabulous burrito."

"I'll be right back, then."

"I'll go with you," James said.

They got up from the table and left. Kirsty looked at me and shook her head.

"Don't. I mean it."

They guys came back and Cameron handed me my burrito. "For you, my lady." He smiled.

There he went again, calling me either "my girl or my lady," like he was staking a claim on me or something. He told me he was okay with our relationship as it is. I hoped for his sake, he was not changing his mind.

"You should've seen Sierra in action today," Kirsty said with enthusiasm.

"I wish I could've. I bet she was great."

"I may just happen to have a video recalling the events of the day."

"Kirsty! Tell me you did not record that."

"Only a portion of it; my battery started to die."

She pulled her phone from her purse and brought up the video, setting it down in front of Cameron as I ate my burrito. When it was over, he slowly turned his head and looked at me.

"Wow, Sierra. I mean, really; wow. I'm turned on right now." He smiled.

I slipped my hand over his thigh and to his crotch and, sure enough, he was as hard as a rock. "We can role play later. I'll be the big bad boss lady and you can be the scheming board member." I winked.

"Deal." He smiled.

"Let's go over to Pacific Park," James blurted out.

"Sounds like fun. Do you want to?" Cameron asked me.

I looked across at Kirsty and she nodded her head yes. I could see the excitement in her eyes, like a kid in a candy store.

"Sure. Sounds like fun," I said.

We got up, threw our trash away, and began walking back to Cam's truck. "Aren't you happy that I made you change into jeans and out of those heels?"

"Of course I am. But you should be the one who's happy because you'd be carrying me the whole time."

"You think so? You mean like this?" He smiled as he swooped his arms underneath my legs and picked me up. I laughed and threw my arms around his neck as he carried me to the truck.

We drove to Pacific Park and it was starting to get dark, so the whole park was lit up with bright lights. The main attraction was the Pacific Wheel that was lit up so bright that it almost hurt your eyes to look at it. We walked past the games and I stopped when I saw a large white cat that looked exactly like Duchess from *The Aristocats*.

"I need to have that cat," I said as I walked over to the ring toss and handed the guy some money.

I threw the rings and no luck. I sucked, so I whipped out some more money and handed it to him.

"Let's try this again." I smiled.

I threw the two rings and nothing. "Babe, you're throwing it wrong," Cameron said.

"Okay, Mr. Smarty. Be my guest," I said as I handed him the ring.

He threw it and that baby landed on top of the glass bottle. "Woo hoo!" I yelled as I kissed Cameron's cheek and the man handed me the white cat.

I squeezed it like a little kid and Cameron hooked his arm around me. "Why that cat?" he asked.

"This is Duchess from *The Aristocats*. It was my favorite Disney cartoon. I've always wanted a real cat like this, but my mom hates cats and my dad always said it wasn't the right time."

"Why didn't you get one when you moved into your own place?"

"I don't know. I guess after a while, I didn't think about it anymore."

We saw James and Kirsty at the tub toss and Kirsty landed a ball in the bucket and won a stuffed animal. She and James started kissing and I turned my head.

"What's wrong?" Cameron asked.

"I just can't get used to seeing them kissing. They're my two best friends and it's weird for me, especially with the age difference."

"James is really cool and he likes her a lot. He told me. He said he had for a long time, but was afraid of you."

"That's nice. So I am scary," I said.

"Sometimes." Cameron winked. "Come on; let's go on the Pacific Wheel. Hopefully, we'll get stuck on top and we can enjoy the beautiful view."

"You and your views drive me nuts." I smiled.

"I can't help it that I enjoy beautiful views."

Chapter 33

Cameron

A week had passed and Sierra and I continued our ballroom dancing lessons and continued to have amazing sex almost every night. I was madly in love with her and I wanted to tell her so badly. This last week, she hadn't been getting home until around ten o'clock. She was worried about the ballroom dance company and securing the account. I made sure that there was a glass of tequila waiting for her when she came home.

"You look tired," I said.

"I am. Today was a tough day. People suck." She smiled. "Delia stopped by the office unannounced and finally confronted me about Ryan. That was the highlight of my day," she said as she drank her tequila.

"What did she say?"

"She told me that she was ashamed and I never should've done what I did. She said that classy women don't do things like that and obviously, she failed as a parent. She also said that she doesn't have time to deal with my immaturity because she's focusing on Ava. She's a real piece of work."

"She said that to you?"

"I had the perfect comeback, but I held my tongue because, even though she's my mother, she's not worth my breath. Let her think what she wants. I'm used to it."

On top of tired, she looked sad. I picked her up and carried her upstairs. There was no sex tonight. We just lay there and held each other without saying a word until we were both sound asleep.

The next morning, I received a call from my brother, Jaden, saying that he was getting married next month and he asked me to be his best man. Sierra was still upstairs, getting ready for work, and I was sitting down for breakfast.

"Morning, Rosa."

"Good morning." She smiled as she handed me a cup of coffee.

A few moments later, Sierra walked down and joined me. "Jaden called me and he's getting married next month. He asked me to be his best man."

"Why?" she asked.

"Why what? Why did he ask me to be his best man?"

"No. Why is he getting married? I didn't know he had a girlfriend."

"He does and they've been dating for two years. She was out of town when we were there. Apparently, he got her pregnant."

"Oh. That's not good," she said as she sipped her coffee.

"What? That he got her pregnant or that he's getting married?"

"Both." She smiled. "Don't think I'm going with you. The last thing I want is to go back there."

"I wasn't going to ask you anyway," I lied.

"Good. I have too much going on around here."

"I know you do. God forbid you think about anyone but yourself," I said as I got up from the table and walked out.

****

Sierra

"What the hell was all that about?" I snapped as I looked at Rosa.

"Figure it out, *senorita*. I have a feeling things are about to change around here," she said as she walked out of the kitchen.

Whatever. I didn't have time to deal with the two of them. I had a big meeting today with Aruelia and Renee. He knew that too. I walked upstairs and found him in my soon-to-be office.

"What the hell was all that about? You know I have that meeting today with Aruelia."

"I know and good luck."

"Good luck? That's it? Were you expecting me to go? Because we're not a couple. You just can't expect me to do certain things because we have sex."

"You're right, princess. We're not a couple and I don't expect anything from you. Shame on me for even thinking you'd be interested in someone like me."

"What the hell is that supposed to mean?" I snapped.

"It means that I love you and that I was a fool for thinking you could ever love me back."

"No. No. No. You don't love me," I said as I covered my ears. "You can't say things like that."

"I can and I will. I love you, Sierra Adams, and I'm not sorry for saying it!" he yelled.

"Stop it."

"No, I won't stop it. You don't rule me, Sierra. I can say whatever I want. I can't help my feelings for you. You're fun and witty and I fell for your high-class ass the minute I saw you. Something inside me needed to be near you and with you. I'd never felt that kind of connection with anyone before. You are the sunshine in my life, Sierra. You are the woman I'm in love with and the woman I don't want to live without."

"No. Stop!" I yelled as I turned around and wouldn't face him.

"I'm only going to ask you this one time, Sierra. Do you love me?"

My heart was aching and my legs were shaking. Shit, my whole body was shaking. The fear of all fears crept up inside me, my future. I'd rather be alone than spend every day wondering if he was going to leave me.

"I guess there's my answer. But, let me tell you something, I know that deep down, you do love me. Either that or you're a really good fucking actress."

I turned around and went to slap him across the face for that remark, but he was quick and grabbed my hand.

"Don't you dare hit me. I have done nothing wrong. The only thing I did was love you and, whether you believe it or not, you deserve to be loved."

"Sierra," Kirsty softly spoke.

Cameron let go of my hand and stormed out. I stood there, frozen, no emotion because I couldn't let it overtake me. I had an important meeting that I needed to focus on and I wasn't about to let him ruin that.

"Sweetie, I overheard some of that. Are you okay?"

"I'm fine. Let's go."

I walked down the stairs, passed Rosa in the foyer, and climbed into the back of the limo. Neither James nor Kirsty said a word to me. THEY. KNEW. BETTER. James pulled up to the building and I flew out of the limo and up to my office.

"Good—"

I put up my hand and stopped Sasha from finishing as I walked into my office and slammed the door. I paced back and forth for a minute before I walked over to the bar and took out the bottle of tequila that Sasha had just restocked. I brought the bottle up to my lips and stopped. Putting the bottle down, I stormed out of my office and across the street to Starbucks for a large coffee. My mind was hazy and I was confused. Damn him. We talked about this. He was fine with our relationship just being about sex. Things were going good and now he had to go and ruin it. I just needed to get through the meeting and I needed to get through the day. *I'll fix this. I'll make him see that we can still have fun together without having anything more than friendship.* I needed to text him. No, I couldn't. As soon as I got back to my office, Kirsty came in and told me that Aruelia and Renee were in the conference room with some of the other staff, waiting for the meeting to begin. I composed myself and took in a deep breath before walking into the lion's den.

The meeting lasted about an hour. Once everyone left, I sank down in my chair and cupped my face in my hands.

"I don't think it went that bad," Kirsty said.

"It did, Kirsty. It went really bad. I wasn't on my game. I really want to be left alone for the rest of the day. I know you understand," I said as I got up from the chair and left the conference room.

****

Cameron

I finally finished up her office. The only thing that needed to be done was the painting and I'd have Paolo do it. I struggled through the day to get this office done because I decided that it was time for me to leave Los Angeles. Our argument this morning and her not being able to tell me that she loved me tore me to shreds. I wanted nothing more than to be with her. I went back to the guest house and packed my bags and, as I was coming out, I saw Rosa standing by the pool.

"Where are you going?" she asked.

"I think it's time for me to head back home, Rosa."

"Don't give up on her, Cameron."

"I told her that I love her and she turned away from me. I asked her if she loved me and she couldn't give me an answer.

After everything we'd been through, she couldn't give me an answer."

"She's scared and she's stubborn."

"There's nothing to be scared of and, if she can't see that by now, then I'm sorry. But I can't stay here and pretend that I don't love her because it hurts too much. She's way out of my league, Rosa, and that's something I knew from the beginning."

I walked up to her, put my bags down, and gave her a hug. "Thank you for being such a great friend and thank you for all the wonderful meals you cooked for me. I'll never forget you, Rosa. If you ever need anything, please call me."

"You're a good man, Cameron." She smiled. "Have a safe trip home."

I smiled back and walked into the house. There was one last thing I needed to do. I went up the stairs and into Sierra's bedroom. I took the neatly folded piece of paper from my pocket and laid it on her pillow. I walked one last time up the spiral staircase and stared at the newly built office that I knew would make her happy and then I climbed in my truck and took off.

Chapter 34

Sierra

After spending the last few hours wandering around Los Angeles, I called James to pick me up and take me home. I didn't have the answers that Cameron wanted and I didn't know what to do. The thing I knew I needed to do was talk to him. If he'd only give me some more time, I knew we could make this work. I sat on a bench and waited for James. When he pulled up to the curb, he got out of the limo and sat down next to me. All he had to do was put his arm around me and I lost it. The tears started to fall uncontrollably as he kissed the top of my head.

"I know it hurts, but you don't have to go through this. Go talk to him."

"He knew the rule. He knew that I wasn't in it for a relationship and then he had to go and fall in love with me. How could he do that?"

I heard him chuckle as he looked at me. "You're a loveable person, Sierra, and I know deep down inside that stubborn little heart of yours, you have feelings for him. I've watched you change since Cameron came into your life. You were happy."

I wiped my tears and lifted my head from his shoulder. "I was, wasn't I?"

"Yes. It was something that came naturally to you when the two of you were together."

"Let's go. I need to talk to him."

We both got up and I slid into the back of the limo and headed home. When we pulled up in the driveway, a wave of nausea overtook me. His truck was gone. I got out and quickly walked into the house and flew up the stairs to my bedroom and then up the spiral staircase with the hope that maybe he was there. He wasn't. I stood in the doorway and looked at my finished room. The windows were all in place and the sunlight was shining brightly through them.

"Sierra," I heard Rosa say.

I turned around and looked at her. The look on her face was sad and I knew in that moment that he was gone.

"He left," she said.

"Where did he go?"

"He went back home. I'm sorry," she said as she handed me a glass full of tequila and turned and walked out.

I took a sip and went down to my room and saw a folded piece of paper lying on my pillow. I walked over and picked it up. Holding it in one hand and my glass in the other, I climbed onto my bed and sat back. It was a letter from Cameron.

"Dear Sierra,

I don't even know what to say to you except that everything that I told you earlier was true. I love you. I know it's not what you wanted to hear, but I can't help it because I wanted nothing more than to tell the world how much I loved you. I'm not going to apologize for loving you. I won't do that because I'm not sorry. We shared some great times together and I will never regret that. But you need to understand that I can't stay because it hurts to see you every day and to make love to you knowing that the relationship will never be anything more. Like the old saying goes: you can't have your cake and eat it too. Life is made up of what you want, and sometimes you need to take a risk, even if it scares the shit out of you because it could be the best and most rewarding risk you ever take. I took a risk coming out to Los Angeles for work, and for me, it was the best decision I ever made. I can't make you love me, but I can wish you the best and all the happiness in the world. I want you to know that I'll never forget you and the time we spent together. Through all your crazy ways and your love for the finer things in life, you swept me off my feet, Sierra Adams. Before I end this letter, I'm asking you to do one thing for me. Go and be happy because you deserve it.

Love forever,

Cameron"

As the tears poured from my eyes, I finished off the glass of tequila and curled up into a ball, trying to shield myself from the pain. This was all too familiar to me. The tears, the curling up, the hurt, and most of all, the ache that my heart felt. I couldn't believe he left. I closed my eyes because I didn't want to deal with the reality anymore. I saw myself from three years ago, holding out my hand, waiting to take me back to that dark place in the deepest corner of my mind. The place that I fought so hard to climb out of. My self was smiling at me and telling me that if I went back, I'd be safe and shielded from the pain. *NO!*

"Sierra, wake up. You're having a bad dream," I heard Kirsty's voice say in the distance.

I opened my swollen eyes; she and Rosa were standing over me.

"Ugh, go away," I said as I rolled over. "Let me wallow in my own self-pity for the next year."

"Absolutely not!" Kirsty said. "You did this to yourself. I'm sorry, but it's true. Fire me if you don't like what I'm saying. Cameron isn't one of your emotionless suits. You hurt him and you have nobody to blame but yourself. He's not Ryan and he never will be. I stood by you through that fiasco because Ryan was to blame for your pain. Cameron isn't to blame here. You are. You're responsible for your own pain and you need to get over it."

Wow. I didn't know she had that side to her. I was a little impressed, but I also hated the fact that she was right.

"Please, just give me this one night. It's all I ask. Just this one night."

"Fine. Just this one night, but I'll be staying here tonight in the guestroom because you shouldn't be alone."

"And I'm staying too," Rosa said.

I rolled my eyes. "Fine."

They both left the room and I curled back up into my little ball.

****

Cameron

I sat on the plane and thumbed through the pictures of us. Her smile was bright and she was happy. Even if she never wanted to admit it, she was happy. It was going to be hard being without her. I'd hoped that being out of L.A. would help lessen the pain, and my parents were thrilled that I was coming home. I wasn't going to tell them about Sierra because as far as they were concerned, she was still the lesbian barista that worked at Starbucks. She was crazy and I loved her, but I had to move on and somehow try to get over her.

Chapter 35

Sierra

I spent the last two slowest weeks of my life buried in my job. I did jobs that weren't even mine to do because I needed to keep busy. I hated coming home every night to an empty house, so I made sure I left first thing in the morning and didn't come home until around midnight. Life was going on as it did pre-Cameron.

"Sierra, Aruelia is on the phone for you," Sasha beeped in.

"Put her through," I replied as my stomach tied itself in knots. "Good morning, Aruelia."

"Good morning, Sierra. I just called to tell you that we've decided to look elsewhere for our advertising needs. I'm sorry."

"Me too. But thank you for letting me know."

I hung up and wanted to die. That account was huge and I should have gotten it. Suddenly, I wanted tacos. I grabbed my purse and did something I hadn't done in years. I hailed a cab.

"Where to, lady?"

"Danny's Tacos," I said with a smile.

"Excellent choice. They have the best Mexican around."

"They sure do."

My phone began to beep and, when I pulled it from my purse, I saw a text message from Kirsty.

"Did I just see you get into a cab?"

"Yes. I have somewhere I need to go and I couldn't wait for James."

"You're scaring me, Sierra."

"I know. Sometimes, I scare myself. I'll be in touch later."

The driver pulled up on the street and I paid my fare, giving him a little extra for lunch.

"Lunch is on me. Go and enjoy some tacos." I smiled as I got out.

"Thanks, lady. That's really nice of you."

I stood in the long line and patiently waited for my turn. When I finally reached the counter, I ordered a burrito, and Danny recognized me.

"Hey, aren't you the lady that made the comment about me not having any tequila?"

"Yeah. That was me. Did you finally get some?" I smiled.

"No. But I never forget a face and I'm happy you came back."

"You do have the best Mexican food in L.A."

I grabbed my burrito and water from the counter, took off my heels, and walked to the park where I ate my first Danny's taco. As I was indulging in my burrito, my phone rang. It was Royce.

"What's up, Royce? You're interrupting me and my amazing burrito."

"Are you at that fine Mexican place on Santa Monica Blvd?"

"No. I'm eating a burrito in a park that I bought off a truck."

"Good God, Sierra. That sounds disgusting."

"Don't knock it until you've tried it. Now why are you calling?"

"I thought maybe we could do something tonight. We haven't really chatted or other things in a while and I think it's time we catch up. How about it?"

I sighed. "Fine. But I want dinner."

He chuckled. "Dinner sounds good. I'll have my driver pick you up."

"No need. I'll have James drop me off at Le Chateau at seven sharp. Make the reservation and I'll see you there."

"You're one bossy lady and you're turning me on," he said in his deep voice. "I'll see you tonight."

I hit the end button and shook my head. Was seeing Royce such a good idea? No. But I needed some normalcy back in my life if I was ever going to stop thinking about Cameron.

****

"What are you doing?" Kirsty said as she scared the shit out of me in my closet.

"Damn you! Stop creeping up on me like that."

"Answer the question."

"I'm going to dinner with Royce," I explained as I pulled out my Chanel dress and looked it over.

"Really? Do you think that's a good idea?"

"No, but I need some normalcy back in my life and Royce is that normalcy."

"No, he's not. He's a suit. Your suits aren't normal. They're freaks!"

"Shush," I said as I slipped on my dress and went into the bathroom to fix my hair and makeup.

"What you need is Cameron. Have you even bothered to get in contact with him?"

"No, and even if I did, he wouldn't get the messages anyway, being up in the non-civilized world he's in. And for your information, I don't need him. He left me."

"He left you because you wouldn't tell him you loved him. He didn't leave you for any other reason."

"Leave me alone before I fire you."

"Sorry if the truth hurts."

"Don't worry about me, Kirsty. I'll be fine. I always am, aren't I?"

I grabbed my clutch and my Jimmy Choos and walked downstairs. "Rosa, is James here yet?" She didn't answer me.

I walked out to the back and noticed the door to the guest house was open. I walked inside and felt nothing but emptiness.

"What are you doing in here?" I asked.

"Dusting."

"Oh. Well, have a good night. I'll see you in the morning."

James pulled up to Le Chateau and the valet opened the door for me. Before I stepped out, James reached back and grabbed my hand.

"Call me if you need me. I'll be wherever you are in a flash."

"Thanks, James, but I'll be okay. It's time to get my life back."

As I walked into the restaurant, Royce was in the lobby, talking on the phone. He saw me, smiled, hung up, and tried to kiss my lips. My quick reflexes stepped into action and I turned my head.

"It is so good to see you. You look gorgeous." He smiled.

Goddamn, that cologne already was beginning to nauseate me. "Thank you."

We were promptly seated at our table, where I downed two cosmopolitans before dinner was even served.

"We are going back to my place after dinner, correct?"

"Of course, Royce. Why ruin our routine?"

"I was hoping you'd say that. I miss my face in between those beautiful legs of yours."

Ugh, his statement made me sick. It never used to. But tonight, it did.

After a wonderful and elegant meal that I barely touched, we climbed in the back of his limo and headed to his penthouse. As soon as I stepped off the elevator, I headed straight for his bar.

"Going for the tequila already?" He chuckled.

"Of course. Must keep up with tradition," I replied as I poured myself a glass.

He walked over to me and softly brushed his lips against the back of neck. His hands wandered down my arms and then up to my breasts, where he cupped them firmly. I closed my eyes and tried to go to that place where George and I always hung out in these situations. It wasn't working. He slowly unzipped my dress and slipped it off my shoulders, letting it fall to the ground. The groan that erupted from his chest made me cringe. His hands caressed my torso as they moved down south and his fingers pushed the edge of my panties to the side. He plunged his finger inside me and I gasped. I was desperately trying to find George, but he was nowhere to be found. Suddenly, when all hope was lost, a man appeared out of the shadows. IT. WAS. CAMERON. I took in a sharp breath as I jumped and ducked under Royce's arm.

"I'm sorry. I can't do this, Royce," I said as I scrambled for my dress.

"What's wrong?"

"I can't do this with you. I can't. I just can't. I'm sorry. I need to leave," I said as I felt an anxiety attack coming on.

"Wait, Sierra. Stop right now!" he commanded.

I stopped and slowly turned around. He walked over to me and zipped up my dress.

"What's his name?" he asked.

"Huh?"

"What's his name?"

"Cameron," I answered as I looked down in shame.

"Go sit down and I'll pour you another drink. You can tell me all about it."

He handed me a glass of tequila and then took his scotch and sat in the chair across from me. I told him everything about Cameron and the times we shared.

"Are you in love with him?" he asked.

"If I say yes, then that means I'm admitting it out loud and, if I do that, then it becomes real."

"It's okay to love him, kid. My advice to you is to go and get him back. You've proven tonight that you're not over him. I personally think you'd be a fool to let him get away. He's one lucky guy to have a woman like you love him."

"You're the same as me, Royce. This is why we do what we do. You don't believe in relationships."

"I do for you, Sierra, because I knew the minute you stepped into that restaurant, you seemed off. You need someone to love, doll. This way of life isn't for you. You're way smarter than that and I knew it was only a matter of time before someone stole your heart. Your dad would have wanted you to find someone to love."

I smiled as I put on my Jimmy Choos. I pulled out my phone and sent a text message to James to come pick me up.

"Thanks, Royce. You're a good friend," I said as I kissed his cheek.

"So are you, Sierra. I'll miss our fun times, but if you ever need to talk, you know where to find me."

I walked to the door and, before I stepped out, Royce called my name. I turned around and looked at him.

"I heard about your board meeting. You've got the eye of the tiger, girl. Your dad would have been very proud of you."

"Thanks. I learned from the best." I smiled as I stepped outside.

James pulled up and opened the door for me.

"You okay?"

"I'm okay." I smiled as I nodded my head. "Royce is a good guy who offered some good advice."

"I give you good advice," James said.

"Of course you do. That's why I pay you. Now stop being jealous." I winked.

****

Cameron

I was sitting at the bar, drinking a beer while Mark was bartending. I had spent my days fixing up some things around the house and helping my parents at their fruit stand. I tried to keep as busy as possible to keep my mind off of Sierra, but no matter how busy I was, I still thought about her. These last two weeks seemed to be the longest two weeks of my life. My family knew something was up because I couldn't fake happiness twenty-four/seven. The only person I could talk to about Sierra was Mark, since he already knew she wasn't a lesbian. I told him what she really did for a living and how she wasn't a barista at Starbucks. He laughed and shook his head because he never would have pegged her for a corporate CEO. I felt a hand on my shoulder and, when I turned around, Jaden, Magnolia, Dallas, and another girl were standing behind me.

"Hey, buddy. Hi, Magnolia," I said.

"Hi, Cam, it's great to see you again." Magnolia smiled. "You remember my sister, Dallas, right? You'll be standing up with her at our wedding."

"I do remember. Nice to see you again, Dallas."

"Thank you. It's nice to see you too."

The last time I saw Dallas was about a year ago and she had braces and short brown hair. Now, her braces were off and her hair was long and curly. She was a cute girl, but nothing compared to Sierra. I told Mark to get me another beer and I went and sat at a table with all of them. Jaden and I played a game of pool and I couldn't help thinking about the time Sierra was here and kicked my ass. No matter what I did, I couldn't stop thinking about her.

Chapter 36

Sierra

I was sitting in my office, staring out the window, when Kirsty walked in.

"I need you to sign these forms."

I was in deep thought about Cameron and how much I missed him. My God, I didn't even miss Ryan this much after he left. I missed his smart comments to me and I missed him making me do things that he knew I didn't want to do. FUCK! I missed him so much that it still hurt as bad as the day he left.

"I love him. I'm in love with him," I blurted out. "I'm Sierra Adams, CEO of Adams Advertising and Design and I always go after and get what I want. And I want Cameron Cole and the account for Aruelia."

I pressed the intercom button on my desk phone.

"Sasha, get in here!"

She ran into my office. "What's wrong?"

"I need you to book me on the next flight out to North Carolina. I'm going after my future."

"I'm right on it, Sierra. I'm so excited." She smiled.

"Kirsty, come with me," I said as I grabbed her hand.

We left the building and I hailed a cab.

"What the hell are you doing and where are we going?" she asked.

"To Aruelia's hotel. I have a few things to say to her."

The cab dropped us off at the Beverly Wilshire Hotel and I had the desk alert Aruelia that we were there to see her. After we were given her room number, Kirsty and I took the elevator up to her room and knocked on the door.

"What's this about?" she asked as she let us in.

"Sit down, Aruelia. I have a few things to say to you."

"How dare you come in here and bark orders at me," she said as she stood there with her arms folded.

"Sit, now!" I exclaimed as I pointed to the wingback chair.

"Well, I never," she said as she sat down.

"I'm not really sure why you didn't choose my agency to represent your company. But I have a good idea. In our meeting, you asked me if I knew anything about ballroom dancing. I told you that I took a few lessons and you gave me a look of disgrace because I didn't love it or know a lot about it. Would you rather have had me lie to you and misrepresent you from the beginning? No. I was truthful and you turned away. Just like I did with Cameron."

"Who?"

"Cameron. The man who told me he loved me that day and I turned away from him. He was telling me the truth and I was hiding. Anyway, life is made up of what you want and sometimes you need to take a risk, even if it scares the shit out of you because it could be the best and most rewarding risk you ever take. I'm asking you to take a risk with Adams Advertising. We aren't one of the top ten advertising agencies for nothing."

"Are you finished?" she asked.

"Yes, and now I have to leave. I have a plane to catch and a man to tell how much I love him."

I began walking towards the door as Kirsty stood there with her mouth hanging open.

"Sierra," Aruelia called. "Good luck." She smiled.

"You too. Kirsty, let's go!" I snapped.

She jumped and followed me out the door. "What the hell was that?" she asked.

"That was me going after what I want," I said as we slid into the back of the cab and I pulled out my ringing phone.

"Tell me you got me on a flight?"

"The only flight available leaves at midnight and arrives in North Carolina at ten a.m. with one stop in Atlanta. They only had two first-class seats left, so I booked it."

"Okay. I wanted earlier, but that will give me a chance to pack and get things in order. Thanks, Sasha."

Kirsty took hold of my hand. "I'm so fucking proud of you and I can't believe you're going to get him. That is so romantic."

Suddenly, a horrific thought came to my mind. "What if he tells me to go to hell or says that he doesn't love me anymore?"

"Stop it. Cameron would never do that. He's so in love with you."

The cab dropped us off at my house and, when we walked through the door, James was in the kitchen, talking to Rosa.

"Do I still have a job?" James asked as he looked at me. "I only ask because it seems that you've been spotted in a yellow cab around L.A."

"Oh, please. I was in a hurry. Don't take offense. You're still way hotter than the cabbie. I have a flight at midnight, so I need you to drive me to the airport."

"Midnight? Where the hell are you going at midnight?" Rosa asked.

"I'm going to North Carolina to tell Cameron that I love him."

Rosa smiled and placed her hands on each side of my face. "You better bring Builder Boy home," she said before she hugged me.

"That's the plan, Rosa."

****

I stepped onto the plane and could barely wait to land in North Carolina. It'd been almost three weeks since I'd seen Cameron and, every day, it was killing me. I couldn't wait to throw my arms around him and tell him how much I loved him. I knew I was in love with him from the beginning, but I kept denying it out of fear. I now realized how stupid I was and if I'd only admitted to myself and him from the beginning, we wouldn't be apart. I drank two glasses of wine to calm my nerves and then fell asleep.

Finally, the plane landed and I couldn't wait to get off and stretch. Shit. I forgot to arrange for a car to pick me up and take me to Cameron's house. Shit. Shit. I didn't have Cameron's address. I exited the plane and threw my head back in disbelief. As I walked to baggage claim, I scoped out where the car rental counter was. Perfect. There was one right across from baggage claim. I grabbed my suitcase and headed to the counter.

"Hello, ma'am. How can I help you?" the brunette asked.

"I need a limo to drive me to Lake Santeetlah."

"Your name, please."

"Sierra Adams."

"I'm sorry, Miss Adams, but there's nothing showing me that you arranged for a limo."

"I didn't. I forgot. But now I'm here and I would like one." I smiled.

"I'm sorry, but I'll have to call and it can take anywhere from two to three hours for one to arrive here. These things must be pre-arranged ahead of time."

I gritted my teeth and now I was aggravated. I hadn't had coffee yet and I was tired.

"I know, but I forgot. So if you're saying it will take that long, then I'll just rent a car."

"Do you have a preference?" she asked.

"A Porsche, please."

She looked at me with narrowing eyes. "We don't have any of those available for rental."

"Then what do you have?" I scowled.

"If you're interested in luxury, I do have one Cadillac Escalade available."

"I'll take it. Do you think we can move this along? I'm in a hurry,"

She glared at me and then asked for my driver's license and a credit card. When I handed her my license, she looked at it and then back at me.

"That explains it," she said.

I rolled my eyes because I knew exactly what she meant. She made a call on her phone and then handed me my license, credit card, and receipt.

"Your rental will be waiting for you outside those double doors. Thank you and enjoy your stay in North Carolina," she said with a fake smile.

I flashed my fake smile back to her as I grabbed my Louis Vuitton suitcase and walked towards the double doors. Sitting at the curb was a black Escalade. I threw my suitcase in the back and got in. Shit. Where was I even going? I pulled away from the curb and into a parking lot once I drove away from the airport. I needed to think where I was going before I lost any kind of service. *That's it!* Jolene gave me her number before I left the last time I was here and told me to keep in touch. I immediately called her.

"Hello," she said.

"Jolene, it's Sierra."

"Sierra! How are you?"

"I'm okay. Listen, I need you to do me a favor and don't tell anyone in your family that I called you."

"Why?"

"Because I'm in town and I want it to be a big surprise!"

"Oh my God. Yay! Cam doesn't know you're coming?" she asked.

"No. He doesn't know and I want to keep it that way. So please, don't mention this to anyone. The reason I'm calling is I need your address."

She rattled it off as I punched it into the GPS with great difficulty.

"Okay. I got it. Thanks, Jolene, and remember, not a word to anyone about this."

"Don't worry, Sierra. Your secret is safe with me."

I hung up and headed on the road to Lake Santeetlah. As I was cruising down the highway, my phone rang and it was Kirsty.

"Hey, girl," I answered.

"I just wanted to make sure your plane arrived safely."

"It did. I did and now I'm driving to Cameron's house."

"You're driving?" she asked.

"Yes. I had no choice. I forgot to tell Sasha to arrange for a driver, so I had to rent a car."

She burst into laughter and then she handed the phone to James.

"Now don't forget, Sierra, the brake is on the left and the gas pedal is on the right," he said.

"Very funny! Can you hear that?"

"Hear what?"

"The sound of me flipping you off. I have to hang up and concentrate. By the way, you're both fired when I get back."

James chuckled. "Bye, Sierra."

It was a tedious drive, but I finally arrived in Lake Santeetlah. I was about ten minutes from Cameron's house and my stomach was a ball of knots. I didn't know how he was going to react when he saw me, and I didn't know how I was going to react when I saw him. *Was I going to break down and cry? Was I going to bust out into uncontrollable hysterics?* I didn't know. With me, anything could go. I pulled up to the house, put the SUV in park, and grasped onto the steering wheel so tight that my knuckles turned white. I took in a deep breath, walked up to the door, and knocked. This was it. My future was going to be determined right this second.

"Eeek!" Jolene squealed when she opened the door and hugged me. "I'm so happy you're here."

"It's good to see you, Jolene. Is Cameron here?" I asked nervously.

"No, he's not. He just left. He took the boat out on the lake to do some fishing. If you go out back, you still might be able to catch him before he gets too far out."

"Thank you." I smiled.

I headed to the kitchen and out the door to the back. I walked down the dock and saw Cameron in the middle of the lake. The boat was stopped. This was it. Time to put my big girl panties on and go for it. I. CAN. DO. THIS.

"Hey, I can think of some better things to do in that boat besides fishing," I yelled to him across the lake.

He turned around and stared at me. He just stood there, not saying a word. *Oh no, maybe he's pissed I'm here. Shit.*

"What are you doing here?" he finally yelled back.

"I missed you."

"Really?"

"Yes! Really!" I smiled.

I couldn't believe what I was about to do, but I couldn't wait any longer to feel his arms wrapped around me. I took off my shoes and threw them on the dock. I jumped in the lake and swam towards the boat. Good thing I was not wearing designer.

"Sierra, what are you doing?"

I reached the boat, completely out of breath. Shit. I really needed to exercise. He reached over the boat with a wide grin and grabbed my arm, pulling me up onto it and wrapping his strong arms around me.

"You're crazy. I can't believe you just did that."

"I had to," I said as I looked in his beautiful green eyes and smiled. "I couldn't wait any longer to tell you that I love you. I love you, Cameron Cole. I'm so in love with you and I was miserable without you."

"Really?" He smiled.

"Yes. Do you think I'd jump in a dirty lake just to say hi?"

"I love you too, baby," he said as his mouth smashed into mine. He broke our kiss and ran his hands down my soaking wet hair. "You're soaked and you're shaking."

"I'm fine as long as I'm with you."

"What's going on out there?" Jolene yelled.

Cameron looked at her and yelled to go and get some help. Apparently, the motor stopped working and that was why he only made it so far out.

"Does this mean you'll be my girlfriend, since you swam in a dirty lake to get to me?" He smiled.

"Are you asking me?"

"Yes, I am."

"Then, yes. I would love to be your girlfriend. Do you think I did all this for nothing?"

He chuckled. "You're amazing, Sierra, and I love you so much."

"I love you more, Cam. We need to hurry up and get off this boat. I'm horny."

"Are you willing to swim one last time?"

"For real?"

"It's either that or we'll be on this boat a while until help comes."

"Let's go, then," I said as I jumped back in the lake.

Cameron followed and we swam back to the dock. Jolene was standing there and handed us some towels.

"I'm confused as to what's going on here," she said.

"We'll explain it to you later. Tell Mom and Dad that Sierra's in town and we'll be back tomorrow. We have a lot of catching up to do."

Cameron took my hand and led me into the house and up to his room. He changed out of his wet clothes and had Jolene bring me one of her sundresses. He threw a few things in a bag and we headed outside. I threw him the keys to the rental car. He looked at the Escalade and shook his head.

"Of course you rented this." He laughed.

"I tried to rent a Porsche, but the girl looked at me like I was crazy."

The minute we climbed into the vehicle, he reached over and kissed me passionately. "I'm so happy you're here." He smiled.

"Me too. I'm just sorry it took me so long."

"I would've waited for you forever if I had to, Sierra."

A tear formed in my eye. "I wouldn't have made you wait forever. Now, where are we going?"

"You pick."

I pulled out my phone and pulled up google. I had only one bar of service and I was going to make this work.

"It looks like the only decent hotel around is the Microtel Inn and Suites by Wyndham."

"I know exactly where it's at and it's only a few miles from here."

"I just don't understand why there aren't any Hiltons or Trump Hotels here."

He laughed as he picked up my hand and brought it to his lips. "I sure did miss you."

Chapter 37

Cameron

I lay there with Sierra wrapped in my arms, cuddled up against me as tight as she could be. The sheets were torn off the bed and the phone and lamp were knocked over on the floor. We had amazing sex. Not once, not twice, but three times in the couple of hours we were in the hotel room. My fingers caressed her bare skin and I was the happiest man in the world. Sierra Adams told me that she loved me. Hearing those words come from her were nothing but sweet music to my ears. I was so in love with her and I was never going to let her go. She lifted her head and gave me a soft kiss on my lips.

"You taste good." She smiled.

"You taste better."

"I want you to know that I went to Danny's Tacos and had a burrito."

"You did?"

"Yep. I missed you so much that going there helped me feel closer to you, if that makes any sense."

"It does, babe. It makes perfect sense. By the way, how did your meeting go with that ballroom dance company?"

"It didn't go well. She wasn't impressed. Right before I left to come here, I went to her hotel room and said a few things to her."

I couldn't help but chuckle because I could just see her doing that. "I'm sorry it didn't work out."

"It's fine. It's her loss, not mine. And, by the way, you have our living room to remodel."

"Ours?" I asked.

She lifted herself up and looked at me. "Yes, ours. That's if you'll move to L.A. and move in with me."

"Back in the guest house?" I smiled.

"No! The main house."

"That means you'll have to share your closet."

She bit down on her bottom lip and made the cutest face. "Oh. That's something we'll have to discuss later. My closet is my—"

I put my finger over her lips. "Shh, babe. I know and I'll do whatever you want."

"We have another problem," she said.

"What problems could we possibly have?"

"Did you forget that your parents think I'm a Starbucks lesbian barista and my mom thinks you're an escort I hired for sex?"

I couldn't help but laugh. "Well, I guess we'll have to tell them the truth because I'm not going to have a lesbian girlfriend."

"*Boom!* Another shock for Delia!" She smiled.

"My brother's wedding is this weekend. Are you going to be okay staying here a few more days?"

"Why wouldn't I be?"

"Because of the cell phone service issue."

"Fuck work. I'm on vacation. Kirsty can handle things. I'm not worried."

I smiled as I placed my hand around the nape of her neck and brought her lips to mine, starting round four.

****

Sierra

Cameron was still in the shower and I was looking through my suitcase for an outfit. I saw something out of the corner of my eye and, when I realized what the white furry thing was, I screamed at the top of my lungs and jumped on the bed. Cameron came running from the bathroom with a towel wrapped around his waist.

"What's wrong?!"

"THERE'S A MOUSE IN HERE!"

"Where?"

"I think it went under the bed. OH MY GOD, do something! There it is!" I screamed again as it scurried out from under the bed and went under the desk. He grabbed a glass from the nightstand and put it over the furry little creature.

"There. I'll call the desk and have someone come get him."

"We're leaving right now. I am not getting off this bed until that door is open and we leave."

"Sierra, he's trapped. It's okay."

"No. It's not okay. Hurry up and get dressed. Hurry!"

I knelt down on the bed, grabbed my shorts and top, and zipped up my suitcase. Cameron went back in the bathroom, collected our things, threw them in his bag, and quickly got dressed. He grabbed my suitcase and opened the door.

"Come on, babe."

"Hell, no. I am not stepping one foot on that floor. You come and carry me out that door."

Cameron laughed. "Are you serious? He's trapped."

"I don't care. Carry me!" I snapped.

He walked over to the bed and held out his arms. I wrapped my legs around his waist and he carried me out of the room. Before he put me down, he brushed his lips against mine.

"You're crazy, but I still love you." He smiled.

"You better. Now we need to find a better hotel, even if we have to travel far."

"We can stay at my house. You'll sleep in my bed and my parents will have to deal with it."

"No. We won't be able to have crazy wild sex and, believe me, I'm nowhere finished with you."

"Right. Start googling," he said as he put me down.

I climbed into the car, trying to calm down from my near heart attack and pulled up a non-list of luxury hotels. *What the hell is wrong with this place?* I ran across an ad for a Smoky Mountain Mansion that was only five miles away from Cameron's house. Now, we're talking! I dialed the number as Cameron climbed into the SUV.

"Hello, I would like to rent your place for the next few days…I see… No, I want the house to myself."

Cameron looked over at me. Poor guy was so confused.

"Well, I'm sorry, but a single room isn't an option. I will pay you triple of what you're asking for the rest of the week if my boyfriend and I can have the whole house to ourselves, plus a nonrefundable deposit. How does that sound?"

I smiled when the man on the other end of the phone agreed to my terms. "I knew you'd see things my way. We'll be by shortly. Can you please send me the address?"

"What was all that about?" Cameron asked.

"I rented us a small house. Here's the address. It's only five miles from your parents' house. We'll have the whole place to ourselves and complete privacy."

"I know these small houses around here, Sierra, and I'm not so sure you'll be happy."

I smiled as I looked over and pinched his cheek. "I'll be happy, honey."

The GPS told Cameron to make a left turn into the driveway. "This can't be right. This damn GPS took us to the wrong place."

I took in a deep breath. "No, this is the right place," I said.

"Sierra, this is a mansion. You said you rented a small house."

We got out of the SUV and I stood in front of the large house and smiled. "Isn't it perfect?"

"Leave it up to you to find something like this in this small-ass town," he said as he shook his head.

The man I spoke with on the phone, known as Blake, walked out and met us in the driveway. He led us into the house and into the kitchen, where I had to sign a rental agreement.

"Would you like me to show you around?" Blake asked.

"No, thank you. We can show ourselves around." I smiled.

He handed me the keys and left.

"I can't believe you did this. Wait; actually, I can believe it," he said as he followed me around.

"Look at this amazing house, Cam. This is way better than any hotel." There were open stairs to a lower level. I walked down them and gasped.

"Look, we have a pool table." I smiled as I climbed on top of it.

"Okay, you've convinced me." Cameron smiled as he held my face in his hands.

Chapter 38

Cameron

After having a make-out session, I helped Sierra off the pool table, which was going to be utilized by us later tonight, and went back upstairs. We reached the third floor and looked in all of the six bedrooms.

"Well, which one are we sleeping in?" I asked.

"Does it really matter? We're going to be fucking in all of them."

"I love the way you think." I winked.

My phone started ringing and when I pulled it out of my pocket, it was my mom calling.

"Hey, Mom."

"We heard Sierra was in town and want her to come over for dinner. It'll be ready in an hour, so make sure you both are here."

"We'll be there, Mom. I know she's really excited to see you."

I hung up and wrapped my arms around Sierra's waist. "We're going to dinner at my parents' house and we're going to tell my family the truth about you."

"Then we better stop on the way and grab a bottle of tequila or two."

"Done. You know I'll always take care of you," I said as I brushed my lips against hers.

We stopped at the liquor store and bought a couple of bottles of wine and tequila. We pulled up to the house and I grabbed Sierra's hand as she took in a deep breath.

"See what happens when we lie?" she said.

"You started it."

She laughed and we walked into the house. Immediately, my mom ran from the kitchen and gave Sierra a welcome hug.

"We are so excited to see you again, Sierra."

"How's the barista business doing?" my dad asked her.

"Both of you come in the kitchen and I'll pour you some iced tea," Luanne said.

"What's in the bag, son?" my dad asked as I set it on the counter.

"Oh, just a couple bottles of wine and tequila for later."

****

Sierra

I felt like I was in the kitchen of Paula Deen. I can say that because I was a few years back when Adams Advertising was a sponsor for her TV show. She invited my father and me to come and watch her cook a meal for her show.

"It smells amazing in here, Luanne."

"Thank you, sweetie. There's nothing like a southern home-cooked meal. I called everyone in the family and they should all be here any minute. Now, you and Cameron go sit down."

I looked at Cameron as he held up the bottle of tequila and smiled. I smiled back as I held up two fingers, signaling to make it a double. The rest of the Cole Clan breezed through the door and hugged me one by one. Mark pulled me over to the side and kissed me on the cheek.

"Thank you, Sierra. You have made my brother very happy."

"He's made me very happy." I smiled.

"What's going on over here? Are you trying to steal my girlfriend?" Cameron whispered to his brother.

"Nah. I tried that the last time she was here. She wasn't falling for it." He winked at me.

We all took our places at the table and Cameron set down the glass of tequila in front of me. I so desperately wanted to give him a thank-you kiss, but the cat wasn't out of the bag yet.

Luanne and Kelly set the food down on the table. "Here we go everybody. We have southern fried chicken, macaroni and cheese, deviled eggs, corn bread, mashed potatoes and gravy, and some sweet creamed corn."

To me, it all looked like a heart attack waiting to happen. A bonafide artery clogging meal. Everyone passed the food around one by one. I took very little of everything so I didn't appear rude.

"You owe me food later," I whispered in Cameron's ear.

"And you owe me a pool table." He smiled. "Well, since the family is all here, there's something I need to tell you."

Oh boy, here we go. I picked up the glass of tequila and threw it back.

"Sierra and I are now officially dating and I'm going to be moving in with her."

The table fell silent and all eyes turned to me.

"But she's a lesbian," Luanne blurted out.

I wanted to crawl under the table and hide.

"No, Mom. She's not. We just made all that up on the spot. You know, like a joke."

"So then she's not a lesbian barista. She's just a barista?" Jerry said.

"No, Dad. She's neither. She's not a lesbian or a barista."

I placed my hand on Cameron's arm and told him to let me as I stood up.

"Cole family," I spoke. "I'm sorry if Cam and I lied to you. It was solely meant for a joke and, to be honest, I didn't think I'd ever really see any of you again. My name is Sierra Adams and I'm the CEO of Adams Advertising and Design. I run one of the top ten advertising firms in the country. I have a home in Hollywood Hills and I'm madly in love with Cameron. And if it makes you feel any better, my mother thinks he's an escort I hired for companionship."

I took another drink of my tequila and sat down.

"Well, I'll be damned," Jerry said. "Look at that, Lu. We have a celebrity right in our very home."

"So you're not a lesbian?" Jolene asked.

"No, sweetie. But I totally support them." I smiled.

The rest of the family was cool about it, but Luanne didn't seem happy.

"Mom, what's wrong?" Cameron asked.

"Nothing. Now that we know the truth and that you're moving away, it's all good." She started to cry as she got up and left the table.

"Aw, damn," Jerry said. "Let me go see if I can talk some sense into her."

Cameron looked over at me with a sad look on his face.

"I'm sorry," I said.

"You have nothing to be sorry for, babe. I'll talk to her later."

A few moments later, Luanne came back and sat down at the table. She wouldn't look at me and I felt horrible. Needless to say, dinner was a silent one. After we ate, and I finished off another double of tequila, I helped clean up the table and the kitchen, and went down by the lake with Cameron.

"I think we hurt your mom's feelings," I said as I ran my hand up and down his back.

"Nah. I think she's upset because I'm moving to California."

"Do you want to move back with me?" I asked nervously.

"Of course I do. I love you, Sierra."

"I love you too. Why don't we go give your mom a drink and talk to her?"

"We can try."

We walked hand in hand up to the house and something was going on in the living room. There was a lot of discussion going on.

"What's going on in here?" Cameron asked.

"It looks like we need to postpone the wedding," Jaden said as he held his crying, I assumed because I'd never met her, fiancée.

"Why?"

"The hall where the reception was booked burnt down this afternoon. Magnolia called all over town and there's nothing available for months," Luanne spoke.

Magnolia? Was that her real name?

"I can't wait months. I'll look like an ole beached whale if we wait and I don't want to look like a whale," she cried hysterically.

Jaden tried to comfort her, but the more he did, the worse she cried.

"I have an idea," I spoke up.

Magnolia looked up at me. "And who are you?" she asked.

"I'm the person who's going to make sure you have a fabulous wedding."

"Sierra, what are you talking about?" Cameron asked with a panicked tone.

"Long story short, I rented Cameron and me a mansion for the next few days and the back yard is huge. It even has a pavilion. It would be the perfect spot for a wedding reception, especially being right on the lake."

"It's too late to plan all that. The hall was taking care of everything," Magnolia cried again.

I walked over to her and grabbed her hand. "Magnolia, darling. It's never too late to plan a spectacular event. Leave everything to me."

"Sierra, I don't think—" Cameron started to speak.

"Then don't, darling. Do you trust me?" I asked seriously as I looked into his eyes.

"Yes, I do."

"Then leave it at that. Now, if you'll excuse us, Cam and I are going to go back to our rental house. I have some phone calls to make."

"Thank you so much. I don't know how to ever repay you," Magnolia said.

"The only payment I'll accept is that you two love each other for the rest of your lives. Come on, Cameron," I said as I grabbed his hand and pulled him along.

We climbed into the Escalade and I pulled out my phone. "Hurry and get me to where I'll have a good signal."

"Do you know what you're doing?" he asked.

"Do you know who you're dating?" I replied.

Once we pulled out of the driveway and were halfway down the road, I got two bars on my phone. I dialed Kirsty.

"Hey, girl! James and I were just talking about you."

"I need you to listen to me very carefully. I'm going to do a three-way call with Sasha, so hold on."

I dialed Sasha.

"Hey, boss lady," she answered.

"Hi, Sasha, I have Kirsty on with us. I need your full attention. I need your help pulling off a wedding reception for this Saturday."

"OH MY GOD! You and Cameron are getting married!" Kirsty squealed.

"No. It's not for me. It's for Cam's brother and fiancée. Their hall burnt down today along with all their plans, so I'm stepping in."

"Oh," they both said.

"I need you both here. Bring James and Rosa too."

"What?" Kirsty asked.

"You heard me. So get on the next flight out here and don't forget to arrange for a car service to pick you up from the airport. I'll text you the address to the rental house Cameron and I are staying at. It has six bedrooms, so you'll stay with us."

Sandi Lynn

"Fine. We'll be there tomorrow."

"Thank you. I love you both. I'll see you soon."

I hung up and Cameron took hold of my hand. "There goes the house to ourselves so we better fuck like rabbits tonight." He smiled.

"We'll start as soon as we get back. Now, I have another call to make."

I pulled up Paul's number and hit call.

"Is that you, Sierra?"

"Hello, Paul. I need a favor."

"Anything for you, darling."

"Can you ship some wedding dresses to North Carolina, like overnight tonight, and also throw in some cocktail dresses for me?"

"Of course. What's going on?"

"Cameron's brother is getting married and there's a problem, so I'm helping out."

"Of course. That's very sweet of you, Sierra. Text me the shipping address and I'll go pull some now. What size is the bride?"

"She's about five feet five inches and I would say she's about a size 6."

"Perfect."

"Oh, Paul? It's an outdoor reception. Keep that in mind."

"Will do, doll. Toodles."

I took in a deep breath as we pulled in the driveway. "A couple more calls, and then I'm all yours." I smiled.

"You better mean that."

"Promise on my Prada."

I pulled up my contacts one more time and dialed Paula St. Hue. Her company supplied the tents, tables, linens, and chairs for events. They were a huge client of Adams Advertising and she owed me a favor.

"Paula, it's Sierra. How are you?"

"I'm good, Sierra. How are you doing?"

"Great. I need a favor. Correct me if I'm wrong, but don't you have a huge warehouse in Knoxville?"

"Why, yes, we do. It's our second largest."

"Perfect. I need about eighteen tables, 150 chairs, and two large white tents. It's for a wedding over in Robbinsville, NC. I'll text you the address. If you can have them here by Friday, I'll be a happy woman."

"Consider it done. I'll call the warehouse now."

"Thank you, Paula. I appreciate it."

Chapter 39
Cameron

As promised, Sierra turned off her phone and devoted all her attention to me and the pool table.

"Come with me, babe," I said with bated breath as I thrust in and out of her from behind while she was bent over the pool table.

Her moans were unbearable and made me come faster than I had wanted. "Oh fuck," I moaned as I pushed deep inside her.

"Are you okay?" I asked.

"Never better." She turned her head and smiled. "I have a little felt burn on my arms, but other than that, I'm great."

I pulled out of her and turned her around. I took each arm and softly kissed where she was sore. "Better?" I asked.

"Much better."

We grabbed our clothes and went upstairs. "We better decide now which bedroom we're taking, since everyone is coming tomorrow. Oh, and why would you have Paul send wedding dresses? Magnolia has a dress."

She crinkled up her nose. "Yeah. Somehow, I think it might not be her dream dress. Don't worry; once she sees these dresses, she'll ditch the other."

I placed my hands on her hips and kissed the tip of her nose. "Have I told you lately how much I love you?"

"No. You haven't. So I think you better." She smiled.

"Do you swear on your Prada that I haven't?"

"Mr. Cole, how dare you bring my Prada into this."

"I love you, babe, and I can't thank you enough for what you're doing for Jaden and Magnolia."

"I love you too. By the way, Magnolia? Really?"

"It's her mom's favorite flower in the whole world. Wait until you meet her sister, Dallas."

"Let me guess. It's her mom's favorite city in the whole world."

"You're so smart." I smiled.

She grabbed a pillow and we had our first pillow fight around the room, which landed us on the bed for another round of sex.

****

Sierra

"Time to get up, sleepy head. We have lots of wedding stuff to do today," I said as I planted little kisses across Cameron's chest.

"We? How did I get roped into this?"

"The gang will be here soon and you can keep James entertained."

He opened one eye and looked at me. "I can take him fishing. We can go fishing and there won't be any whining or complaining."

"Yes, the two of you can form a little bromance, but you better remember who swam in a dirty lake for you."

"You're never going to give up on that, are you?"

"NEVER!" I smiled.

After we finally climbed out of bed and got dressed, my phone rang.

"Hey, Kirsty. What? You're breaking up. I can't hear you. Where are you?"

"Judging by that conversation, I'd say they're almost here." Cameron laughed.

I opened the front door and, sure enough, a black sedan pulled up. Kirsty flung open the door, got out, and ran to me.

"Look at you two. I'm so happy for you," she said as she hugged me and then turned to Cameron.

After I hugged James and Sasha, Rosa walked up and Cameron took her bags.

"Rosa, thank you for coming." I smiled.

"Look. Look at this house. Are you expecting me to clean this house? This house is huge."

"Yeah, Sierra. How the hell did you get a house this big out here?" Kirsty asked.

"It's a long story."

"No, it's not." Cameron smiled as he pulled out his phone and I heard myself scream. "This is what led us here."

Apparently, he recorded me screaming and jumping up and down on the bed after the mouse incident. Everyone busted into laughter.

"You're all fired. Each and every one of you."

"I don't work for you." Cameron smiled.

"I'm breaking up with you," I said as I nodded my head.

"The hell you are." Cameron threw me over his shoulder and slapped my ass as he carried me into the house.

He was in his glory because he got to take James fishing while the girls and I planned the wedding. I had Cam get Magnolia's number and I called her and asked her to come over. She said she would and that her mother, Peggy, and Luanne would be coming too. We almost had everything arranged, right down to the caterers, when the doorbell rang. Magnolia had arrived, as well as the boxes from Neiman's.

"Oh my God, look at this house," Magnolia said.

"I guess the smaller things just aren't her style," Luanne said.

What crawled up her ass? How dare she make a comment like that.

After I introduced my friends to them, Rosa walked in the room with a tray of lemonade.

"This is my housekeeper, Rosa."

"Of course she would bring her housekeeper," Luanne said to Peggy.

"Rosa, could you get me a glass of water please?" I asked with a smile.

****

We spent the rest of the afternoon going over the plans for the wedding. Magnolia cried when I showed her the wedding gowns and veils that Paul sent. She found her perfect style and perfect fit. She looked beautiful in it and Jaden was in for a treat. Comment after comment was made by Luanne and she would barely look at me the whole afternoon. When Cameron and James walked through the door, she asked Cameron if she could speak to him in private. I was positive it was about me and there was only one way to find out. I snuck up the stairs and listened.

"This is way over the top, Cameron. Who does she think she is coming here and doing something like this? Our family isn't into this fancy stuff. We could have had a nice reception at our house. But no, she had to turn your brother's wedding into a production."

"Mom. Sierra's only trying to help and this is the way she knows how. I think she's doing an excellent job."

"Of course you do because you're blinded by her. I don't think she's right for you, Cameron."

"Stop right there. I love Sierra. Where did all this come from? You sure as hell loved her when you thought she was a lesbian and worked at Starbucks."

"Because I thought she was a simple girl."

"She's the same girl she was not too long ago. I'm really ashamed of you, Mom."

"I'm sorry, Cameron, but that's how I feel. I will never welcome her into our family."

Whoa. Hearing his mom say that about me really hurt deep down. I couldn't listen anymore, so I went downstairs and poured another glass of tequila. A few moments later, Cameron and the spawn of Satan II – Delia was spawn of Satan I – came down, and I said goodbye to Magnolia and Peggy. I became quiet and took my glass outside on the patio. Kirsty joined me and we both sat and watched the calmness of the lake.

"I like the ocean better," Kirsty said.

"Me too."

My phone beeped and alerted me that I had a voicemail. I punched in my pin and put it on speaker as Kirsty and I listened to Aruelia speak.

"Sierra, it's Aruelia. After careful consideration, I've decided to hire your firm to represent my dance company. I feel that we'd make a great team. I know you're out of town and I hope things are good for you. Call me when you get back and we can discuss the specifics."

"Holy shit! You landed the account!" Kirsty screamed.

I smiled. It wasn't my happy smile and it wasn't my fake smile. It was an in-between smile that said I was thrilled, but I had another issue to deal with first.

"What's going on out here?" Cameron smiled as he strolled out on the patio.

"Your girlfriend just landed one of the biggest accounts. We have to celebrate. What do you guys do here for fun?" Kirsty asked.

"That's great, Sierra. I'm so proud of you. What made her change her mind?"

"Probably the fact that Sierra sort of told her off."

Cameron sat down on the edge of the chair and placed his hand on my leg. "What's wrong? You should be jumping up and down right now."

"Nothing's wrong, and I am very happy. I just have a lot on my mind right now with the wedding."

"Let's forget about the wedding for tonight and go hit the bar. We have some celebrating to do." He smiled.

"Sounds good." I smiled back. I had a date with tequila.

✶✶✶✶

"A round of shots for everyone! Woo hoo!" I yelled.

We'd been at the bar for about an hour and I already had my fair share of liquid courage. The guys played pool. Sasha was admiring a country boy from across the bar, and Kirsty was talking to the DJ. Suddenly, the song "Turn Down for What" started playing. Kirsty ran over to me and grabbed my hand.

"Let's show them how we do it L.A." She smiled as she dragged me and Sasha to the dance floor.

The entire bar stopped and all eyes were on the three of us as we moved our bodies to the music. Here we were, three girls from Los Angeles in this small country town, getting down to a song that I'm sure was never played in this bar. My friend, Tequila, had settled inside me and I let go, dancing and grinding up against Kirsty without a care in the world. Cameron and James were standing to the side with wide grins spread across their faces. The three of us definitely showed this town how we partied. After the song wrapped, "All About That Bass" began to play. I climbed on top of the bar and starting moving my hips back and forth. Kirsty and Sasha joined me and the three of us started laughing as we stared out into the bar and stared at the faces of the patrons. The men were howling and, before we knew it, a couple more girls got on top of the bar and joined us. The song ended and Cameron grabbed my waist and took me down.

"You sure know how to liven up a bar." He smiled as he kissed me.

"Someone had to," I slurred.

We walked through the door of the house or, should I say, I stumbled through the door and almost fell on my ass. I would have gone down if Cameron didn't have a tight grip on me. As he picked me up and carried me up the stairs, I yelled and waved to Kirsty, James, and Sasha.

"Shh. Rosa's sleeping," Cameron said.

"Your mom hates me," I slurred as he sat me down on the bed and I fell back.

"No, she doesn't. Why would you say that?"

"Oh fuck." I bolted from the bed and into the bathroom, barely making it to the toilet.

Cameron walked in and, like the gentleman he was, held my hair back while my friend, Tequila, decided to leave my body.

"I heard everything she said about me," I replied with my head down in the toilet.

"She doesn't hate you, Sierra. She just doesn't like the fact that I'm moving to L.A. permanently."

"No. She thinks I'm high maintenance," I squeezed in before I vomited again.

"You are high maintenance and I love you. That's all that matters, babe. She just doesn't understand. Do you think Delia's going to be happy when she finds out I'm a builder and not some corporate suit with money?"

"Screw Delia."

"Exactly, and screw Luanne. She's my mom and I love her, but she's not telling me who I can and can't love. Now, are you finished?"

"Yeah," I said as I took the towel from his hand.

He helped me up and lifted my shirt over my head.

"Fuck me." I smiled as the room spun.

"Are you going to throw up on me if I do?"

"I shouldn't, but you never know. Are you willing to take the chance?"

"I'm willing to take any chances with you, babe." He smiled as his lips brushed against mine.

Chapter 40

Cameron

I went downstairs and poured a cup of coffee for Sierra. The aroma of pancakes filled the kitchen as Rosa stood by the stove, flipping them.

"Breakfast is almost ready," she said.

"Rosa, you're not here to cook us meals. You need to go sit down and let me wait on you."

"You're very sweet, Builder Boy, but I like to cook food. Besides, you have Miss Hangover-pants upstairs to deal with."

"True. Let me take this up to her and I'll be back down for those delicious-smelling pancakes."

I went back upstairs and set the cup on the nightstand. "Wake up, babe. The trucks will be here soon with the tents and stuff."

She moaned and rolled over, pulling the pillow over her head. "You deal with it. I'm not getting out of this bed today," she mumbled.

"Nope. This is your project and you're going to follow through with it and make it perfect!"

She rolled over and opened her eyes. "Is that coffee?" she asked.

"Yes. Freshly brewed just for you." I handed her the cup as she sat up.

"I'm sorry I threw up on you."

"Yeah, well, it was bound to happen at some point in our relationship." I smiled. "Why don't you go and take a hot shower and I'll meet you downstairs."

"Okay. Thanks for the coffee."

"You're welcome. I'll have the aspirin waiting for you when you come down," I said as I got up from the bed.

"Hey."

"What?"

"Aren't you going to give me a kiss?" she pouted.

"I am. As soon as you shower and brush your teeth." I winked.

She picked up the pillow and threw it at me as I walked out the door.

****

Sierra

I showered, brushed my teeth, and threw on a maxi dress. The shower didn't help. I still had a bad taste in my mouth and my head was pounding. Shame on you, tequila. You failed me this time. I went downstairs and the smell of the pancakes cooking was almost as nauseating as Royce's cologne. Rosa handed me two aspirin and a glass of juice.

"Why? Why do you do this to yourself?" Rosa said.

"Why? Why do you keep asking me that?" I replied.

She mumbled something in Spanish like she always did, and she did it because she knew that was the one language I didn't study in school.

"If you have something to say, I'd prefer you say it in English!"

She looked at me with her sinister smile. "Where's the fun in that?"

I rolled my eyes as I popped my aspirin and finished my juice.

"The trucks are here, Sierra," Sasha yelled from the foyer.

Good God; why does everyone have to be so damn loud? "Come on, my little drunken minx. Let's go decide where we're going to set up."

"What did you just call me?"

He smiled and walked out of the kitchen. I followed behind and walked outside to talk to the drivers about the set up.

I had a vision. Creativity was my thing and I was about to unleash it with this wedding, regardless of what Luanne Cole thought of me. I directed the men on the set up of the beautiful, elegant white tents. Lights were strung throughout and a chandelier hung in the middle of the dance floor. Tables and chairs covered in white linens and light pink bows graced the tents with elegance. It was all starting to come together perfectly, after a bit of crazy from me.

"Sierra, we need to start getting ready for the bachelor/bachelorette party."

"And where is that again?"

"On the boat that Magnolia's parents rented."

"Big boat or small?"

"Big." He chuckled. "I think you'll like it. It has an upper deck and a lower deck. Can you believe it?"

I rolled my eyes at his sarcasm. "Okay, I'm in."

I high-fived the drivers and told them they did an excellent job. I gave them a little cash on the side for putting up with my craziness.

Cameron and I got ready and headed to the marina for the party.

"No more than one or two glasses of tequila for you," Cameron said.

"Aw, you're no fun! Besides, I drank enough last night for the next week."

As soon as we stepped on the boat, Luanne shot me a look.

"Hi, Luanne. Do you like my Prada bag?" I smiled. Bitch wouldn't know a Prada bag if it slapped her in the face.

The party wasn't as bad as I thought it would be. There was plenty of alcohol (I only had two cups – yes, I said cups – of tequila) and there was plenty of food. Everyone mostly talked about the wedding and had a good time. I sat and watched Cameron talking and laughing with his brothers and realized how much his family meant to him. I saw Luanne talking to Magnolia and I asked her if I could speak to her for a moment. Maybe it wasn't the right thing to do at that moment, but being Sierra Adams, I often didn't wait for the right time.

"What is it?" Luanne said.

"What is your problem with me?"

"I don't have a problem with you, Sierra."

"Yes, you do, Luanne. Ever since you found out who I really am, you've been avoiding me like the plague, and I heard you and Cam talking upstairs yesterday. You said some pretty mean things."

"I just don't think that you and my son are right for each other."

"Why? Because I run my own company? Well, guess what, Luanne, so does Cameron."

"Cameron isn't like you and doesn't belong in your world."

"Who are you to decide what world Cameron belongs in? I love him."

"I've googled you. I saw the photo of you attacking that man and I've seen the men you've been photographed with."

Here we go again. Damn that photographer who took that picture.

"First of all, that was no man. He's a cowardly boy who hurt me very deeply and I took three years of anger out on him. And, as for those other men, Cameron is more of a man than those men will ever be."

"What's going on over here?" Cameron asked as he walked up and placed his hand on my shoulder.

"Your mother is telling me how much she doesn't care for me and I think she implied that I am a whore."

"Mom!" Cameron snapped.

I put my hand up. "It's okay. She doesn't have to like me, but let me tell you something, Luanne Cole," I said as I pointed my finger at her. "Your son is thirty years old and can make his own decisions. He fell in love with me. Yeah, that's right; me! And if you don't like it, that's too damn bad because this high maintenance, corporate CEO, Prada-carrying, Chanel-wearing, and Jimmy-Choo-walking bitch isn't going anywhere."

I stomped away and went below deck. Cameron followed. "Sierra, stop."

"Leave me alone, Cam."

He grabbed my arm and pulled me into him. "I love you and that's all I'm saying."

The anger that had erupted inside me began to wither away the longer Cameron held me.

"We need to talk about tonight," Cameron said.

"What about it?"

"I'll be spending the night at my parents' house with my brothers. Are you coming to the church tomorrow?" he asked.

"Nah. I think it's best that I stay back at the house and make sure everything's ready for the reception. Plus, your mom wouldn't want me there anyway and I don't want ruin her day."

"It's not her day, Sierra. It's Jaden's day and I know he'd want you there. I want you there," he said with a sadness in his voice.

I brought my hand up to his face and softly stroked it. "I love you, Cameron."

"Does that mean you'll come to the church?" He smiled.

"No." I laughed.

The boat had docked, which meant the party was over. Thank you, God. Cameron said his goodbyes and I got off that boat as fast as I could and high-tailed it to the Escalade. Cameron followed behind and we drove back to the house so he could pack a bag.

"I don't want you to worry about my mom," Cameron said as he softly kissed me goodbye.

"I won't anymore. I said what I had to say to her and, if she can't accept me, then I'm over it."

"She'll come around, Sierra. I promise. Just give her some time."

"She can take all the time she needs because I'll be about three thousand miles away."

He took my hand and placed a folded piece of paper in it. "This is the address of the church, in case you change your mind," he said as he kissed my forehead.

"Thanks, but I don't think so. Have fun with your brothers. I'll miss you."

"I'll miss you too. Maybe we can have text sex."

"You mean sexting? You dork." I laughed.

"Same thing. I like my name for it better. I have to go. I love you."

"I love you too," I pouted as he walked down the driveway.

Chapter 41

Sierra

I set the alarm to go off at six a.m. because the decorators and the florist were supposed to be here around eight. I grabbed my phone from the nightstand and smiled when I saw six text messages from Cameron. Shit. I fell asleep on him last night during our sexting.

"Hello?"

"Sierra, why aren't you replying?"

"You can't leave me like this, babe. Not fair."

"I bet you fell asleep or you're passed out drunk."

"Babe?"

"Good night, sweetheart. I love you."

I quickly sent him a message.

"I'm so sorry I fell asleep. I don't even remember falling asleep."

"I have blue balls."

I laughed out loud.

"I'm sorry. I'll massage them later."

"Promise?"

"I promise on my Prada."

"Church?"

"No."

"Have to go. Mom made breakfast."

"I feel like we're in high school."

"Yum. She made French toast with strawberries. Why don't you ever make that?"

"Do I cook? Why don't you ask Rosa?"

"I want you to make it."

"Silly boy."

"I'm serious."

"Tell Luanne I said GOOD MORNING!"

"Let's not stir the pot."

"Bye, lover."

"Bye, babe."

I climbed out of bed and headed downstairs for some much-needed coffee. Kirsty and Sasha were still asleep and Rosa was making French toast.

"Morning. Do we have any strawberries to go with that French toast?"

"Yes. Would you like some?"

"Yes, please."

I walked over to the refrigerator and noticed a can of whipped cream in the door. Perfect! I took it out and waited for Rosa to fix my French toast. As soon as she put two slices on a plate with the strawberries on top, I squirted some whip cream on them. I took my plate to the table, pulled out my phone, and took a picture.

"Does your French toast have whip cream on it?"

"Lol, no. I wish."

"MINE DOES!"

I sent him the picture of my breakfast.

"I officially hate you."

"Don't hate me because I have whip cream."

"Lol. Gotta go, babe. Hide that whip cream in the back of the fridge for later.

"Already thought of it."

Kirsty and Sasha came down just as the florist pulled in the driveway.

"Do you need our help?" Kirsty asked.

"No. You two enjoy your breakfast. Come outside when you're done."

There were five trucks in the driveway and each one was filled with flowers arrangements, flowered trees, archways, and swags of magnolias to be hung from the top of the tent. Each table was elegantly decorated with a centerpiece made of magnolias and floating candles. The swags of magnolia and ivy were hung from the tent and woven with white lights. Damn. This was going to be beautiful tonight. As I was standing there, making sure everyone was doing their job, my phone beeped with a text message from Cameron.

"Church?"

I sighed.

"No."

"What wrong?" Kirsty asked as she stood next to me.

"Cameron wants me to come to the church and I don't want to."

"Why wouldn't you go?" she asked as she looped her arm around mine.

"The main reason is Luanne, and the second reason is because I need to stay here and make sure everything goes smoothly. The caterers will be here and the DJ and, most importantly, the booze will be delivered. I need to make sure they sent plenty of bottles of tequila."

She laughed as she looked at me. Sasha and Rosa walked over to where we were standing and the four of us watched as a future was about to unfold.

"You did good, Sierra," Rosa said.

"Yeah. I can't believe you pulled this off in such a short period of time," Sasha chimed in.

I looked at her in disbelief. "Do you not work for me?" I asked.

We all laughed and Kirsty and Sasha went back inside.

"Rosa, Luanne doesn't like me and she said that she doesn't think Cameron and I are right for each other."

"Does it matter what she thinks?" Rosa asked.

"No, but she is his mother and I'm sure it bothers him."

"Why wouldn't she like you?"

"Because of my lifestyle. She said that Cameron doesn't belong in my world."

"Since when do you care what other people think?"

"Yeah, since when does Sierra Adams care?" James said as he sat down next to me.

"It's just—"

"It's just nothing. She doesn't know you. She hasn't bothered to get to know you since you've been here because she's full of judgment. Let her judge. If she can't see how happy you make Cameron, then that's her problem, not yours." James smiled as he took hold of my hand. "You're Sierra Adams and you're an amazing woman. Any person who has an ounce of a brain can see that from a mile away. Screw her, Sierra. You and Cam are starting a life together, and when I say together, I mean the two of you doing things together and respecting what the other wants."

I look at him and cocked my head. "Are you referring to the church?"

"Yes. Cameron wants you there. He wants you to be a part of his brother's wedding. You sitting there and watching his brother marry the love of his life means something to him and for you not to attend because of Luanne is just ridiculous. The two of you are a couple now. What you do affects both of you."

"Screw Luanne," Rosa said. "You walk into that church and you show Builder Boy that you're there for him and nobody's going to stop you."

"You know that Kirsty, Sasha, and especially Rosa will be here to oversee things while you're at the wedding," James said. "Now go get ready. Put on that Vera Wang dress of yours and those Jimmy Choos and show Cameron how much you love him. I'll drive you."

I put my arm around both of them and gave them each a hug. "You two are getting a raise when we get back," I said as I kissed them on their cheeks.

"You keep saying that, but I have yet to see it." James smiled.

****

Cameron

Jaden was literally shaking as we stood in the waiting room at the church. My mom walked in and straightened his bow tie and then walked over to me and straightened mine, even though it was already straight.

"I need to talk to you for a moment," I said to her.

"About what, dear?"

"Sierra."

"She's off topic right now. I have other things to think about."

"I don't care what you have to think about. The way you treated her was extremely rude. You don't even know her. You only know what you saw on the internet."

"I'm not doing this right now, Cameron."

"Well, I am and you're going to listen to me. I love that girl with all my heart. I've never been this happy before and for you to try to ruin that for me by telling her that we're not right for each other really sucks, Mom."

"Cameron!" she exclaimed.

"Now, if you want things to be bad between us when I leave for California, then so be it. You're my mom and I love you, but I will not let you treat my girlfriend that way. I am thirty years old. Don't you think it's time that I deserve to be in love?"

"You need to get to the altar. The wedding is going to start soon. We'll talk about this later," she said as she left the room.

I shook my head and Jaden put his hand on my shoulder. "Ignore her, Cam. She's just upset because you're moving away. Now come on; I have a woman to marry." He smiled.

We walked through the back and took our places at the altar. I looked out into the crowded church with the hopes that Sierra had changed her mind about coming. But I didn't see her. The bridesmaids began to line up and the wedding was about to start when the side door to the church opened and Sierra walked in. A huge smile splayed across my face when I saw her. She looked at me, flashed her beautiful smile, and made everyone in the row behind my parents move down so she could squeeze in. That was my girl.

After the ceremony ended, I met Sierra out in the waiting area of the church and gave her a big kiss. "Thank you for coming. You look gorgeous."

"Thank you. You look good enough to eat; with a dab of whip cream, of course." I winked.

"Why did you change your mind?"

"I wanted to be here for you because I love you and it wasn't fair of me to put that aside and not attend because of what people think of me."

"I can't wait to get back to California with you," I said as I wrapped my arms around her.

"You and me both. I think I've had enough of your hometown for a while." She smiled.

"I have to go. I'm being summoned for pictures. I'll see you back at the house," I said as I kissed her goodbye.

Chapter 42

Sierra

As soon as I got back to the house, I walked around and inspected every nook and cranny of the back to make sure everything was perfect for Magnolia and Jaden. I walked over to the bar area and introduced myself to the bartender.

"You have plenty of tequila, right?" I asked.

"Yes, ma'am."

"Good, and when you see me, make sure you have a double ready and waiting." I winked.

Everyone started to arrive and cocktails were being served. Finally, the wedding party arrived, and when I walked over to Magnolia and Jaden to congratulate them, she began to cry.

"What's wrong?" I asked.

"This. This. This is all so beautiful. It's like a dream. I will never be able to thank you enough."

"You're welcome and no tears. You'll smear your makeup, and there's nothing worse than a bride with smeared makeup."

She laughed.

"That's better." I winked. "Now go and enjoy your wedding reception. We have lots and lots of alcohol."

As they walked away, I felt strong arms wrapped around my waist and a kiss on my cheek.

"This is beautiful, Sierra. I had no doubt that you'd pull this off, but this is beyond amazing. I think I may keep you around."

"Thank you, Mr. Cole. I was thinking that when we get back home to L.A., we could go furniture shopping for the living room."

"It's not remodeled yet."

"I know, but I like you, and I want furnish the room with things we pick out together. It'll be our special room." I smiled.

"I like that idea. What if we can't agree?"

I grabbed hold of his hand and pulled him along. "If we can't agree, then we'll do it my way."

"Somehow, I knew you were going to say that." He laughed.

Night had fallen, dinner had been served, alcohol was being consumed, and everyone was having a wonderful time. While Cameron was talking to some friends, Luanne walked up beside me.

"I want to thank you for doing this for my son and daughter in-law. It was very kind of you."

"You're welcome."

"Listen, Sierra, I'm sorry for the things I said. I want you to know that I'm very happy that Cameron has finally found someone he loves. I will admit that I'm not happy that my son is moving so far away. It was hard enough when he was there working, but I knew he would come home. Now, he's moving there permanently and it's not like this place is a hop, skip, and a jump away. He's my first and oldest child and it's hard."

I felt bad for her because it had to take a lot of courage on her part to tell me these things. I took her hand and squeezed it.

"I know it's hard, but we'll visit. In fact, we'll visit so much you'll get sick of us and want us to leave, plus you'll come visit us in California. I think you'll like it there. I would like to take you shopping on Rodeo Drive."

"I think that would be quite an experience." She smiled. "Excuse me, Sierra. Jaden is calling for me."

The corners of my mouth turned up as I took a sip of my tequila.

"Did I just see you and my mom holding hands?" Cameron asked.

"Yes. She apologized. I accepted. I told her we'd visit and that she needs to come to California. All is good."

The DJ called all couples out onto the dance floor for a romantic dance. Cameron placed his hand on my waist and placed his other in mine.

"We can dance right here under these beautiful lights." He smiled.

I stared into his beautiful green eyes. The same green eyes that caught my attention and piqued my interest a few months ago, and the same green eyes that agreed to a sex-only relationship. As we slowly moved to the music, a thought came into my mind.

"When we get back to L.A., let's just tell Delia that I hired you for the year."

"Really, Sierra? I think, sooner or later, she'd figure it out. We need to come clean about who I really am." He smiled.

"But that's no fun," I whined. He kissed the tip of my nose and told me to shush.

Cameron Cole walked into my life and turned my world upside down. Tomorrow morning, we would get on a plane back home and he'd move all his things into my house. My house would become our house and we'd start our life together as a couple of thirty-year-olds who finally figured out life.

My name is Sierra Adams, CEO of Adams Advertising and Design. This was my story about being a single woman who wanted a sex-only relationship and how one man changed all that.

The Upside of Love

Chapter 1

Lily

"Have I told you how much I love you, Luke Matthews?" I asked as I ran my hand across his chest.

"You have, babe, and I don't ever want you to stop telling me."

I lifted my head from his chest and kissed his lips – the lips that devoured every inch of my skin last night from head to toe. The lips that made me warm when I was cold, and the lips that gave me the security I desperately needed.

It had been two months since Sam's and Gretchen's accident. Gretchen's leg was healing nicely and Sam waited on her hand and foot, practically never leaving her side. Luke pretty much moved into my apartment, since Sam moved Gretchen into his. Lucky was staying with Giselle at her place because his apartment building had a flood and it was being renovated. Their relationship was still weird. Even though Giselle was pregnant with Lucky's kid, it didn't stop the two of them from seeing other people. It was awkward when one of them would bring the other out with us.

"I guess I should get up and head over to the bar," Luke sighed.

I tightened my arm around him because I didn't want to move. "No," I said.

"What do you mean?" Luke laughed.

"I think we should stay in bed all day and do nothing but have wild sex." I smiled as my hand traveled down to his hard cock.

"You sure know how to turn me on, babe," he said as he rolled me over and hovered over me. "I have to go to the bar. You have to edit those photos for Mrs. Braxton, and we have a lunch date with Charley today." He smiled as he took down my panties.

"You're right. But, promise me we'll schedule a day when we can just stay in bed all day and not worry about the outside world."

"You got it." He smiled as he plunged his finger inside me. "Now, give me your lips and shush. I'm going to make sweet love to you."

After a sweet round of lovemaking, Luke took a shower and I made a pot of coffee. As I waited for it to finish brewing, I stared out my window at the perfectly blue sky and the sun that was shining brightly into my living room. Settling in Santa Monica was the best decision I ever made. Lost in my thoughts, I felt strong arms wrap around me. I tilted my head back and looked up at Luke's smiling face.

"What are you doing?" he asked.

"Just admiring the beauty of the day."

He was wearing only jeans and his hair was still soaking wet. He was the sexiest man alive, as far as I was concerned, and I couldn't seem to get enough of him.

"Well, I'm admiring the beauty in front of me." He tilted his head and softly kissed my neck.

I giggled. "You sure have a way with words, Mr. Matthews."

"And you have a way with those lips." He smiled as he kissed me again.

Luke walked to the coffee pot, poured a cup of coffee, and sat down at the table.

"Do you want me to make you breakfast?" I asked.

"Nah, I'm good, babe. I'll grab something at the bar."

There was a knock at the door and Sam's boisterous voice came through loud and clear. "Dude, are you up? Are you decent?"

Luke sighed as he got up from his chair and opened the door.

"Morning, Sam. Morning, Gretchen."

I smiled as my best friends walked into the apartment. I immediately grabbed two cups and poured coffee in them.

"Sit down," I said to Gretchen and I lightly took hold of her arm and led her to the table.

"Thanks, Lily." She smiled.

"Have you talked to Giselle?" I asked.

"Yeah. She said that she and Lucky were going furniture shopping for the baby's room."

"For both places?" Luke asked.

"I'm not sure. She didn't say and I know his apartment still isn't ready. To be honest, I think she likes having him around."

"They're weird." I laughed.

Luke got up from the table. "Okay, friends. It's been fun seeing you, but I have to finish getting dressed and head over to the bar. Maddie and I have some liquor orders to go over."

"We playing tonight?" Sam asked.

"Yeah. I already talked to Lucky and he said that he and Giselle will be there. I'm also interviewing new bands to play on the weekends after we play our gig. I want Lily to play and she won't," he said as he pouted.

"Get over it, Matthews." I winked.

Luke headed to the bedroom to get ready, and Sam and Gretchen got up to leave. "I can't wait to get this cast off today. So, when you see me tonight, I'll be strutting in."

I laughed as I hugged her.

"I can't wait to finally make love to her without that cast getting in the way." Sam smiled.

"Just keep it down," Luke yelled from the bedroom.

"Paybacks, bro. Paybacks." He laughed.

****

Since I couldn't get another teaching job right away, I decided to make photography my full-time work. I mostly just worked out of my apartment, but I wanted to rent a small space and turn it into a studio. It was something that I'd thought about over the past couple of months and Luke was extremely supportive. He told me that I needed to follow my dreams and just go for it like he did with the bar. I did a photo shoot with Rory Braxton and her twin girls. It was a surprise gift for her husband's birthday. I photographed them at the beach and then Rory wanted some sexy pictures for Ian. I brought her back to the apartment once I set it up with the backdrop. I had never photographed sexy pictures like the ones I did for her and I was nervous at first. But after seeing the photographs, I knew she'd be more than pleased. I met Rory through Giselle. Rory's husband's best friend, Adalynn, owned *Prim* magazine, for which Giselle did a lot of modeling. When she overheard Rory and Adalynn talking about finding a female photographer, she instantly thought of me. Since the pictures that Rory wanted for Ian were of her practically naked and very seductive, she thought it would be best to have a female photograph her, so as not to upset her husband.

As I was sitting at my computer, editing the photos, Luke walked up and gave me a kiss.

"Bye, babe. Have fun today and I'll see you later at the bar for lunch with Charley."

"Bye, baby." I smiled.

I looked at the photos of Ashley and Ariel Braxton and smiled as I envisioned a family like Rory's and Ian's one day. I picked up my phone from the desk and called Rory.

"Hello," she answered.

"Hi, Rory. It's Lily. Your pictures will be ready by tonight, so I was hoping we could meet for lunch tomorrow and I can show you the final shots."

"Excellent, Lily. Tomorrow will be perfect. If you're in the mood for Mexican food, we can meet at the Border Grill, say around noon?"

"Sounds great, Rory. I'll see you tomorrow."

As I was editing the photos, one popped up of Luke. I smiled as I ran my fingers across his perfect six pack on the screen. It was one of him lying on the bed in only a pair of unbuttoned jeans. His arm was behind his head and he was looking out the window. I was the luckiest girl alive to be loved by him and my life was perfect. More perfect than I had ever dreamed it would be.

About The Author

Sandi Lynn is a New York Times, USA Today and Wall Street Journal bestselling author who spends all of her days writing. She published her first novel, Forever Black, in February 2013. Her addictions are shopping, romance novels, coffee, chocolate, margaritas, and giving readers an escape to another world.

Please come connect with her at:

www.facebook.com/Sandi.Lynn.Author

www.twitter.com/SandilynnWriter

www.authorsandilynn.com

www.pinterest.com/sandilynnWriter

www.instagram.com/sandilynnauthor

https://www.goodreads.com/author/show/6089757.Sandi_Lynn

Playlist

She's So Mean ~ Matchbox Twenty

Through Glass ~ Stone Sour

Country Girl (Shake It For Me) ~ Luke Bryan

Endlessly ~ The Cab

Miss Independent ~ Ne-Yo

Wish You Were Here ~ Avril Lavigne

Boom Clap ~ Charli XCX

All About That Bass ~ Meghan Trainor

Before It's Too Late ~ The Goo Goo Dolls

Turn Down For What ~ DJ Snake, Lil Jon

She's So High ~ Tal Bachman

The Queen and I ~ Gym Class Heroes

Life Of The Party ~ Shawn Mendes

14859825R00205

Printed in Great Britain
by Amazon.co.uk, Ltd.,
Marston Gate.